FINDING PEACE

B. E. BAKER

For Emma

You lift me up. You support me. And you bludgeon anyone who doesn't with a club. . . or vicious rhetoric.

So, basically, you're the best sister ever.

❦   I   ❦

ANICA

I used to have a poster that hung above my bed that said, "Shoot for the moon. Even if you miss, you'll land among the stars."

I believed that down to my perfectly polished toenails.

It's the reason I sent a bold one-page query letter to my top ten agents with my very first novel.

Because of that poster, I wasn't even surprised when three of them offered to represent me.

When my book went to auction and sold for six figures on the second week it was on submission, that made perfect sense to me too.

After all, I'd shot for the moon, and I hit it, dead in the center.

What Norman Vincent Peale's inspiring quote neglects to address is that there's no oxygen on the bloody moon. That's probably why I asphyxiated up there.

"Uh, I'm sorry." I blink. "Can you repeat the question?"

Ursula, general manager of the only Fogo de Chão in Atlanta, purses her lips. "I asked you what your greatest strength is."

I'm not off to a great start, clearly. "Right. Duh. That's

like number one in the interviewing handbook, right?" I chuckle.

She doesn't.

I lick my lips. "Okay, well, my greatest strength is that I pay attention to details, which is pretty helpful for a job as a waitress."

She jots something down.

I resist the urge to lean toward her and try to read it.

"And your greatest weakness?"

"Sometimes I just can't suppress the urge to light things on fire." I can't quite keep the half grin off my face.

Her eyes widen and she clutches her pencil until her knuckles turn white.

"I'm kidding," I say. "I'm not really a pyro. Clearly my biggest weakness is a propensity to crack jokes before I know the person well enough to pull them off."

"You do realize that you'll be asked to interact with a wide variety of people. They'll be from all sorts of back-grounds—"

"But it's Fogo de Chão, so no matter where they're from, the customer is always correct. Right?" I try one last time.

She grunts. "If I may be blunt, I'm concerned that you'll be offensive."

"You can call my references," I say. "They'll tell you that the customers love me." I *don't* explain to her that most people have more personality than a toothpick. . .

"I'm not sure that even strong recommendations from —" She glances down at my job application and scrunches her nose. "IHOP and a place called 'The Little Door' will convince me."

I sigh. "Alright, I started my waitressing career at IHOP, which has a surprisingly robust number of options on their menu, I might add, but 'The Little Door' is a Parisian—"

Ursula stands up and extends her hand. "I'll let you know."

My mouth snaps shut. I'm sure that she will, with some kind of awkward text or a brusque, early-morning voice-mail. "Thanks, I really appreciate it."

On the way home, I give myself a little pep talk. There are plenty of restaurants around that will have less obnoxious general managers. Plus, I don't *need* a job. My royalty checks may not be as hefty as they once were, but I've got a free place to stay right now, and Mary and Luke seem to enjoy having me around to help since Mary had the new baby. Plus I'm getting to know Amy and Chase better, which is also great.

By the time I reach Luke's house, I've already gotten a text message from Ursula, thanking me for coming in and letting me know they've decided to go another direction to fill their open server position. Apparently I'm not even qualified to carry drinks to the table and tell people about the salad bar.

Another warning I wish good old Norman had included alongside his dumb old quote is that once you've hit the moon a time or two, falling short when you're aiming for a bush twenty feet away really stings. Falling among the stars? I wish.

The front door isn't locked, and when I walk through I realize why. The sound of murmuring voices emerges from the office. Clearly Baby Jack is taking a nap and Mary's meeting with Paisley about their new startup firm. Paisley has been here almost every day for a week now. If I'm quiet, maybe I can sneak past them and reach my room without being asked about the interview.

But one little overheard word from Mary stops me in my tracks. *Anica.* I freeze on the opposite side of the entryway and strain my ears to catch a hint of what they may be saying about me. "—space. It's not like we can ask."

"But she can't be planning to stay here forever, right?" Paisley laughs. "I mean, imagine this one. She meets a new guy, and he asks her out, and she says, sure, pick me up at my brother-in-law's house. The one he shares with his new wife."

I stiffen. So much for a free place to live as long as I want. I can't quite make out what Mary's saying, but I can imagine.

"Sure, but you could use it, right? I mean, until we rent an office, we're kind of crammed in this library."

My face floods with heat. They want me out soon—of course they do. This house is big, but between the nursery, Chase's, Amy's, and Luke's rooms, well, it's not the White House. The guest room is the obvious place for Mary to use for her new startup. I run my hand through my hair, forgetting my sunglasses are on top of my head, and knock them to the ground. Drat.

"Hey, Anica." Paisley's leaning against the doorway into the library when I turn around. "How'd the interview go?"

I force a smile. "They decided to take the restaurant personnel decisions in a different direction."

She frowns. "What does that even mean?"

"The manager hated everything about me."

"So that means we won't be going to Fogo de Chão every week?" Paisley's shoulders slump. "That stinks, because I straight up love their grilled pineapple."

Twenty types of steak and she likes the pineapple? That's *so* Paisley. "I'm sure I'll find another restaurant you'll like almost as much," I say. "Speaking of, how do you feel about IHOP?"

Her eyes light up. "Their lingonberry Swedish pancakes." She groans. "Yes. Do IHOP. Plus, it's way closer than all that fancy junk downtown."

This time, my smile is real. "Duly noted." It's awfully hard to stay irritated with Paisley.

"I'm sorry it didn't work out." Mary steps into the doorway, leaning on the opposite side of the frame from Paisley. "But you'll find something, and you already know that there's no pressure from us."

Right. At least, none you'll admit to applying. "Thanks." I duck into my room as quickly as possible, drop my purse onto the end table, sink into the armchair in the corner, and open my laptop out of habit.

My fingers freeze on the keyboard when my new email loads and I notice a certain name in bolded letters.

I haven't heard from Henrietta Blake in over a year.

Not since the day last spring when she fired me and stopped being my agent. I swallow once. Twice. There's no obvious reason for her to be emailing me. I close my laptop, my heart hammering in my chest cavity. I stand up and do ten jumping jacks.

That was dumb. Between the email and the unnecessary physical activity, I'll probably give myself an actual heart attack. I sit back down and flip the top of my Mac Air back up. I force myself to read the subject line. "Long Time."

Yes, more than a year is a long time, that's true, but it tells me nothing about what she wants.

Has she changed her mind about my last manuscript? Maybe Veronica reached out to her—maybe my editor changed her mind! Could she be looking for a book just like the last one I sent, right this very moment? Is she regretting dumping me?

My fingers tremble as I click on the email. As it opens, I consider throwing my laptop across the room. It seems safer than reading the tiny pile of words currently blurring in front of my face.

But of course, I'd still read it—just on my phone—and then I'd need a new laptop, which I can't afford. I sit on my hands and focus on the email until the words un-jumble enough that I can make sense of them.

D*ear Anica:*

I'm sorry I haven't emailed you before now. I promised we'd stay friends, and clearly I've failed to keep my word. I hope you're doing well, and that you've found some measure of peace and balance in your life.

In the spirit of friendship, an opportunity crossed my desk today that felt like a perfect fit for you. Avon sent me some requests for new IP project submissions, and look at the description on one of them:

- *Cripplingly shy MC forced to administer crazy spinster aunt's will; battles the local pastor to whom the aunt promised the entire inheritance, to rebuild a chapel burned in a fire. MC makes great strides in overcoming shyness and asserting herself, and learns to trust the pastor . . . and to love him.*

For this particular brand, we're seeking fun, quirky, upbeat tales of love, perseverance, and devotion in the face of bizarre twists of fate. The light tone and situational and conversational humor should underscore serious issues that modern women face.

If you have any interest in submitting a sample for any of these, let me know. You should know that I still haven't read a single book in the romantic comedy genre that had the spirit, sense of relevancy, and humor that yours embodied. Your writing is missed.

Whatever you decide, I'd love to chat.

Best,

Henri

An original, publisher-generated intellectual property story? They call them IP projects, which sort of feels like the opposite of what it really is. But why she thinks that I'd want to write a story wrapped around a plot line that Avon hand-fed me for peanuts that wouldn't even come out under my name is beyond me. And she thought of me when they asked for bubbly, ridiculous, romantic comedies?

I slam my laptop shut and toss it onto the bed. My room is a little too small to pace in a satisfying way, but I can't go out into the family room, not with Paisley and Mary already frustrated about the space I'm taking up.

I need the money if I want to get my own apartment, but I can't do it. Not that. I'd rather work at McDonald's taking drive-thru orders than write a story someone else cooked up under a name other than my own. I wouldn't even own the story at the end. IP projects pay a single, upfront lump sum, because Avon's paying to own it outright. I can't think of a bigger step back I could possibly take.

No thanks.

I haven't fallen *that* far.

Except I don't even have a friend to call about this latest indignity. I don't have anyone I can ask for advice. Mary has taken my sister's place, and she wants me gone. My mom is insufferable. My dad won't even understand why I'm upset. *Money is money is money*, he'd tell me.

The less I write, the less I keep up with my writing friends. Besides, many of them do several IP projects a year, so they're unlikely to understand my reaction.

I've never been someone who makes friends easily. I never minded before—I had my books, my online writing friends, my boyfriend, and my sister. That was more than enough for someone who didn't love socializing most of the time anyway.

But then Lizzie died.

And my boyfriend left me.

Since my writing career sank, well, my writing friends . . . I can't even talk to them, not right now.

I used to be able to read and read and read whenever the world seemed too hard, but even that is denied me.

Every book I've picked up has hurt lately. If the book is lousy, I can't read it, and if it's great, I'm consumed with jealousy.

I curl into a ball in the middle of my bed and cry for far too long. "Ah, Lizzie. I miss you," I whisper.

And then I wipe my tears, and I open up my dumb old laptop. And I apply for a dozen more jobs at every restaurant that's hiring in a ten-mile radius. Once I get a job and save enough for a deposit and first month's rent, I'll get an apartment of my own, but I'd still like to be close enough to Luke and Mary that I can visit Amy and Chase regularly.

At least my niece and nephew still like me—and it's looking like I better soak up the next few years. I doubt they'll worship me once they're old enough to recognize me as the cautionary tale that I've become.

ETHAN

Most people wait to ruin their lives until they're in their twenties. Not me. I made the biggest mistake a person could ever make at the tender age of twelve.

My mother died because of my selfish cowardice.

That might be the reason I work so hard to avoid even the smallest mistakes in every aspect of my life. It's also what makes me such an excellent manager. I never underestimate the impact of even a moment's delay or a tiny omission. "I noted three errors on the quarterly report." I drop it on my assistant's desk. "Can you talk to Bryce about them and get me an updated version?"

Genevieve nods. "You're heading out?"

"For the day." The Billabong Pipeline Masters is only a few months away. If I get home and take Partner for a quick walk, I should have plenty of time to change and catch a few waves.

"Weather says it's supposed to be a glorious day." Genevieve stands up, the report in hand, but she waves at me as I leave. "And maybe when you get back you'll be in a good enough mood to call your dad back. He's called twice more."

Doubtful. I know exactly what he wants, and my answer is still no. "When is it not glorious here?"

Her laugh follows me out of the room and down the hall.

After I release the latch on her crate, Partner, my Border Collie, shoots out like a rocket and nearly jumps high enough to reach my face, her tongue lolling from the side of her mouth. I've been told that once they're not puppies anymore, they calm down. So far, at two years old, she's as energetic as ever. "Alright, alright," I say. "Let's go." Her backside wiggles so forcefully that I can barely clip the leash to her collar.

So much for a leisurely walk down the beach to scope out the waves. Partner pulls the entire four and a half miles, never once letting up, even though I'm jogging at a brisk pace. Perfect weather notwithstanding, I'm drenched in sweat when I reach my beach shack. "Alright, girl. You had your fun. Now it's my turn." I wish I could trust her to play in the waves while I surf, but it's just not safe.

I grab the mail as an afterthought on our way inside, flipping through the thick stack of letters as I walk up my creaky wooden front steps. Junk mail, catalog for boring business wear, warranty offers for my brand new car.

Until a plain white envelope with a return address marked Sparta, Georgia. My adrenaline spikes, even after all this time.

For years, every Tuesday I threw away a letter from Hancock State Prison. But I haven't gotten one for more than five years now. He gave up on me thirteen years to the week from the day it happened. He actually lasted way longer than I expected, but then again, I suppose there's not much for him to do in there.

The sender is different than the one marked on all those letters I threw away unopened. This letter says it's from the 'Prison Warden.'

My hands shake and Partner circles my legs, tangling the leash. I drop it numbly and unwind the cord, stumbling over my agitated canine pal and dropping the mail onto the weathered wooden floor. The letter lands face up, staring at me like a coiled serpent, ready to strike.

What could it say? Why would the warden write to me? Is it some kind of ploy—change the sender so that I'll open it? Another option rises unbidden in my mind, and I shove it downward with more violence than I've felt in years. I thought I'd let that part of my life go. I thought I'd expunged the anger it generated thoroughly and completely.

But one letter and it all comes rushing back.

The guilt. The terror. And as always, stronger than anything else, the rage.

I redo the math I already know in my bones. From 2002 to now. His first fifteen years was up three years ago, which means he could be out on parole any time. This letter could be the worst news I've had in eighteen years. I lean over slowly and pick it up. My phone rings, and I almost ignore it, assuming it's just Dad. Again.

It's not. Adriana. My sister has been almost as annoying as Dad lately, but I can't ignore her like I do him. "Hello?"

"Did you get a letter?" Her voice trembles.

I don't bother asking what she's talking about. If it's about what I fear, they'd have sent one to both of us. "Yeah."

"Did you open it?"

I grunt.

"Me either."

"How long have you had it?"

The sound my sister makes could be a laugh or it could be a cry. "Two days. I figured your mail would lag."

"Good old Hawaii."

"That's another reason you should move home," she wheedles again.

When Dad asks, my jaw locks and my fists tighten, but when Adriana asks, guilt wells in my chest and tears at my heart. She wants me to come home because she misses me. Dad wants me there so he can control me more easily, direct me toward the path he chooses, and make me into the man he wants me to become. "I'm not talking about that right now."

"Fine." She always gives up that easily—one of the reasons I don't get angry with her. I can't fault her for wanting to see me more. I miss her, too. "So do we open it at the same time?" Hope. Her voice practically vibrates with the same emotion she always feels when she asks me to move back to Atlanta—only this time, it's about the terrible, gut-wrenching letter from a prison warden.

"Ana, please tell me you're dreading this news. Please tell me you're not . . . excited."

"We never lie, not to each other."

I can barely breathe. "If they parole him—" I can't say anything else. The world only makes sense because he's not free.

"I know how you feel. But you and I aren't exactly the same in every way, and that's okay."

Exactly the same? I would write a check to the warden for the entire contents of my checking and savings, right now, if he'd lock *him* up and throw away the key. Ana's *hopeful* he'll be paroled and she thinks *we're not exactly the same?*

"Ethan? Are you still there? Let's open it on three, okay?"

I grunt again. My feelings, her feelings, none of it will change what *is*. No point in arguing until I know the truth.

"One, two, three." I hear the ripping of the paper, and a small inhalation of breath. She must have put me on speaker.

When she claps and coos, the bottom drops out of my stomach.

"Oh, Ethan! He's getting out! Finally."

I crumple the letter in my fist.

Her voice is at least an octave higher than it usually is. "I can't believe he didn't say a word to me about it, not once. He must not have wanted me to get my hopes up. They denied his first request, you know."

"They must be out of their minds not to have denied this one." I hate the growly way my voice emerges. It's almost as bad as her squeaky excitement. I flatten the anger out of my voice. He doesn't have that kind of power over me, not anymore. But I can't quite ignore her implication. "You've been writing to him?"

"You said you didn't want me to talk about him to you," she says. "Ever. Or I would have told you that."

I shouldn't have said that—knowledge is always better than fumbling around in the dark. "You shouldn't have been writing him, and you shouldn't be happy he's getting out, either. He's evil incarnate." My hands shake as I think about that night. And the many, many nights that came before it. So many horrible memories I've been forced to suppress.

"He said he wrote you for more than a decade and you never once replied." She's chiding me. My own sister.

"More than a decade."

"Not one response, Ethan?" She tsks. "That's not like you. You're not hateful."

My own sister doesn't know me at all. "Not responding

was the kindest thing I could have done." The words barely escape through gritted teeth.

"Well, now you can talk to him in person. Our father will be released on August 28th! Now you *have* to fly back stateside, even if it's only for a visit."

I don't crush the phone. I don't throw it against the wall. I don't even swear at my little sister. I'm kind of proud of how much I've grown. "Phillip Sims is not your father, and he's not mine. Never say that again."

"Fine," Adriana says. "Fine. I forgot how touchy you get about it. Uncle William may have adopted us, and yeah, I think of him as our dad, but we still have a biological father, and he's going to be free for the first time in eighteen years. You have to at least come back." I can practically *hear* her rolling her eyes. "Even if it's only to yell at him."

"How can they be freeing him at all?" I practically shout into the phone. "How? After what he did?"

"He was terribly drunk the night he—the night it happened. He has given up eighteen years for taking things too far. How much more do you want?"

I want him dead. Like our mother is dead, thanks to him.

Thanks to me.

"I won't be coming home, not to see him. Not now, not ever."

I grab my board and sprint toward the reprieve of the ocean waves. My assistant Genevieve was right about the weather—the waves are perfect, but it doesn't matter. I've never needed the peace of standing in a perfect barrel of ocean movement more than today, so of course, I wipe out over and over. Finally, after a particularly rough blow from my surfboard to my head, I cough out a bucket of saltwater and trudge my way back to my beach house, dragging my board behind me in a breach of every kind of surfer etiquette I ever learned.

Every time I try to recall the feeling of pure bliss that always surrounds me inside a perfect wave, fury battles its way back upward. My little sister Adriana doesn't have ANY idea what a particularly deadly form of cancer Phillip Sims becomes if you allow him any place in your life. He's a blight on humanity. She was so young that he never beat her, but I remember every single blow, every single strike, and how it always felt justified, like it was my fault for displeasing him.

I learned how to dodge and weave at the age of seven. By eight, I could curl into a tight ball that protected most of my vital organs. I had identified dozens of hiding places all over the apartment. And I had gotten believably creative with the stories I told at school to cover my injuries.

Mom told me the only thing worse than Dad hitting us would be *losing* Dad. He was a jerk, but he paid the bills and put food on the table.

Most of the time.

I may have been taking a beating every night, but by the time I started Junior High, not a single kid at school could whip me. I'd like to think it was because I was stronger, faster, and smarter, but the reality was that none of them knew how to take a punch like I could. I'd basically been trained since birth to take a punch. Bob and weave and take my licks and keep on going. By seventh grade, I won every single fight I fought—and I finally felt ready to take on Phillip Sims. But when the time came, I hid in the last hiding space that was large enough, Ana in the space right next to me.

I failed my mom that night, but I've been preparing to redeem myself ever since.

The same thought keeps running through my head, over and over. I'm ready, but Adriana isn't. She can't take a hit, and she has no idea what kind of person our biological father really is. By the time I shower and eat dinner, I'm ready.

When Dad calls for the third time today, I answer.

"You're finally going to talk to me?"

"Didn't seem to be much point before," I say.

"Why's that?" Dad's voice is low, gruff, scratchy.

"I had no intention of coming home."

"But now?"

I shrug. "Dunno."

"Adriana called you."

"I got the same letter she did," I say. "I assume you're going to stop her from going to see him."

"She's an adult. I can't keep her from meeting him when he's released."

I swear loudly, angrily. "Are you kidding me right now?"

"She doesn't listen to me," he says. "But she might listen to you."

"Are you really trying to leverage the release of that pile of trash to get me home?"

"You've played in Hawaii long enough, far longer than we ever agreed."

"I'm not *playing* here," I say. "I've rehabbed two hotels, and I've brought the botanical gardens into profitability, which you didn't think would be possible."

"All of which is still far below your capacity, as you well know."

"We don't all have to conquer the world," I say. "Some of us are happy just living in it."

"That's how you'd describe yourself?" Dad asks. "Happy?"

"Would Annelise say that you're happy?"

"Touché," he says. "But promise me you'll think about it. I'm still in a bind with the Riviera Grand, and I need you here."

"Whatever," I say. "You can whip a mismanaged hotel into shape with your eyes closed and one hand tied behind your back."

"I'm not as young as I was." He drops his voice. "I can't pull the hours I used to pull, and things are rough here right now."

He's far from a perfect man, but my mom's brother became my dad by *choice*. He could have surrendered me and Adriana to the state or tasked a nanny to raise us. Instead, he stepped in and parented us to the best of his limited ability. I'll always be grateful. His repeated attempts to convince me to come back to Atlanta and run a newly acquired hotel there have been more obnoxious than anything else, but I never thought he actually needed me.

And Adriana definitely needs someone to talk some sense into her.

"Fine," I say. "Fine."

"Wait, you'll do it? You're coming home?"

I swallow. My life here is practically perfect. Two beautiful hotels and a fabulous botanical garden. Wonderful staff. Perfect weather. All the surfing I could want. I was making plans to expand to Oahu... but if I'm honest, Hawaii has always been an escape, and escapes are fairly close to hiding places. Both of those things are for cowards. Which means, I can't come back to Hawaii until I'm doing it for the right reasons.

With Phillip Sims being released, staying here feels a little too close to climbing into the bathroom cabinet. Maybe it's time for me to rectify the error I made eighteen years ago when I failed to protect my own mom. If I'd stood up to him, if I'd stopped him from hurting her that night, maybe she wouldn't have died. Maybe I could sleep without nightmares.

I imagine Adriana lining up to take Mom's place by his

side, and my hands curl into fists and adrenaline floods my body.

"I'm not saying it's permanent, Dad. Don't replace me here, but tomorrow I'll be on a flight home to Atlanta." And I'm going to ensure that Phillip Sims never harms Adriana or anyone in our family ever again.

I've got one arm around Amy's bony, fragile shoulders, and one arm around a humongous bowl of popcorn. My finger presses the play button and *Ratatouille* roars to life in all its vibrant, gluttonous glory. Mary may be eager for me to leave, but Amy and Chase and Troy are happy to have me here, at least. Even little baby Jack is snoozing away in his glider, which I take as a quiet vote of affirmation.

I may have no professional life to speak of, but I'm rocking the aunt gig.

"Uh." Mary's head pops around the corner. "You started the movie already?"

I pause it. "Were we supposed to wait?"

Chase is already bouncing next to me. "I want popcorn."

I hand him the bowl.

"Oh, it's fine that you've started it, but—"

Paisley shoves past Mary, her hands wrapped around her tiny belly. "You're taking forever. Just ask her."

Mary rolls her eyes. "James can't be here tonight—business—and Paisley was hoping you'd come down and play with the adults for once."

I like the kids, and the kids like me. Furthermore, I like *Ratatouille*. I frown.

"I hear you're, like, *amazing* at charades." Paisley beams. "And I *really* want to win for once."

"James isn't a great charades partner?" My eyebrows rise. "I'd have thought—"

"He's fine at guessing. He sucks at acting things out, and if I don't guess it from the *one* thing he tries. . . " She tosses her hands in the air. "Plus, when we lose, he gets all glowery and refuses to play charades the next time, and it's my favorite." She leans closer. "Don't let that group fool you, either. They *seem* like a nice bunch, but Geo is unbelievably smug."

"She and Trig win a lot?" I ask.

"Is every week a lot?" Paisley's eye twitches.

I laugh. "But Amy needs me here."

Amy smiles at Mary. "Aunt Anica hogs the popcorn."

My jaw drops. "I can't believe you'd sell me out like that."

She giggles.

"For food." I shake my head slowly.

"So will you do it?" Paisley bites her lip. "Come help me destroy Trig and Geo."

"If it was anyone else, I might feel bad," I say. "But Geo—"

Paisley nods. "Is ridiculously smug? You've seen it?"

"I was going to say is prettier than anyone should be, so why should she always win charades, too? The universe needs a little balance."

"Oh." Paisley rolls her eyes. "I'm so used to that, I don't even let it bother me anymore."

I lift one eyebrow. "Not even a little bit?"

She shrugs. "Maybe a little bit."

"Oh fine," I say. "Let's go beat them."

When Paisley slides her arm through mine, I almost feel like I have a friend. I mean, I know this is probably a pity move. She's probably here because I've officially become one of Mary's charity projects, but right now, I can't think of a reason that should make me upset. Assigned friends are still friends, aren't they?

Actually, having an adult ask me to come hang out feels nice.

My social anxiety flares a little when we walk into the living room and every single set of eyes swivels toward us, but Paisley appears to sense it.

"James looks a little different this evening." She bumps my hip with her own. "But I'd say it's probably an upgrade."

"Why do I feel like we're in the presence of a ringer?" Geo presses her lips together and arches one perfectly curved black eyebrow.

"There's no rule I can't use a dear friend when my husband's out of town," Paisley says. "If she happens to be a professional writer and tonight's theme is literature, well, that's just too bad."

"Oh, come on," Trudy says. "Like being spanked by Trig and Brekka every week wasn't bad enough."

"It's not our fault that none of you were grilled about academic topics every night while you were in diapers." Brekka wheels herself toward the big blue armchair easily even on the plush carpet, and her husband Rob darts around and drops into it next to her.

"Your mother is a singular delight," Rob says. "But as pleased as I am that my wife destroys everyone at Trivial Pursuit and charades, we may decide to forgo that kind of training with our children, don't you think?"

"Children?" Brekka raises her eyebrows. "I'm still working on this one. Can you maybe not mention having more until we survive the first?"

Paisley has been spluttering since Rob's comment. "Did you say Brekka destroys everyone?" Paisley releases me. "Prepare to be dethroned, nerd spawn."

"Dethroned? That's a mighty big prediction," Trig says, "but at the end of the day, it's only empty smack talk. Care to make things more interesting?"

What does that mean?

"What did you have in mind?" Paisley asks.

"How about a friendly wager?" Trig beams.

Geo whaps him on his arm. "Stop."

"Hey, you drag me here every week." Trig tilts his head toward his wife, his eyes soft. "You may as well let me have a little fun while I'm here, being a good sport."

"You like it as much as I do." Geo smirks. "Don't even try to act like you don't."

"I like a good wager," Paisley says. "But for what?"

"If you win, you pick our Halloween costumes this year," Trig says. "You can dress Geo and me up as Bo Peep and Woody from Toy Story."

"Or Peter Pan and Tinker Bell," I whisper.

Paisley laughs out loud. "You've caught my interest. Go on."

"But if you lose," Trig says, "then—"

"You get to dress James and me?" Paisley frowns.

Trig shakes his head. "That's too easy. James will find some way to weasel out of it."

"Okay," Paisley says. "What then?"

"We get to choose what you two wear for your Christmas card photo," Geo says with a twinkle in her eye. So much for her objections to his idea of making a wager.

Luke laughs. "Oh, I like this, but I feel like, to make things fair, Pais has to send the cards to a list of your choosing."

"Thanks a lot." Paisley scowls at Luke.

"And it wouldn't be even," Luke continues, "unless Trig

and Geo had to come to a Halloween party here, at our house, with as many guests as we invite."

"Plus, they have to stay for the entire party," I say.

"I like you," Paisley says. "Did I already mention that?"

A warm feeling spreads through my chest as my social anxiety melts away. No one is teasing me, or prodding me, or asking me why I'm single, or why I'm unemployed.

"Fine," Paisley says. "It's a deal."

"This is going to be fun." Brekka's eyes sparkle.

"Keep your mouth shut," Rob says, "or we'll end up having to dress our little girl up as Baby Yoda for her birth announcements."

"Wait, we aren't already doing that?" Brekka asks. "Because I already bought that tiny Baby Yoda costume. . . "

"Alright, alright, let's get started already," Trudy's husband Paul says. "Some of us still get up and work on Saturdays."

"And some of us stay up all night with babies," Trig says. "Cry me a river."

"I think Troy is trying to prepare us for what it will be like if we ever have more." Paul groans.

"It's a phase," Trudy says. "I'm sure of it."

"He keeps waking up in the middle of night and trying to sneak food," Paul says. "Like, he thinks that if he eats at night, it doesn't count or something."

Luke's passing paper around to everyone in the circle, and he freezes. "Whoa, so what are you doing about it?"

"So far Winnie has alerted us every time he's gotten up, we think." Paul rubs his eyes. "Which is great fun."

"It's a good thing you've got Winnie," Mary says, "because with his diabetes, eating in the middle of the night could be really bad for him."

"Thanks a lot for that insightful warning," Trudy snaps. "That hadn't occurred to me a hundred times."

Mary's eyes widen.

"I'm sorry," Trudy says. "I know you're up a lot with Jack so this seems minor, but I've been a little stressed. That makes me crabby."

I suddenly love Trudy. She's the first person in this entire group who has actually seemed a little bit flawed, and consequently *real*.

"It's fine." Mary sits next to her, and like the saint she is, wraps an arm around her sister's shoulders. All is already forgiven.

Luke hands me some paper and a pen.

"Sorry if this is dense, but what's the paper for?" I ask. "I thought we were playing charades."

"Ah, right," Paisley says. "I forgot to explain. This is a special kind of charades called Fishbowl. Each person writes down five different submissions. This week, they're about literature. So you could write down, like Keating. Or Hemingway. Or, I don't know. Hester Prim."

I can't quite help my snort. "You mean Hester Prynne. Right?"

"I'm a little sketchy on American literature." Paisley bites her lip. "See why I need you?"

"Sure, sure. But then once we write them down?"

"Oh, right," Paisley says. "We drop all the papers into a fishbowl. Or in our case, a blue mixing bowl."

Mary sets a large, sky blue, ceramic bowl in the middle of the coffee table with a flourish.

"And then on the first round," Paisley says, "you draw as many papers as you can in one minute. You can say anything except the word or phrase that's on the paper."

"Okay," I say. "And?"

"And however many your team gets, you get a point for. You can't skip any. Then in round two, you can only say one word to describe the phrase."

"But it's easier, since you've already heard them all," I say.

"Exactly," Paisley says. "And then on the third round, you can't say a word. You can only act out what is on each slip of paper."

"Okay, so there are. . . " I tap my lip. "The two of us. Mary and Luke. Paul and Trudy. Rob and Brekka. Trig and Geo. Ten of us. How does that work?"

"We'll divide into two even teams, obviously," Trig says.

"But. . ."

"Mary and Luke usually end up getting split," Paisley says. "And we insist on Brekka and Trig being on opposite teams."

"Which makes our team Mary, Brekka, and Rob, and you and me," Paisley says. "And they'll have Paul and Trudy, Luke, and Trig and Geo."

"Alright," I say. "I think I get it."

Luckily, it's fairly straightforward. And even more luckily, I'm definitely, hands down, the most well versed in literature. The group consists of a tax pro, a tech nerd, an event planner, and a bunch of business experts, leaving me as the only writer. Our team is way ahead after round one, and I haven't even gotten up to read off any words yet.

"How did you know every single one?" Trig grumbles. "This isn't fair."

"I've been thinking," Paisley says. "I feel like Adam and Eve in fig leaves would be a pretty neat outfit. What do you think, Mary?"

"I was thinking Leia and Jabba, personally," Mary says. "I think it'll be pretty easy to find a gold and white bikini, and with Geo's dark hair." She shrugs innocently. I find that I like Mary more than I thought I ever could.

But Trig's team does much better on the one word round, and Paisley stops making jokes. By the time it's my turn to act out the words, we're tied. And we're entering the third round. The bowl is only half full. Paisley grabs my hand. "Girlfriend, I need you to rock this. James is going to kill me if we have to wear one of those awful costumes for our holiday cards."

I really wish I performed well under pressure. But when I draw Don Quixote, for which Trig said "windmill" last round... no one has any idea what I'm doing. I try jousting into a windmill. I try shaping one out in the air. But before I know it, my minute is gone and I've gotten . . . zero.

So of course, when Geo pops up, I hand her my slip of paper, the one that destroyed me, and she beams. "Oh." She spins her hand around in a circle and Trig immediately says, "Don Quixote. Good one, babe."

They proceed to get every other slip of paper in the entire bowl. Twenty-three points in one round.

And we're tanked.

I feel like I might puke. I can't believe I lost the whole thing for my team, and now Paisley is going to hate me. Trig and Geo are discussing options for the holiday card with Luke, and my panic deepens.

"I'm thinking Rudolph and Clarice," Geo says.

Trig taps his wife's nose with his index finger. "Oh, no, that's far too cute. No, we owe them something better. Maybe the Grinch and what's that little dog named?"

Now I know I'm going to puke. Paisley is going to kill me, and her husband is legitimately a scary person, even when you haven't caused him social pain.

Except, for some inexplicable reason, Paisley's dying laughing. She slaps her knee. "Yes. Yes! Do that one. I can see people opening those cards right now!" Tears steam down her face. "The Grinch! Green paint. Fluffy green tufts, and I'll have dog ears and antlers wrapped around my head. It's perfect."

I don't understand. "I'm sorry I screwed up," I whisper.

But Paisley doesn't even hear me, she's laughing so hard.

"Okay, we need to come up with something even better to bet about next week. Who has ideas?"

"I'm not sure that's a great plan," Trudy says.

"Oh, it is." Paul is beaming. "This is the best thing that has happened at a game night in a very long time."

"How long?" Trudy raises one eyebrow.

Paul squeezes her hand. "Of course I'm excluding our engagement, weirdo. And that wasn't really an official game night."

"And you know James is going to want a chance for revenge once he's back," Paisley says. "Some things never change."

"You have got to be kidding," Trig says. "Without Anica, you're dead in the water."

I inhale sharply to keep from crying. Is he mocking me?

"Hey, are you alright?" Paisley's eyebrows draw together, and she turns toward me slightly.

"I should go check on the kids," I say. "I'm really sorry about that last round."

She puts a hand on my forearm. "Um, we've all been stuck—but we're the ones who let you down, girl. No one blames you. You named like ninety percent of the other answers for our team. You know we'd have lost without you too, and much worse, right?"

I stand up, trying my best not to start crying in front of all these people right here. "Sure. Totally."

"Seriously," Geo says. "Once Trig drew the word 'Snickers.' No one could figure out what he was trying to do. A full minute of him scrunching his face up and grabbing his belly."

"He looked so constipated," Mary says. "Oh man."

Paul and Luke start laughing, talking about when Luke got stuck on the word 'scrum,' whatever that even means. And for the first time, I wonder if maybe they're serious. Maybe they really don't care.

"Are you leaving?" Trudy stands too. "I'm sure the kids are fine. Believe me, Amy knows how to work the remote when the movie they're watching ends. She might be better with it than I am."

I blink. "Well, I mean, I figured once charades was over—"

"Oh, we'll play Balderdash next," Paisley says. "I bet you're pretty good at that one too. Have you ever played before?"

I shake my head, but don't confess that I don't have many friends.

"We'll explain it," Mary says. "It's really fun."

So I stick around and let the laughter and smiles wash over me. In a strange way, it's exactly what I needed. To be surrounded by people who seem to genuinely want me around, even if I don't have a job. Even if I'm a sponger. Even if I can't even get hired as a waitress.

When Trig yawns and Geo stands up, I'm surprised at how disappointed I am. "We better head home. The sitter has some kind of yoga class in the morning."

"Plus, I need to sleep," Geo says.

"Beauty sleep?" I ask. "How long do you sleep, exactly?" I shrug. "I'm asking for a friend."

Trig's laugh is so loud, I actually jump. Seconds later, everyone is laughing. "Good one," Brekka says. "Because you're not the only one who wants to know. Unfortunately, I doubt any of us could sleep long enough. Ever."

"Right?" I say. "So unfair."

"Totally," Mary says.

"Hey, what are you doing Monday?" Trudy asks.

"Monday?" I frown. I can't very well say I have absolutely zero plans for the next . . . forever. "I, uh—"

"Yes," Geo says. "You should totally come with us!"

"Come with you?" I repeat dumbly.

"Geo has to go try out restaurants before big events and

report back to her clients, so the meal is totally free," Trudy says. "It's like my new favorite thing. She introduces me to all the best places, for free. And they thank us for going!"

"You're kidding," I say.

Trudy shakes her head. "Now you're wondering how she's so skinny eating out for free all the time, right? We all want to know."

"Oh please," Geo says. "Stop. But seriously, we're going to lunch at that place off Peachtree with the gorgeous fountains in the gardens."

"I'm not super familiar with Atlanta yet," I say. "It's changed a lot since I was here last."

"I'll send you the address," Trudy says. "If you want to come."

I really shouldn't go when it's clear they're inviting me out of pity, but saying no feels rude. "Sure," I finally say. I can always cancel Monday morning. Stomach bug, sore tooth, hangover, car trouble. A million ways to get out of it that don't involve looking them in the eye and saying no.

"Wonderful," Geo says, like she really means it.

For the first time in a long time, after I help get Amy and Chase to bed, I don't have any trouble falling asleep.

The next morning, when I open my laptop, my hand hovers over the Scrivener file, interested in opening it to start writing for the first time in a very long time. Thinking about last night makes me want to write witty banter, for some reason. Or a story about flawed characters who still deeply love someone else. Probably a person who's as broken as they are—a pair of bookends who heal the pain in the other effortlessly.

But then Patrick's words the last time he saw me open up Scrivener to write leap into my brain, like a punch in the gut. *Oh, wait, are you going to write something meaningful this time?* He was so hopeful. So desperate for his girlfriend to write a book that wouldn't be embarrassing for him to share.

Witty banter, redeeming love—another romance. So no, nothing meaningful, not me. My excitement fizzles like stale soda.

I close my laptop and spend the day with Amy, playing with Alpha, a bossy Rhode Island Red chicken, Hope, her miracle Andalusian grey hen, and Midnight, the black and white striped Cuckoo Marans, who really is a little cuckoo. She pecks at everything, but especially my toes. "Who would have thought chickens would be so much fun," I ask.

"I knew," Amy says.

"You didn't." I roll my eyes. "You were just like me, blithely eating eggs with toast, with no idea how funny the critters who made them really can be."

"I didn't know the eggs came in so many colors," Amy says. "But I knew they were funny little critters. I've seen *Moana*."

I laugh. "Good thing they aren't as dopey as that rooster."

"Right?" Amy pets Hope's back, and her little dove grey hen makes a funny clucking sound that obviously means she's content.

But on Sunday, when Amy and Chase, Mary and Luke, and baby Jack all go to church, I'm left alone. Just me and my laptop. I really should try and write the story I've been working on for the past few years.

"Your words matter," Lizzie told me right before she died. "They have more power to change this world than anything I'll ever do."

Except she was wrong. My words are crap, and her two children are already changing the world for the better. She bet on the wrong horse—her faith in her little sister clouded her judgment. Guilt hits me like a two-by-four to the face and I drag myself to my room and force myself to open up the file on *Ashes,* a story about the fleeting nature of life and the absolute certainty of death.

No words come easily. I struggle for every single one, but I don't give up. I grind them out, one agonizing thought at a time.

When Amy comes to tell me that dinner is ready, I can't shut my laptop down quickly enough. But afterward, when I return to my room, I check the total word count at the bottom of the scene I worked on for most of the day.

Six hundred and twelve.

In six and a half hours, I wrote a little over two pages. At this rate, I'll finish the novel in . . . ninety-six and a half years. I slam the laptop closed, trying to ignore the nagging fear that they aren't even very good words.

My book stinks.

Just like me.

My watch buzzes, and I realize I've got a new email. I don't bother opening my laptop. I check it on my phone. An interview to work as a waitress at one of the restaurants I applied for—Golden Gloves. That sounds promising. I agree to meet them after the lunch rush on Wednesday, and then I look them up online. I applied to so many, I can't recall details about any of them, but fancy gloves sounds promising. The nicer the place, the better the tips.

Unfortunately, inexplicably, it's a *diner*.

What kind of diner calls itself Golden Gloves?

Ugh. This is my life now. A failed writer turned diner waitress. But at least it will pay me something, and then I can be a failed writer turned diner waitress who has her own apartment instead of one who sponges off her brother-in-law.

Former brother-in-law?

Am I still Luke's sister-in-law now that my sister has died? The idea is so horribly depressing that I throw a blanket over my head and go to sleep without even brushing my teeth.

The next morning I wake up before six a.m. I know I ought to write again. Even six hundred words is better than no words, and once I finish this manuscript, I can start querying and find a new agent. I need to get out there and try to turn my real career around.

But I ought to feed the chickens, and let them out of the coop to scratch around the back yard before I start. And then Andy needs food. And I hear the chickens singing, which means they've likely laid, at least one of them. When I find a dark speckled brown egg sitting right alongside a white egg, I decide I ought to go ahead and make breakfast for everyone. I mean, what's better than fresh eggs?

But finally, once Luke is at work and Mary is working away in her home office, and Jack is asleep, and Amy and Chase are busily coloring, and even Andy has closed her eyes with a sigh, I have no more excuses. I trudge toward my room, preparing myself mentally to write the words. The epic, important, meaningful words that I need to write so that I can prove Patrick wrong and prove Lizzie right and everyone will finally see that I'm not a fluff writer. I have value.

Except the very second my fingers touch the laptop, my phone bings. It's Trudy, with the address for lunch.

I totally forgot to cancel on her. I should cancel right now, even if I'm rudely late. My fingers itch to type the words that will get me out of another awkward social interaction. There's pretty much no chance that Mary's *sister* and her friend really want to have lunch with me. They're trying to help the poor pathetic mooch who won't leave Mary's house.

Ugh.

But if I stay home, I've got to write the words. Epic

words. Words that will awe and inspire. Words that will change the world.

ON MY WAY, I type instead, trying not to think too much about why.

And then I'm stuck going to lunch with two people who don't want to see me at all.

When I park my battered little Honda Civic, Cashew, in between a Mercedes convertible and a BMW SUV, I begin to wonder whether my pink blouse and dark jeans are going to be far too casual. As I pass grand fountains and perfectly manicured hedges, and as my black flats squeak across the white marble floors in the foyer of the Riviera Grand, I *know* I'm underdressed.

I whip out my phone and start to tap out a last minute excuse. CAR TROUB—

"Anica!"

I whip my head toward the yell.

"Hey girl, I'm over here." She waves. Even Geo's shouting doesn't seem vulgar. How is that possible?

I delete the text with trembling fingers. It would be just like me to send that text half written, like a moron, and then scramble to try and explain it away unsuccessfully.

Of course Geo's wearing a white sundress that perfectly shows off her gorgeous tan, bright blue eyes, and raven's wing black hair. If I didn't know it for a fact, I'd never believe she had a baby two and a half months ago. Some things in life are unfair, but other things, like Geo's existence, are *monumentally* unfair.

"Oh, you made it!" Trudy's white high heels clack loudly against the marble. Somehow, even though she looks cute and casual in her handkerchief dress and heeled sandals, I feel more at ease. Trudy just projects a sense of normalcy wherever she goes.

"I did, thanks for the address," I say.

"I've heard their strawberries wild salad is to die for," Geo says.

"Of course she loves salad." Trudy winks at me as she pulls out a chair and plonks down on it.

"It's got a poppy seed dressing and candied walnuts," Geo says. "It barely counts as a salad—it's almost a dessert."

"I like my desserts without a side of spinach," Trudy says. "But you've sold me on trying it as a side."

"How are their burgers?" I sling my purse over the back of an unclaimed chair.

"Amazing." A squatty waiter with a shock of blonde hair that sticks straight up in the air hands me a menu. "As are our sweet potato fries."

"I *love* sweet potato fries," Trudy says.

"So do I," I say.

And lunch is so much better than sitting in front of my laptop—from the juicy cheeseburger, to the cinnamon and sugar sprinkled sweet potato fries, to the conversation.

"So what are the odds you choose this venue?" I ask.

"The bride and groom wanted me to be sure and try the stuffed mushrooms and the strawberry salad," Geo says, "and I thought both were excellent."

"So will you do the wedding here?"

"I'll need to bring them to confirm that they like the lighting and the banquet hall I have in mind, but I think it's likely."

"Not a waste of resources by the restaurant then," Trudy says. "That makes me feel better for being completely stuffed and not spending a dime."

Geo waves the waiter over. "I absolutely loved the food. I'd love to set up another lunch for next Tuesday, so that the bride and groom can make a final decision."

"I'm so happy you were pleased," he says. "But unfortunately, after this Saturday, we'll no longer be serving lunch. Could I reserve a dinner time?"

Geo blinks. "Not serving lunch? Why ever not?"

The pinched look on the blonde, puffy-haired waiter's face makes it clear he's not a fan of the new plan either. "Apparently the profit margins aren't high enough to justify the expense."

"That's a terrible decision," Geo says. "Lunch isn't about the profit margin on the particular meal as much as it is about keeping your clientele happy."

"Well, maybe you can march into his office and tell our new manager that, because everyone else is afraid of Mr. Trainor."

Geo's full lips part and her eyes widen. "Wait." Her eyes narrow. "Mr. Trainor? Is his name, by chance, Ethan Trainor?"

Blonde puff nearly drops the mostly empty pitcher of water he's holding as his arm goes slack. He's lucky the pitcher wasn't full, or he'd have soaked Geo. "I think it is."

"Does he look like a blonde surfer-guy?"

He nods dumbly.

"Tell Mr. High and Mighty Ethan Trainor that a patron would like to file a formal complaint. Tell him I'm livid and insist on speaking with him personally."

"Should I tell him your name?" Blonde puff's eyes tighten and the water at the bottom of the pitcher shakes a little, betraying his hand tremble.

Geo bites her lip. "What fun would that be?" She beams, and I suddenly can't wait to see how this plays out.

❊ 4 ❊

ETHAN

The air in Atlanta hits me in the face like an open-palm slap.

I'd almost forgotten how hard the summer in Georgia tries to suffocate me, but the dense, heavy air as I walk down the steps of the plane reminds me right quick.

"You made it." Dad's standing at the bottom of the stairs.

"You're here, waiting on me?" I narrow my eyes. This is not typical behavior for him. Not at all. "What's going on?"

Partner barks and barks and barks at him, until I command her to stop and sit. Dad uses the distraction to grab one of my suitcases, which is already resting on the ground. His flight crew is efficient—no surprise there. "There has to be something wrong for me to be eager to see you?"

I shake my head. "I mean, no. I guess not, but it's weird that you're here waiting on me in the middle of a business day."

"You arrived on my jet. I figured the least I could do was ensure it actually arrived safely."

One of the greatest perks of having a rich adoptive

father: use of a private jet. "Thanks for sending it for me."

"I'm glad you're here." He'll never say that he's missed me and he loves me, but I know that's what he means.

I expected him to have aged in the twelve months that have passed since I last saw him, especially with his talk of the years catching up to him, but he looks and sounds exactly the same as he did when he came out to Hawaii last summer: broad shoulders, thick, wavy, dark brown hair, and small, delicate wrinkles framing his bright, golden eyes. He looks and sounds as strong and steady as ever.

"I'm not relocating permanently," I remind him. "I'm here until I'm sure Adriana is safe from *him* and this new hotel is in good shape."

"I know."

"Alright, then."

"You packed pretty heavily for someone who isn't staying." He rubs Partner's head. "And you brought your dog."

"I couldn't just leave her in Hawaii for an undetermined period," I say. "And if I'm here for very long, I'll need cold weather clothes too, so I brought some. Sweaters are bulky."

"You had sweaters in Hawaii?" Dad asks.

"It's not like I was going to rent a storage unit when I moved," I say.

"If you really didn't mean to come back, why didn't you toss them?"

He's trying to distract me, which means. . . "Something else is wrong," I say. "Just tell me what it is."

"Nothing's wrong," he says. "But I do have a small bit of news."

"What?" I knew it.

"I called the warden."

My grip tightens on both my suitcase handle and the end of Partner's leash. "Why?"

"Your sister is giddy about meeting *him* on his release

date."

"I know. That's the real reason I came."

"I thought it prudent to arrange an earlier release—one she's not aware is happening."

I've never wanted to hug Dad more than I do right now. "Brilliant," I say. "Did it work? Did the warden agree?"

"For a generous donation to the facility, he was willing to release Phillip three days early."

I blink. "That's tomorrow."

"I'm glad your flight made it without any hiccups and that you're here. I imagine you'll have a few things to say to him when he's released."

I've been planning to see him, but I thought I had more time to prepare. Knowing he'll be released tomorrow, well. I'm just surprised, that's all. "I do."

"Good. Well, I won't bother you more, then."

"Can your driver take me to the Riviera Grand? I'd like to check in today."

"Actually, I arranged to have your car brought here. You can drive yourself."

My car? "I don't have a car here, remember? I need to call Enterprise."

Dad smiles. "No, you don't. Let's call it a welcome home present."

Oh, no. This is the man I remember. Overly generous, with a strong dose of heavy handed. "Please tell me that you didn't buy me a car."

"Why would that upset you?" He shakes his head. "I swear, it's like you look for reasons to get mad."

"I told you I'm not staying. I don't want to own a car here, but if I did, I could buy one for myself. I'm thirty years old, Dad."

"Well, once you're done with your hissy fit, you can follow me to the car I bought you in an unparalleled act of heinous villainy."

I sigh. How does he always succeed in making me feel like a petulant baby when I'm in the right? I grit my teeth and follow him to the parking lot, where a dark blue Porsche 911 Carrera 4S Cabriolet waits for me, the top already down. All it's missing is a neon sign that says "midlife crisis underway—trying way too hard to act like a high-roller."

But I don't sigh or make a fuss. It wouldn't matter if I did.

"I know how you hate red, so look. I bought you a blue one."

"Red is just fine. It's Porsches I don't like," I can't quite keep from pointing out. "And my suitcases won't even fit inside it."

"Oh, please. Everyone loves Porsches once they get behind the wheel. Drive this one for a day, and if you still hate it, I'll take it back for myself. I don't have this one in blue." He hands my suitcase to his driver, Raul. "My driver will drop your suitcases off for you. Don't worry about that."

Sometimes I wish he could step out of his body and listen to the words coming out of his mouth. How practical is a car that won't even hold my *two* suitcases? And he doesn't have this one . . . *in blue*?!? But pointing those things out as excessive is pointless. "Thanks, Dad. I'm sure it's wonderful." And the second I leave, he can have it back. At least it'll spare me the trouble of renting something. "I'm really grateful."

"I'll text you the address of your house."

I nearly choke. "My what?"

"You said you were bringing your dog." He tries not to stumble over the word, but not quite hard enough. He hates pets and always has. "You can't keep that thing at the Riviera Grand, obviously."

Is he serious? "I'll tell people she's a service dog." When

I open the door, she races up and into the passenger seat, drool slinging across the dash and onto the seat with a plop.

Dad shudders. "I will never understand why you want . . . that bouncy, slobbery *thing* with you."

"No, and it's okay that you don't understand all the human things. Cyborgs often struggle with ideas of affection and connection."

He rolls his eyes.

Well, even if he thinks my dog is bizarre, plenty of things about him make no sense to me either. "I appreciate you lining up a rental home, but I can find my own lodging —even with my dog along."

"Now who's being bullheaded? I found a nice, clean, comfortable house less than five miles away from the hotel."

"And you rented it for me."

"Of course not. We don't *rent*."

"Please tell me you didn't buy it for me." My tone is as flat and calm as I can make it.

"Of course I did. I'd hardly buy it for myself." It never even occurred to him that I might not want him to buy me a house, as a thirty-year-old man. Clearly he doesn't believe that I can take care of myself in any way.

"Well, I'll let you know how it goes with Phillip tomorrow." I start to slide into the driver's seat of my new, ridiculously shiny sports car.

His hand grips my shoulder. "Be careful," he says. "He's a dangerous man."

"So am I." I shake him off.

"I know you are," he says. "But I didn't mean physically dangerous. If you need to talk, tell me. I'll meet you wherever, whenever."

I swallow, buckle up, and drive away.

Dad hasn't ever lived in the real world with us plebeians, but he means well. And he might be on to something with this overpriced convertible. The wind in my hair doesn't feel nearly as humid racing past at eighty. The roaring of the engine makes my heart accelerate pleasantly, and the looks of envy from passengers in the cars I pass lift my spirits.

I don't want to keep it, but it's fun on a temporary basis.

"What do you think, Partner? What will this house look like?"

She barks by way of response, her eyes as happy as I've ever seen them, checking out every single thing we pass with a lolling tongue and rapidly billowing fur. I'm pleasantly surprised when the house is large without being ostentatious, and it's centrally located, in an older but well maintained neighborhood, the central streets all lined with huge, majestic live oaks. You can't even see the neighborhood from the main roads, it's so tucked into a tiny corner.

Plenty of dogs bark at Partner, and she barks happily back. There's even a dog door that leads into the securely fenced back yard of the new place.

All in all, I don't feel too bad about leaving Partner while I check out the state of things at the Riviera Grand. Dad wasn't exaggerating that it's a mess, but it's nothing I can't handle.

Which leaves me more time than I wish I had to think about Phillip's release tomorrow.

But no amount of thinking leaves me feeling prepared. The next morning, I try on six different things before settling on a black t-shirt and jeans with heavy black boots. I'm not dressing up for him, and I don't want him thinking any part of me is happy to see him. Funeral garb, without being nicely respectable, it is.

The entire drive, no matter how hard I try, memories keep popping into my mind like a miserable game of past horrors whack-a-mole.

Christmas morning, when he gave me a bright green

guitar and showed me how to play a few power chords.

New Year's Eve, when he let me light off fireworks, and then cheered as they exploded overhead.

My eighth birthday, when Mom and Phillip took me to adopt a dog. I loved that beagle puppy more than anything.

Until Adriana was born the next year.

Two weeks after Adriana came home, Philip used my green guitar to smash a hole in the wall right next to Mom's head. Even the good memories are twisted with the bad. My hands grip the steering wheel so tightly, I wonder if I'll damage the leather.

I'm close to the prison when the night I'll never forget flashes across my mind. Phillip, his lip curled, his teeth shining brightly in the dark, yelling at Mom for flirting with the fifty-year-old neighbor who had cleared the driveway of snow. I should have stood up for her. I should have told him she wasn't flirting, that she was just grateful that he had helped her out so she wouldn't be late for work.

But I was too afraid of Phillip to defend my own mother.

I shake my head. It's been eighteen years. I'm bigger, and Phillip is older. Unlike Dad, he's probably aged significantly. Of course, there's a chance he's gotten tougher and scarier in prison. He's only fifty. He was only two years older than I am now when he was locked up—

But even if he's just as tough, just as scary, I'm not a little boy anymore. I'm a champion boxer. I'm a successful businessman. A college graduate. A son. And most importantly, a brother. That's why I'm here. To make sure Phillip never hurts another woman close to me. Never again will I fail to protect a woman I love.

My hands shake when I shove the Carrera into park outside Hancock State Prison in Sparta, Georgia. It looks nothing like I imagined it would. The drive took longer than I expected, thanks to the Atlanta traffic, and I'm ten minutes late. I assume the prison warden will wait until I arrive to release him, seeing as Dad made a huge contribution to the prison for an early release.

But, of course he didn't.

Phillip is standing near the bus stop at the edge of the parking lot when I step out of my car. I might not have recognized him, except that he's wearing the same shirt he had on *that night*. It's clean—no blood at all—but it's the same navy blue polo shirt he was wearing when he killed my mom.

I've imagined this scene a million times. A billion. The moment I come face to face with my horrifying birth father —the man who raised me until I was twelve years old—as an adult. He was a scrappy musician who fought better than he rocked and drank better than both combined. I would finally punch him in the nose, shattering cartilage and bone, repaying him in small part for the pain he has inflicted on my world.

But he's not the man I remember.

He smaller. He's covered in tattoos. And he looks so sad and . . . so broken. And when he hears me walking his direction and he turns to face me, his eyes widen.

Not with fear, like I hoped. Not with guilt, or remorse, or anger. No matter how many times I imagined this happening, I never considered he'd look at me with joy or hope.

"Son?" He sets a small black canvas bag on the concrete bench.

My lip curls when he calls me son.

"They changed my release date. I didn't know if anyone would even realize. . . I'm surprised you came for me."

I've probably imagined this moment a thousand times. Ten thousand. But now that I'm here, every single plan I made, every single cutting word I imagined that I'd eviscerate him with . . . evaporates. Vapor. Mist. Smoke. Gone.

"I didn't *come* for you." I'm not sure why I'm focusing on that word, but it's what caught my attention. "I wouldn't have come at all, if it was up to me."

He frowns, the hopeful look sliding off his face in a very satisfying way. I didn't realize how badly I wanted to hurt him, not just physically, but in every single way, until right now. I want to laugh with complete joy at the raw, baffled injury.

"I'm here for only one reason."

"You're angry."

"You killed my mother," I whisper. "Of course I'm angry. Did you think I'd bring flowers?"

He shakes his head.

"I came here to tell you that Adriana doesn't see you for who you are. You've been writing her, but that's not the same as *knowing* you like I do. You may have duped her, but you'll never fool me."

He looks at his feet, his shiny black shoes shifting. Something about the submissive gesture hurts me, like I'm kicking a puppy, or crunching a beetle.

Like I'm the villain.

"Do you hear me?" My hands ball into fists. "Do you understand what I'm telling you right now?"

He clears his throat. "You don't want me to see Adriana."

"I arranged for you to get out early so she wouldn't be here. I'll ensure that they don't share your parole information and your whereabouts with her. I don't want you to see her, and I don't want you to call her. Is that clear?"

He looks up at me, his eyebrows drawing together. He holds his hands out, palms up. "Do you know how men come out of Hancock State Prison?"

"Excuse me?" I ask.

"They come out three different ways. Better, worse. Or not at all."

I swallow. "Clever. Since you're here, why don't you tell me how you're coming out."

"I wouldn't presume to tell you anything at all. You're all grown up, no thanks to me. But I think you'll agree I had no way to go but up when I was locked away. I was about as bad a person as they get."

I can't argue with him there. "If you think I'll forgive you—"

His laugh is bitter. "I don't expect miracles, son."

I flinch. "Stop calling me that. I am not your son. You are not my father. I have a father, a legal father, and it's not you."

When I look up at him, his hands are trembling and his lip wobbles. "Okay."

"I want you to promise me that you won't attempt to contact Adriana."

His face falls, his eyes shining with unshed tears. "I promise."

Good. "For whatever your word is worth."

"My word is all I have," he says. "I won't try to contact her, but I also won't turn her away if she finds me."

Every muscle in my body tenses, and a familiar feeling rushes through me. An overwhelming urge to hit something. To crush, and destroy, and shred. My heart thunders in my ears, and my breathing become shallower. I haven't suffered from a fit of uncontrollable rage in a very long time, but I remember what to do. I don't get in my car. That much speed is too dangerous right now.

No, I take off down the street that runs alongside the prison at a jog.

Phillip calls after me, but I ignore him. I run past the battered silver bus that will carry him to whatever crap hole they lined up for him. I run past the miles of sweet corn, and cotton, and wheat fields, almost ready to be harvested. I run past a small gas station, and then I keep running. I run until a blister rises on my heel, and sweat circles form under my arms, and finally, finally my heart rate steadies and my fury is contained.

By the time I finally turn around and head back toward my car, my anger is all but gone. I'm worried that if Adriana doesn't keep her distance from Phillip, it'll return, maybe even stronger. Or maybe in a place where I can't simply run away.

Which means I have to talk to her, but not today.

After I drive home and shower, I throw myself into repairing the mess at the Riviera Grand. The next day, I keep on working. I should call Adriana and explain that Phillip has already been released and beg her to stay away, but I can't quite bring myself to do it. I have another day before I really *have* to call her.

I'm reviewing the updated marketing plan when a ridiculous looking man with a huge fluff of blonde hair on top of his head knocks on my door.

"Yes?" I shouldn't scowl, given how terrified he already looks.

"Sir, um, there's a woman in the restaurant complaining. Loudly. She'd really like to talk to you."

"To me?" I can't help my frown. "How does she even know who I am?"

"Well." When he swallows, his Adam's apple bobs prominently. "I might have mentioned—"

Never mind. I stand up. I'd like to set someone down, as it happens. Might as well be this woman, demanding to talk to the manager for some idiotic insufficiency. "It's fine. Show me to her."

The idiotic looking waiter bobs his head. "Right this way."

I run through a list in my head of the things a dissatisfied customer might complain about as we approach, and I dig deep for a little extra patience. I really shouldn't spend my third day in a new place screaming at a customer. I'll apologize, no matter what she's angry about, but I'm not comping her meal unless we've actually done something wrong.

And the manager of the restaurant is going to get a piece of my mind about his wait staff hunting me down and paging me like I'm some kind of runner-monkey. What's the point of even having a restaurant management team on site if they don't handle this sort of thing? We approach a table with three seated women. A very attractive blonde, a remarkably cute brunette, and a shining black haired woman whose back is to me. They're all very nicely dressed, which means the odds of the upset woman being an entitled whiner just doubled. I try not to groan preemptively.

I clear my throat instead. "I hear one of you wanted to talk to me?"

The blonde meets my eyes, and then ducks her head immediately. Not her, then. The brunette smiles broadly, but she doesn't reply.

"I'm very, very unhappy with the service we received today," the dark haired woman says without turning. "I demand you fire the chef, the wait staff, *and* the hostess. I'm not sure that *you* should retain your job, frankly, if what I've seen so far is any indication of your skill level."

The brunette bites her lip and looks down at her feet.

The blonde looks like a deer about to be hit by a car. A very large, very horrifying truck.

Who is this woman who shouts at me without even facing me?

"Ma'am, if you could turn around, it might be easier for you to tell me why you want me to fire my entire staff and hand in my own resignation. What exactly did any of them do wrong?"

The woman stands up melodramatically, squares her shoulders, and then spins around with a smile on her stunning face. The laugh starts in my belly and then moves upward. I don't even realize how badly I need a comedic break until this very second. "Done," I say. "I'll fire them immediately, and once I get things in order, I promise that I'll quit too."

"Was that so hard?" Geo asks.

"Actually, I've been looking for a reason. We're cutting lunch next week, so I won't need as many servers, chefs, or hosts."

Geo puts a hand on her hip. "And now you've hit on what we need to discuss. How can you cut lunch when I've only just found this restaurant? I love it, you big dope. Don't eliminate it."

"What?"

"Sit down here with us so we can convince you to change your mind." Geo sits and points at the chair next to the blond, who still won't meet my eye.

I comply. "Who are your friends?"

"My friend Trudy." Geo gestures at the brunette. "She's a computer whiz, in case you need some freelance—"

"I have zero time for extra work," Trudy says. "If I even tried to take on another client, Paul would never talk to you again, G, but thanks for the attempted referral."

"The best ones are always already taken," I say.

"There are exceptions to every rule," Geo says. "And on that note, let me introduce Anica. She's a single, New York Times bestselling novelist, and she agrees with me. You shouldn't get rid of the lunch here."

"The burger was great," Anica says.

"And the strawberry salad is the best I've ever had," Geo says. "It would be practically criminal to limit it to dinner alone."

"I do want to stay out of prison." I can't quite help making a reference no one else will understand. "And I love keeping beautiful ladies happy." Even if there's no way I want to get involved with anyone in Atlanta. I'm getting this mess sorted and flying back to Hawaii ASAP.

"Actually maybe you *should* shut it down," Geo says. "Anica said she's been dealing with some writer's block on her current novel."

"How are those two things related?" I glance around to see whether Geo's been downing a lot of wine with lunch.

The blonde blushes in an adorable way. I doubt most bestselling novelists get embarrassed about writer's block. I think it's probably a pretty common thing. I would have expected her to be an insufferable snob, not a nervous, blushing lady.

"Well, if you insist on shutting down lunch, the terrible decision could inspire her. She might even write you into her next bestseller. I can see it now. The villain will be a handsome, blonde, corporate suit who fires a bunch of people to finance his second Porsche, leaving the waiters and hosts and chefs unable to make rent."

I try not to cringe over the Porsche stereotype I now fit, thanks to Dad. They have no way of knowing about that. "You really are a novelist?" I ask. "What kinds of books do you write?"

Anica blushes again and knots the napkin in her hand. "I'm working on a general fiction novel right now about surviving loss and grief. I'm not sure I'd be able to work corporate greed into the plot without overbalancing the narrative pretty badly."

"Wow, deep stuff," I say. "Well, I'd hate to inspire another novel in which I'm the villain. I can hear the reveal you'd make now, from a couch across from Oprah, that I'm the inspiration for your modern day Jean Valjean. Then instead of just hating myself, the whole world would hate me, too." I shake my head in what I hope is a very self-effacing way. "What if you ladies give me some suggestions for how to draw a larger lunch crowd, and in exchange I'll keep lunch around for another month while I try implementing them?"

"I'll accept that." Geo stands up. "But we've got to head out right now. If you want our thoughts, maybe you can set something up with Anica. We'll pass all our ideas along to her, and you can pry them out of her over lunch. She *did* say she'll need more strawberry salad very soon."

Geo couldn't be more obvious, but I don't mind being set up, even if it's highly unlikely to go anywhere with me moving back to Hawaii. "I think I could do that." Anica still isn't looking at me. "If she wants to meet me for lunch, that is."

She finally looks up, her cornflower blue eyes widening when they meet mine. "Sure, if you're not too busy."

"Never too busy to spend an hour listening to ideas on how to improve my business." I wink. "How about Wednesday?"

She nods, and as if I've missed some secret signal, Trudy and Anica stand up in unison.

"We won't keep you any longer," Geo says. "I'm sure you're very busy." She leans closer. "I'm proud of you, Ethan. You look as if you've finally grown up."

Hiding from my sister, threatening my father, and going for a five-mile jog to keep from beating him to a pulp. . . I wish she was right, but I'm fairly certain she's dead wrong. I wave as they walk out. "See you Wednesday," I say.

When she turns back to return the gesture, Anica's eyelashes flutter and she half smiles. I've taken out women who seemed less excited to spend time with me, but not many.

I'm almost back to my office when I hear a voice I've been dreading. "How long have you been in town? Dad didn't say a word."

Adriana.

So much for having one more drama-free day.

$\maltese$ 5 $\maltese$

ETHAN

"Hey, there," I say.

My little sister pounces immediately, hugging me with all the excitement of a new college grad. She really does act her part perfectly: the fresh-faced college graduate with her entire life spreading out before her. "You should have texted me. I'd have met your plane."

"How did you even know I'm here?" Phillip better not have called her. I walk into my office and she follows.

"Dad." She rolls her eyes. "Duh."

I blink. "You said Dad didn't say a word."

"About you coming early, I mean. He let it slip today that you had a meeting with him at three, so obviously. . ."

"Ah, right." I forgot how Ana skips from topic to topic like a bumblebee in the spring. They used to think she suffered from a learning delay, but she aced all the tests. She just thinks faster than she talks, which leads to some disconnects for the mere mortals around her.

"So why'd you come in early? And why didn't you tell me?" She puts one hand on her hip and arches an eyebrow imperiously. "Confess."

I should just rip the Band-Aid off, but I'm worried

about how she'll react. I sit down, but not in my desk chair—I collapse into one of the heavy leather wing chairs facing my desk and point for her to take the other one.

"Oh, no. This is one of those sit down kind of discussions?" She sighs heavily and plops into the chair. "Spill already."

I've thought of a dozen lies, some of them fairly convincing, but I can't do it. After what we've endured, I can't lie to her. "Dad got Phillip released early."

Her brow furrows. "Wait, when? Today? Is that the meeting at three? Why?"

I hold up one hand. "Slow down, officer."

"How about you speed up, tortoise." She leans toward me. "What's going on?"

"You don't know Phillip," I say. "Not like I do, and not like Dad does."

"Dad doesn't know him at all. Dad cut Mom off when she married Phillip. Did you know that? Dad's not the nice, perfect guy he wants us to think he is."

"You know, we may be the only people in America with our mom and her *brother* on our birth certificates." When I realized that adoption by Dad changed the name of the father on our birth certificate, I looked at mine. It's true. Mother, Juliette Trainor. Father, William Trainor. Kind of gross, honestly, even though I know that biologically we're not Dad's kids.

"What are you even talking about? Stop blathering and tell me what's going on with Phillip." She stands up and begins to pace. "And don't try to pre-explain or justify what you've done. Just tell me what it is and let me decide what I think."

"It's not an explanation of what I did," I say. "It's history, plain and simple. Phillip beat us—not once or twice, but regularly. He killed mom, Ana. And he'd have done the same to you and me if Dad hadn't gotten us out of there."

"Dad's not perfect either."

My laugh sounds more like a bark. "Do you think I don't know that?" I stand up, too. "But he convinced the warden to let Phillip out early so I could talk to him alone."

"You had no right to do that. You don't know him at all, not anymore. Do you honestly think that eighteen years in prison wouldn't completely transform him?" Her eyes flash. "Inmates only come out of prison three ways. Better, worse—"

"Or not at all?"

Ana splutters. "What—look—"

"He fed me that corny line too, okay? Listen, he's always been charming. Why do you think Mom married him? He was the life of every party, but he had a temper then, and that kind of thing doesn't just disappear. He's not safe, and you need to promise me not to see him or talk to him."

She folds her arms. "No."

"What do you mean, no?"

"Dad took him away from me when I was little, but I've been writing him for years, and I know him, and he's changed and you've ignored it. Fine, that's your choice. But I don't have to do what you say." She narrows her eyes at me. "I'm twenty-two, and I have my first real job and you're not my boss or my dad. Actually, Dad isn't either, for that matter."

"He is, in every way that matters."

"You're worse than he is," Ana says.

"Which he?" My nostrils flare.

"Take your pick."

"I'm nothing like any of our parents." But as I say the words, I'm not entirely sure. I've got Phillip's anger, Dad's manipulation, and Mom's avoidance issues. What if I'm the worst of all of them?

"I know you love me, Ethan, but you can't control me. I'll call the warden and find out where Dad is, and I'll go see him myself, and there's nothing you can do to stop it from happening."

"I'll kill him myself to keep you safe if that's what it takes," I say. "And there's not a man in America who would convict me." I was bluffing, but as I say the words, I realize that part of me is entirely serious.

Ana steps toward me and grabs my forearm with her small hand. "You'll do nothing of the sort, and furthermore, you don't need to. Phillip isn't a threat to me, I promise."

She can't know that—he turns on the flip of a coin. Happy, exciting, and fun, and then a split second later, angry. Terrifying. Always predictable in only one way: his unpredictability. "Ana, I know you think—"

"I'm done talking about this." She crosses her arms.

She's right that if I don't respect her wishes, I'm as bad as our dad. And if I try and stop her physically or by threatening or attacking Phillip, I'm as bad as our sperm donor.

After I saw Phillip, I literally shook with rage. But now, knowing that Adriana is giving him a second chance he doesn't deserve, I practically quiver with it. I need to surf, badly. I need the perfection of a long, calming tunnel. I need the peace of the ocean and surf and sun. But there's no way to find that, not here. A run doesn't feel like it will be enough, not by a long shot, but I don't have any better ideas. After Ana finally leaves, I change into my gym clothes and head out the front door of the Riviera Grand.

About two miles from the hotel, I realize I've turned down a street I knew well eight years ago. Too well.

Even so, the sight of the dark red brick facade—the same bright golden letters across the front window—the sweaty guys streaming in and out, it stops me dead in my tracks. I spent every afternoon here while I was attending

Emory. Before I have time to rethink, my feet carry me inside.

The smells crash over me, each of them attached to a memory. Sweat. The speed bag. Leather. A glove connecting with my jaw. Blood. Spit from my mouth on the mat. Dirt. Under my nails, on the side of my face, and clinging to every part of my body. Spit. Never on the mat, or Harrison would gut us, but outside, or on an opponent's face if no one is watching. And on the heels of all that, my worst failure since that night.

I turn to leave as quickly as I entered.

"You look like you've seen a ghost," a scratchy voice says. I scan the room, my eyes sliding past the same four rings I knew, the same aluminum ductwork ceiling, the same huge fans overhead, and finally I spot the guy who spoke. He's clean-shaven, bald, and lean—obviously a fighter, which makes sense given my location. He's probably middleweight, maybe a hundred and eighty pounds.

"Oh, no, nothing like that," I say. "I just got lost. Pardon me."

"Got lost." He snorts. "Sure you did."

My hands clench into fists reflexively, my heart accelerating against my will.

"How'd you like to go a few rounds? I love trying my luck on fresh faces. They're in short supply around here lately." He stands up straight, and I revise my assessment. He's closer to 200 pounds. Light heavyweight, just like me when I was fighting.

"I was just going for a run," I lie.

"But you're a fighter," the man says. "I can see it in your stance, in your hands. And in your eyes."

I don't argue. "I haven't been in a ring in years."

"Boxer, I bet."

I shrug.

"You used to train here?"

"Maybe."

"So what will it hurt to go a round or two?"

Nothing. That's what. And it might ease the ache in my heart and the strife in my soul. "Okay, sure. You're a boxer?"

"Started out there, yeah." He steps toward me and holds out his hand. "Name's Chad. Chad Greene."

"I'm Ethan Sims," I say out of habit. I never used my legal name boxing. No one in my real life would ever connect that name to me—to Ethan Trainor, heir to the Trainor family fortune. It felt appropriate somehow, using Phillip's name to flush the anger he engendered out of my system. "What do you do now?"

"UFC, man. It's almost all anyone watches anymore."

"I don't have gear. Can I borrow some?"

Chad nods. "Holden. Get me some gloves and a mouth guard, will you?"

A flyweight stops working on the bag in the corner and walks toward us. His nose was badly broken—recently. "You gonna fight this guy?" When he smiles, his nose looks even worse, like a smashed plum above a completely normal mouth.

"Yeah, if you ever shut up and get him some gear."

"Fine, geez." Holden trots toward the lockers in the back and emerges a moment later with battered black gloves. He holds them out to me.

"Thanks." I put them on. They're a little small, but they'll work for a few rounds, which is all this is. "These are light."

Chad shakes his head. "Boxers."

"I heard that UFC gloves were thinner. I forgot."

"You've done UFC?" Holden cocks his head and frowns.

"Nah, but I've watched some matches." All the rings are occupied. "Where are you thinking?"

"Jared. Logan." Chad tosses his head. "Get out."

The huge black guy in the ring closest to me releases his rear choke on the poor guy he's destroying and they both climb out of the ring.

"Don't worry," Chad says as he climbs in. "I'll go easy on you." When he smiles, it's with a cockiness I didn't notice at first. Judging by the way he orders people around, I'm guessing I've managed to draw the attention of one of the top dawgs here.

Just my luck lately.

Getting an epic beat down should remind me why I quit boxing in the first place.

Holden hands me a mouth guard that doesn't look altogether clean, but I can't really complain about a little pocket lint when I'm about to get my face slammed against a dirty canvas mat. I wipe it against my shorts surreptitiously as I climb into the ring.

"It's clean, man, I swear," Holden says.

"Of course," I say. "Habit."

"I thought you ain't fought for years." Holden frowns.

"Some things are embedded in the muscle memory." I close the gap, and notice that only two of the rings still have guys fighting in them. Five or six people have gathered to watch. That's not normal for a random match with a walk-in. Who exactly am I about to fight?

"How long has it been?" Chad asks. "You know, since the last time you punched someone?"

I act like I have to think about it. Like I haven't missed it every single day in the last seven years, nine months, and fourteen days. "Close to eight years."

The heavyweight black guy slouches against the same wall Chad was leaning against and whistles. "So you climbing into that ring is like Rocky or something."

Gosh, I hope not. "Sure. I'm thirty now, but this isn't some kind of comeback." I laugh. "I just had a bad day, and I'm looking to blow off a little steam."

"Right." Chad says. "Let's go, then." He circles me, and I follow suit, keeping my space for now, watching how he moves.

He's light on his feet. He's definitely in active training and it shows. He also loves fighting, which matters more than people realize. In my experience, the very best fighters are the ones who love doing it. The only thing that beats love of the sport—in terms of sharpening someone's skillset—is rage.

Unfettered, unadulterated rage.

At least I have that going for me, even after all these years.

Chad doesn't wait, advancing with a jab right off. I weave to evade it pretty easily.

That's when his half smile spreads into a full one. "Nice. You got some legs on you still, old man, huh?"

And I pop him in the jaw. He flies backward almost a foot, and flies right back up.

At least that stupid smile is gone.

UFC or not, it's clear in the way he moves, the way he holds his shoulders, the way he feints, that Chad started as a boxer. Fine, well, I'll treat him like one. My best move has always been my hook. Every TKO I ever got came from my left hook. I pound him with my right-left-right, and then swing with the left. He shifts enough that it connects with his shoulder instead of his face, but judging by the way he dances back, I haven't lost all my power.

When Chad circles this time, all the friendly banter is gone. From the corner of my eye, I notice that now, no one else is fighting. Everyone is watching us. More than a dozen guys stand around the ring. My adrenaline spikes and I start pushing him around a little to see what he'll do. Jab cross, jab cross, jab cross, shuffle. He defends, he circles, he defends and circles more.

Why's he defending? Why isn't he attacking?

"What'd you say your name was?" Chad asks.

"Ethan Sims," I say. "I'm a nobody."

"I ain't heard of you." Chad spits. "But that hook, man, it's raw." And he drops his hands. Not very much.

But enough.

I hammer his abdomen with a round of blows, and I can feel it. I've got this. I'll soften him a little more, and then I'll take him out with a real hook, full force.

But then my head dips a little too low, and he drops his arm around my neck. He locks it by grabbing his wrist with his free hand and flips me to the mat. Suddenly, I can't breathe. Like, at all.

A moment later, the world goes black. When light comes back, I blink and blink and blink until my vision clears. I'm staring up at the slow-turning giant fans. When I swear under my breath, my voice is rough. I thought I had him.

Chad's beaming face looms over mine, and he offers me a hand. "Not bad, old man, not bad at all."

I drag in a breath and force myself to take his hand even though I'm not really ready to stand up. As he yanks me upward, I notice with no small amount of joy that his jaw is swollen and he's got a black eye. He might have won, but I did some damage on the way down.

And it felt good. Maybe too good.

"Thanks," I say. "I think I needed that."

"Ethan Sims," a low voice rumbles at the edge of the ring. A voice I'll never forget, no matter how many years and months and days pass. A frog crawls up in my throat.

I haven't seen Harrison Lunger since the night I lost.

"What are you doing in my gym?" My old trainer's standing at the exit for the ring.

"I had a lousy day," I say.

"I heard you was in Hawaii." He scowls. "Surfing."

"Surfing?" Chad laughs. "Are you kidding? That's why you're so tan?"

I cross my arms. "Don't knock it until you've tried it. There's something about surfing and boxing—they're both all encompassing—consuming somehow."

The guys gathered around scoff and mutter. I doubt any of them have ever touched a surfboard, much less been in the tunnel.

"You know this surfer guy, coach?" Chad asks.

"He used to train me." I climb out of the ring, but Harrison doesn't move, and I bump his shoulder as I walk past. "But don't worry. I didn't come to bother you. I happened past on a jog—I won't be back."

"What makes you think I don't *want* you back?"

I freeze.

"I've been waiting eight years to see you walk back through that door."

"I'm too old," I say. "And I lost."

"Thirty is too old?" He laughs. "It's the new twenty-five."

I turn around slowly. "I'm here for a family thing. I'm going back to Hawaii soon. To surf my life away." I stare at him.

"Well," Harrison says. "If you think you can just stroll in here and rough up my guys—"

"I beat him," Chad says. "You saw that."

"I was going to say," Harrison nearly shouts, "that you'd always be welcome." He smiles. "I've missed you and that killer left hook."

Chad looks like he wishes he'd held that lock a little longer.

"You're doing UFC now?" I can hardly believe it. No one was more method than Harrison. No one was a more irritating boxing purist. If he's sold out, it's the end of an era in Atlanta.

He shrugs. "Times change. If you don't change, you die off. The people want UFC, so we give them UFC."

I know a lot about giving the people what they want. In fact, it's kind of my whole job. "Well, if I have another crappy day," I say, "I might come back."

Harrison smiles. "We'd love to see you again. Wouldn't we, Chad?"

"Sure," Chad says. "The mat has been dirty. I'd love to mop it with your face again."

I hope I wasn't that idiotic at his age. "I'll remember that." But even if I come by every now and then for a match to blow off some steam, I'm not training again. That was another life, another me. That was old Ethan—which is why I need to get this Phillip situation resolved and go home as soon as possible.

❧ 6 ❧

ANICA

Setups are for total losers. Always.

Which is probably why I didn't cancel. I mean, that's basically me to a tee, right? Unemployed, homeless, thirty, and single.

Trudy and Geo convince me to wear my favorite sky blue dress and strappy white sandals, like I'm some fresh-faced college student. I swing into a spot as close to the back of the parking lot as I can, in case Mr. Hotel Manager insists on walking me out. Surely he'd give up on any gentlemanly resolve before we would reach my 'nearly at the end of its life' old car way back here at the very far side of the lot.

No self-respecting bestselling author would drive Cashew, a fifteen-year-old, banana yellow Honda. At least, no *currently* bestselling author would.

The best thing my new friends can tell someone about me is so far removed from the present that it's basically a lie at this point.

I'm about to open my door when someone screeches around the corner in a blindingly shiny, royal blue Porsche.

I hate Porsches.

My ex drove one. I don't really have any other good reasons for disliking them, but I feel like that's enough. Back when we were dating, I thought it was amazing that he drove a Porsche. Now I see them for what they are: a cry for attention and validation.

Maybe I could include that in my book somehow, subtly, and if he reads about it, he'll feel my jab. Not that he'd read anything I wrote. Which is totally fine.

Of course the driver of the Porsche throws his door open immediately and hops out.

And...it's Ethan.

I should have guessed. Why else would he park way out here? To hide, or to keep his pristine car from getting dinged. I suppress a groan, because if he hears that, he'll notice I'm here and I might not be able to text him to say I'm cancelling.

Even though not a peep escapes my lips, he still notices me. "Anica?" He taps on my window.

How?

Bionic ears? I almost can't suppress my groan this time.

"Oh," I say as brightly as I can manage. "Hey."

His face registers relief, as he's technically five minutes late. "Phew. I was worried you'd be waiting on me."

I swallow and force myself to climb out of Cashew. This is going about as perfectly as I expected it to go. "Not at all. In fact, I should probably confess that I'm chronically about ten minutes late."

He beams. "Me too. Well that's a relief."

I'm not chronically late. In fact, I hate people who are always late, and now he's failed a second of Anica's tests—drives a Porsche, *and* he's late all the time. I'm beginning to think we have exactly zero in common.

And now I've officially started dating people on the basis of one single criterion: we're both single.

"Did you want—" Ethan says at the same time as I say, "Well, should we—"

He laughs. "After you."

Awkward. I walk toward the hotel, acutely aware that I'm overdressed compared to his dark jeans and polo shirt.

"You look nice," he says. "Like a lily or something."

A lily? He thinks I look like a flower? I try not to cringe. "Thanks."

"So how do you know Geo?"

I should have expected this question. After all, it's the reason I'm here. Somehow, I find myself singularly unprepared to answer him. Do I tell him she's friends with my ex-brother-in-law's new wife? And then confess that I'm currently sponging off of said ex-brother-in-law and sort of helping with things while they deal with a new baby?

It's all too weird.

So I do something crazy. Clearly this date's not going anywhere, so why invest in it? I just take the easiest path: a complete and total lie, one that won't make either of us edgy or nervous.

"I'm new in town and I met her at a game night my friend threw."

"Oh, so you barely know one another."

"Basically." I shrug. "Geo and Trudy are just really nice and insisted I come along for their lunch."

"I haven't seen her in years, but she used to be pretty particular about her friends." Ethan's brow furrows. "She's never been much of a social butterfly." We've reached the entrance and he motions for me to go ahead. "After you. You've got some strawberry salad to eat."

"Actually, about that."

"Yes?" Ethan smiles, and I notice that he's got two adorable dimples. It's too bad we have zero in common, because he's almost painfully hot.

"Never mind." No reason to confess that I'm more of a

burger and fries girl than a spinach and fruit one, not when this clearly has no future. "Let's go."

Once we sit and I order the obligatory strawberry and spinach salad with grilled chicken, as well as a side of French fries because, well, French fries, I decide to go on the offensive. If I don't want to answer awkward questions, better to push those his direction. "So you were in Hawaii, and now you're here? What prompted that terrible step down?"

I expect him to laugh. He frowns instead. "I'm not staying."

"Oh." It kind of makes me feel better to know that even if we had hit it off, he's splits-ville the second he does whatever he came here to accomplish. "Well, why did you come, then?"

"I have family here."

Since our food isn't here yet, there isn't even a strawberry salad I can dive into to escape the terribly empty space that has opened up between us. I don't want to share what a clusterous mess my life has become, and he won't tell me why he's here in Atlanta. This may be the worst date I've ever had, and I've had some doozies.

"What books have you written?" he finally asks.

I try my best not to frown. I know he's just trying to make conversation, but it feels a bit like we're both drowning on dry land. "Uh, nothing you've read, I'm sure. I write romantic comedies, like the kind of movie Tom Hanks and Meg Ryan would star in."

"Ah." He nods. "Okay."

"When will you be heading back to Hawaii?"

"As soon as I possibly can." He's staring at his phone without even looking up to answer.

I laugh. I can't help it. "Well, I'm sorry I didn't go with my gut, for your sake as well as mine."

"Excuse me?" Ethan drops his phone to the table and

braces both his hands on the table's edge. "I'm sorry. That was my sister. She's just gone to meet someone I don't want her seeing."

"It's cute, the protective older brother thing." I shake my head. "What I meant was, I usually duck this kind of thing—setup attempts and the like. But you're so good-looking and you have a respectable job, so I figured, why not?" I snort. "Lesson learned, right?"

When the waitress shows up with our meals, I stand up. "I don't even like sugary salad. Actually, I don't like salad that's not sweet either." I point at the fries. "But can I get these to go?"

Ethan stands up, too. "Did I say something that offended you?"

I shake my head. "Not at all. You haven't said a thing, really, so there's no way you could have offended me. But when I turned thirty a few months ago, I've realized something, Ethan I-gotta-get-back-to-Hawaii-as-soon-as-possible."

"You did?" He even has dimples when he half smiles.

"I realized that my most valuable commodity is time, and I should be smart enough by now to know not to waste it. Don't you agree?"

"You're saying lunch with me is a waste of time?"

I point at him. "You drive a Porsche." I scrunch my nose. "Sorry, but for me, that's strike one." I extend a second finger. "Number two, you aren't sticking around Atlanta, and I just moved here. I don't want to leave any time soon, so that's another strike." I point at the table. "And for the last one, you're too cute for me to be comfortable admitting that I don't like salad. Not your fault, but that's still strike three. I'd say three strikes in less than half an hour isn't an auspicious start to any kind of relationship."

"Relationship?" He looks like he's suppressing a laugh.

"You do appear to have a sense of humor, the lack of which is my only absolute deal-breaker, but let's save us both some time and call this now." I point from his chest back to mine. "We're not ever going to work out. I'll save you another hour of awkward conversation in which I try not to let on that I'm a washed up author who can't sell the kinds of books she wants to write, and you're forced to keep evading questions about the real reason you're here, which I'm now imagining has something to do with a dead body and a shovel."

His mouth hangs open for a moment, but when the waitress arrives with a styrofoam container for my fries, he starts to laugh.

I dump the fries into the container and close it. "Judging by your reaction, we can still both leave this interaction in a good mood. I got some delicious fries, and you didn't offend your friend Geo by turning me down flat."

I spin on my cute, not-at-all-like-a-lily heels and walk away.

At least I ended the date well. I check my watch. I've got almost an hour to kill until my interview for a waitress position at Golden Gloves, which is only a few miles away. I decide to eat my fries in the park and watch people.

I love watching people.

Most authors I know do it. It's almost the perfect writing exercise, honestly. I make up conversations for the couples, mostly, which makes sense given my romantic comedy background.

I start with the long-haired hippie and his sweater-set-wearing girlfriend. Like, how did that happen? Maybe the barista at Starbucks mixed up her non-fat latté and his soymilk blondie? Their eyes locked, and his hair reminded her of that one crush she never spoke to in high school? He secretly craves someone who will scold him like his mother always did, but even more secretly longs for her acceptance?

Or then there's a forty-year-old woman who's clearly meeting the twenty-something guy in this park because it's really, really far from anyone she knows. Is she divorced? Widowed? Was he her kids' babysitter a few years ago, and they bumped into each other cycling in the park?

Is the college-aged jogging couple as perfectly in unison as they look, from their matching Nikes all the way up to their sweat soaked brows? Or perhaps she's thinking, even now, about her boss. And he's trying to figure out how to break up with her and not lose his favorite jogging route.

When did I get so jaded?

I close my eyes and eat the last French fry.

I force myself to think up happy endings for the next half dozen couples, and something odd happens. A weight lifts from my chest. A chef that bakes his girlfriend a baguette that says, "Marry me." She swoons with joy. A marathon runner who finds a diamond ring in the toe of her shoe early one morning. "Run through life with me," her hunky body-builder boyfriend says as he hands her a Gatorade.

Sometimes I wish the world thought it was okay to be in love with *love*. Why does a story have to be 'deep' and 'meaningful'? If my love stories make me happy, why isn't that enough?

I sigh as I force myself to head to my interview.

Because in the real world, not everything ends with happily ever after. People leave, and people die, and even when they stay, it's all shades of grey and tan and taupe. No matter how much I wish it was, the real world isn't full of sparkles and glitter. It just isn't, no matter how much I wish it to be true. That's why I should be writing about more important things and not 'fluff' as Patrick always called it.

I'm not as excited as I ought to be when I arrive for my

interview, ten minutes early as usual, but maybe that's good. Hopefully I won't make stupid jokes and tank this one. I really need a job.

As I approach the diner, it's clear that the golden gloves are, in fact, *boxing* gloves. The image of huge golden boxing gloves is larger than the words on the sign overhead as I walk into the diner. That's a plot twist. The entire front of the diner is glass, and only a handful of customers are present right now, which is probably normal for three p.m. on a Wednesday, hence the interview time.

When I walk through the door, a little bell jingles brightly, and a woman with her hair pulled into a loose bun on the top of her head looks up. She's probably in her fifties, but her eyes are kind, and she's in great shape. "Are you Anica?"

"I am."

"This might be a little odd, but my waitress called in sick at the last minute. Any chance you'd be okay with your interview being more of a hands on variety?"

"Will this interview come with tips?"

She beams at me. "I can already tell that you're my kind of girl."

"I'll take that as a yes," I say. I grab a menu and start scanning. Pretty standard stuff. Burgers, fries, including sweet potato, my favorite, and milk shakes. A decent sampling of normal diner options, including breakfast all day, and a variety of basic salads. I snap it shut.

"You ready?" The woman bobs her head at a table in the corner with two teenagers sitting at it. "I'm Barbara, by the way."

"Great," I say. "And sure."

I stroll across the shiny tile floor and stop in front of them. "Can I help you?"

They both blink at me. "Do you work here?" The gangly boy asks.

I have to work not to stare at the impressively large pimple on his forehead. "Maybe. This is my trial run."

"Oh." He looks down at his menu. "Well, we're not sure what we want yet."

I slide into the booth next to the girl. "Tight budget?"

The girl's eyes widen.

"Believe me, I've been there." I smile. "I'm Anica, and I have a little secret for you. Your best option if you've got limited cash is almost always breakfast food. You can get a pancake combo for under six bucks, and it's usually enough food to share."

"Can you bring two plates?" The girl gulps. "Or do they charge more for that?"

I don't laugh, but I do smile. "Absolutely I can, and there's no extra charge. I'll even throw in two sets of silverware."

"We'll tip you well, I promise." The boy's voice cracks when he says promise, and I just want to hug them both.

"I'm sure you will."

When I pick up the order and grab an extra plate, the cook tosses an extra piece of bacon on. That's when I know this is a decent place to work. "Thanks," I say.

The kids split everything right down the middle when it comes, and I revise my original assessment. "Brother and sister?" I ask.

They both bob their heads. When it's time to pay, I refuse their money and pay for their meal myself. I need money, but not as badly as them. "Don't take each other for granted, okay?"

"I'd never do that," the boy says. "Lauren's my sister, but she's also my best friend."

"Good," I say.

When I get back to the register, Barbara watches me closely. When I grab menus for the trio that just walked in, she says, "You're hired." She touches my shoulder. "Not many people are kind anymore."

So she noticed that I refused their money. "Not nearly enough."

When the first dinner waitress, Pearl, shows up just before five, I'm almost sad to leave. "Thanks for helping me out today," Barbara says. "I know it was unorthodox, but I wanted to let you know that the customers have all loved you so far. Any chance that you can work a double tomorrow and lunch Friday?"

"Sure," I say. "I'll see you then."

My heart is decidedly lighter when I walk out, with a spring in my step that I've missed. I shouldn't be embarrassed when I tell people I'm a waitress. Serving people has value, and bringing food to hungry people does, too. I'm almost to my car, which looks pretty much like every other car in the parking lot, when I notice another car. A very conspicuous one.

A bright blue convertible Porsche.

Did Ethan follow me here for some reason? I look around but don't see him. There's a shipping kiosk, a corner market, and right next to the Golden Gloves, a red brick building with a sign above that says "H. Lunger Gym."

There's a gym here? Ethan could have passed two other grocery stores to come to this one, but it seems more likely, given his delicious build, that he's at the gym. A sudden desire to make sure he's not a stalker grips me. One little peek into the gym should confirm that he's actively engaged and not following me around. Plus, he's easy on the eyes. I wouldn't mind seeing him work out, as long as he doesn't notice me looking.

Then he might think *I* was the stalker.

I cross the street again quickly and poke my head around the corner. Luckily, the door of the gym has a big window on it. I'm peering through when a huge bald man's face appears just in front of mine. He smiles at me and shoves the door open.

"You lost?" He grins, and even though I know it's idiotic, my heart races. I have a serious soft spot for alpha males, the kind that are all wrong for a soft-spoken, introverted writer like me.

"Uh, no. I'm new in Atlanta, and I was just looking for a place to work out."

"We don't train ladies here," he says. "But I'm Chad. I'd be happy to work with you in my free time."

"Oh, well thanks, but—"

"What's going on?" A gruff voice asks.

"Nothing, Coach. Just getting a number. I'll be right there." Chad smiles at me and I almost consider giving him my number. Almost, but not quite. As wrong as Ethan was for me, this guy is probably worse.

Ethan! I was supposed to be looking for him, not flirting.

"I'd better go," I say.

"Anica?"

Ethan's standing behind Chad, just tall enough to see me over his shoulder.

"Oh." I want to die on the spot. What was I thinking coming over here? Now he's definitely going to think I'm following him.

"Wait, are you pretty boy's girlfriend?" Chad asks.

"No," I say at the same time that Ethan says, "Yes."

Chad's grin couldn't be bigger. "Well, you know where you can find me if you decide you want some—" he wiggles his eyebrows "—training, sweetheart." He turns around and walks past Ethan and the older man toward the back of the gym.

"What are you doing here?" Ethan asks, walking toward me quickly.

"I saw your car," I admit. "And I was hoping you were in here, and not. . . "

His eyebrows rise. "Creeping on you?"

It's my turn to laugh this time. "It seems ridiculous when you put it that way, but kind of."

"Well, you're safe. This is a bizarre coincidence, nothing more."

"What kind of gym is this?" I ask, peering around his broad shoulders. "Are you a fighter, *pretty boy* Ethan?" I swallow. "Is that your big secret? Are you here to train for something?"

"Not hardly," he says. "But I do enjoy an occasional sparring match when I have a rough day."

"Why was today so rough?" I can't help asking, even though I know he'll dodge the question. "Our date wasn't great, but it wasn't *that* bad."

"What are *you* here for?" he asks.

I point to the left. "I just got a job next door."

"A job? Writing?" His nose scrunches and it makes him so cute I wish I could grab him and kiss him.

What is wrong with me? "When I get stuck, like I've been for, I don't know, the last few *years*, I wait tables. Glamorous, right?"

"Well, it's real," Ethan says. "And in my experience, real beats glamorous every single time."

"Yeah—I'm the queen of real. I prefer burgers over salad, remember?" I glance behind him. "And it looks like you prefer controlled brawls in a gym to a good bar fight. Seems smarter." I tilt my head. "I might have been a little hasty. We might have more in common than I realized."

"And to set the record straight on one point, I don't even like my Porsche. That's my dad's fault—he's obsessed with them. I haven't had time to do much about his overly generous gift yet."

A dad who gives Porsches as a gift? "I'm feeling a little

unloved. Last year my parents gave me a Nook e-reader for Christmas."

He snorts. "I would have preferred that, actually. Look, maybe we could try this over again," he says. "You can struggle to tell me the truth in spite of my beautiful face, and I can try to use more than three or four words to answer when you ask me a question."

An above average sense of humor, seemingly. "Alright, sure," I say. "But on one condition."

He lifts one golden eyebrow. "What's that?"

"You let me stay here and watch you pummel someone."

"I'm not even sure whether I'm—"

"You can," the Coach says. "I'd like to see you up against Flint."

"I knew it," I say. "You are training."

"Totally wrong," Ethan says. "I used to train with Harrison, but right now I'm just blowing off steam."

"For now, that's true," the Coach who I assume is Harrison says. "But if you stay and watch, you'll see that this boy is really something special."

"Or you'll see me lose a tooth, and everyone will stop calling me pretty boy. You never really know how a fight is going to go."

I can tell that's one of the things he likes about it, this baffling Porsche-driving Hawaii fanatic, who's not at all what I thought he was.

"If I let you stay, then you have to let me take you out tomorrow." Ethan lifts one eyebrow questioningly.

"Assuming you're not busy getting emergency dental work, you mean?" I ask.

"Exactly," he says.

"I'll be working tomorrow, next door. Sorry."

"Lunch and dinner?" His eyebrows rise.

"Check and double check."

"Right, well, how about Friday?"

"I'm only working lunch, but I kind of promised I'd babysit my niece and nephew that night. Their parents have a standing game night with a bunch of friends."

"I like kids."

Huh? "Are you saying you'd be fine having our redo date be . . . babysitting?"

"I doubt there would be any awkward conversations," he says. "Or any lulls. Kids kind of iron that sort of thing out."

"Well, we are supposed to be watching the second *Incredibles* movie. When Chase found out I hadn't seen it, I thought he was going to explode."

"Now I really want to come." His dimples should be licensed as deadly weapons.

"Alright," I say. "If you let me watch yours, you can come see mine."

Ethan's grinning as he walks away.

And I can't seem to stop smiling as he pummels the huge guy Harrison sends into the ring to fight him. His old coach is totally right about his hook. It's killer.

He leans against the edge of the ring as I leave and waves. "See you Friday," I say.

"I look forward to it," he says.

Bizarrely, so do I.

ETHAN

"I'm telling you, you're a natural. Are you sure you don't want to train?" Harrison hands me an ice pack for my eye.

"I shouldn't have even come in today," I say. "It's just that I've been dealing with some stuff."

"As I recall, you were *dealing* with stuff for all four years of college." Harrison folds his arms and leans against a locker. "No pressure, but I'll just say this. You always had it in you to be the best, not just alright, but The Best."

"I'm a boxer, not an expert at this mixed martial arts stuff you do now."

Harrison guffaws. "That's what they want, son, boxers. Believe me. The wrestlers, they win a lot, don't get me wrong. You'd need to learn holds and a wider array of strikes, but that's not the sexy part of UFC. Wrestling holds are not what draw the crowds. Do you know what clips from UFC get millions of views? It's the good old-fashioned KOs. The knock outs in five, six, seven seconds, those are watched and talked about, and they're what keep the franchise hot." He unfolds his arms and leans toward me. "Do you know who does those, what kind of fighter?"

"Boxers?" I roll my eyes. "Look, I get it. I missed my shot before, yadda yadda. It's just, that's not where I see my life going. I've never been someone who bets on the long odds."

"Are you sure?"

"Absolutely positive."

Harrison shrugs. "Fine. But if you change your mind, I'd be happy to help you put in some work on holds. You're about fifty times smarter than any other fighter I've ever had, and you take a punch like no one I've ever trained. Those things combined with your left hook?" He whistles. "I'm really not trying to sell you on it—your head has to be in it. But if it ever was. . ." He walks away, shaking his head.

I head for the locker room to change. I'd be lying if I didn't admit, if only to myself, that it's nice to hear. No matter how long I've been pretending to be a surfer, deep inside, I've always been a fighter, not a peace-loving hippie.

Some things never change.

And if Anica's working next door. . . On my way out, I pause near my old coach. "Maybe I could come by and work on holds tomorrow afternoon, on the late side, after work."

Harrison doesn't smile, but his lip twitches like holding a straight face is costing him. "Sure. And if you suck at them, I'll stop bothering you about it."

"Deal."

The next day, I show up for work early and get right down to business. By three, I've only got loose ends to tie up. Which is good, because I'm antsy, and I keep thinking about blushing cheeks and cornflower blue eyes.

Harrison's ready when I get there around four. "The first thing we're going to do is show you how effective holds can be. You're unlikely to win with one given your background, but you need to learn to avoid them, and they can be used effectively to apply pressure in most any fight."

He throws his best wrestlers my direction, one at a time. I tap out from dozens of armbars, and an embarrassing number of guillotine chokes. "The rear naked choke is the worst." I rub my neck.

"That's because it doesn't rely on cutting off your air supply," Harrison says.

I blink and blink and blink until my vision goes back to normal. "You don't say."

"It cuts off the carotid."

"I hate it."

"You ready to learn how to do them?" He lifts his stupidly bushy eyebrows. If I'm still in Atlanta, I'm buying him a personal trimming tool for Christmas.

Why would I be here at Christmas? What a stupid thought. I shake my head to clear it. "Yes, I'm ready. Let's go."

An hour and a half later, my arms feel like jelly and the outside of my left thigh is swelling from a particularly brutal take down, but I think I've improved, at least a little. "So what's the verdict?"

"On what?" Harrison asks, like he has no idea. Sometimes I can't stand him.

"You said you'd stop bothering me."

"If you really suck."

"Right."

"You did suck," Chad says. He's been unbelievably annoying since the very first time he locked me into a choke.

"But no worse than any other boxer I've seen on day one," Harrison says. "Too early to tell. Come back tomorrow."

"Tomorrow's Friday," I say.

"Oh," Harrison says. "Never mind. I'll see you whenever it's convenient, then."

"You will?"

Chad snorts.

"Tomorrow," Harrison says. "At three this time."

I sigh. "Fine."

But as I turn, I notice he's grinning.

Practicing holds isn't quite as good as riding a perfect wave, but it's better than a long jog. I walk really slowly to my car, peering into the well-lit dining room of the Golden Gloves. Even if Anica wasn't there, I might want to stop—I'm starving. But my creeping pace pays off.

She looks up from a table in the corner and our eyes meet.

Hers light up and she smiles and waves.

Good enough for me. I showered, so my hair is dripping on my collar, but at least my clothes are clean and I don't think I've got any bruises on my face. I hang a quick right and yank open the door with a typical diner jingle of bells.

"Anywhere is fine," a woman behind the counter with a poofy bun says.

"Are the burgers here any good?" I ask. "Because I can't really handle salad. I'm more of a burger and fries kind of guy."

A guy with one chipped tooth waves at a table right by the door, encouraging me to take it.

I compress my lips. How can I say this? Eh, may as well just come out with it. "No offense dude, but I want to be in her section." I jerk my thumb toward Anica.

He rolls his eyes. "Join the club."

I look around and notice that nearly every youngish guy in the place is seated at a table or booth on Anica's side. Well, that's annoying.

But the mother of a small family is gathering things into a diaper bag. I hover while they pack up, and before the table has even been cleaned, I slide into the booth.

"Hey, stranger. What're you doing?" Anica wipes the table off. "Are you actually hungry?"

"Always," I say. "But I'll admit—I also wanted to see you."

And she blushes. Which I love even more now that I've heard the sharper side of her tongue. She's such an interesting mix of conflicting behavior. "Well, I'm working, so I can't really chat."

"What time are you off?"

She scrunches her nose. "Ten, when it closes."

"That's rough," I say.

She shrugs. "It's not so bad. I like the work, and I can use the cash."

"I'm a really generous tipper."

"Generous is good, Mr. Porsche, but keep it under the 'creepy' line, alright?"

"What's the creepy line?" I can't keep the curiosity out of my tone.

"Anything over fifty percent starts to feel . . . yucky. Especially when it's a guy tipping me."

"So if I were, say, an elderly woman, a two-thousand percent tip—"

"Would be mostly fine, yeah." She shrugs. "I might be worried you can't quite figure math right and confirm, but I wouldn't be uncomfortable otherwise."

"That's hardly fair," I say. "And it's kind of sexist."

She shrugs. "I don't make the rules."

"Oh, fine. Well, until I can pass as an elderly woman, or if I'm being waited on by an elderly man, I assume, I'll keep my generosity under the fifty percent mark."

"Sure," she says. "Good enough. Now what do you want?"

"Two cheeseburgers with lettuce, grilled mushrooms, and swiss. And lots of pickles."

She's not writing it down.

"Should I repeat it?"

She snorts. "Only if you're bored or if you've changed your mind."

"Alright. I also want a chocolate milkshake, and a plate loaded with French fries."

"How is that possible?" She asks.

"How is what possible?"

"How do you eat all that, and look like this?" She points to me and wiggles her finger around.

This time I'm the one whose cheeks are heating. "I'm blessed, I guess." And I like that she thinks I look good.

"I'll say."

Strangely, I've never felt very blessed. At least, not before she walked into Harrison's yesterday. My life has been a sequence of near misses and utter catastrophes, and I'm never quite sure which it'll be next. Even now, I'm holding my breath, figuratively anyway, hoping the excitement I feel for her doesn't die on the vine—or that she doesn't suddenly change her mind and find me repulsive. "You aren't secretly married or anything, right?"

She blanches.

"What?" I shift on the smooth vinyl upholstery of the bench seat. I splutter. "Are you married?"

Anica shakes her head. "No, nothing like that."

"A secret fiancé or boyfriend, then?"

She laughs this time. "No, no boyfriends or fiancés, secret or otherwise. Why?"

I shrug. "I'm not usually very lucky, so meeting you. . . I can't explain it. I guess I don't trust it."

She rolls her eyes, but when she walks toward the kitchen, she looks back at me over her shoulder with a strange look I can't place. I figure that's not a bad sign. For once, a girl I like might actually like me back.

The burgers she brings a few moments later are perfect, as are the fries and the milkshake. She's busy tonight, which is probably good for her. Judging by the flirting looks the guys at her other tables keep shooting her, she'll do pretty well in tips, but she doesn't ignore me even though she probably could. It's not like I'd stiff her, even for bad service.

"How're the burgers?" She pauses near my table, close enough I can smell the apple-y smell that must be coming from her shampoo.

"Perfect," I say. "I was nervous when you didn't write my order down."

She snorts. "I have a pretty good memory. I never write anything down."

"You might be underemployed, working at a diner."

Her face immediately shutters, and I make a mental note to avoid disparaging her job here. "Sorry," I say. "My mom spent a lot of years waiting tables when I was a kid, and she hated it."

"Your mom was a waitress?" The walls come down just a hair.

"She was," I say. "At a diner sort of like this one, but she didn't want to be."

She shrugs. "I like it, quite a lot, actually. I like the people, mostly, since I don't have to work at figuring out what to say to them, and it's cathartic, filling a need so simply. I can do a good job, brighten people's day and fill their bellies, and that's the end of it. No unmet expectations, no complicated issues, no awkward silences I need to fill."

It feels like a puzzle piece drops into place about her. She likes people, but she needs to have a purpose with them. She doesn't want to just sit around with nothing to do or say. "Well, the food is pretty good. I wouldn't be surprised if I find myself eating here pretty often."

She smiles then. "Really?"

"Since I agreed to do a little bit of training next door."

"Whoa," she says. "You're going to be fighting again?"

"Not sure, but I'm going to look into it anyway."

She bites her lip, spins on her heel and heads back to the kitchen to grab a few more orders. When she comes by the next time, even eating as slowly as possible, I'm done with my food. "All finished? Want your check?"

"Yeah, I figure after the milkshake, the two burgers and the fries, I might skip the pie." I lean back and pat my belly. Her eyes follow my hands and she blushes again. This is too much fun.

"You'd probably survive a slice of pie."

I stand up and drop some bills on the table that I figure can't be much over fifty percent. I lean close enough that she'll hear me even though I'm whispering. "I always think it's better to leave when you're still wanting more, don't you?"

Her breathing hitches.

"We're still on for tomorrow?"

"If you still want to watch *Incredibles Two*." She looks up into my face, her bright eyes wide.

"I'd like to spend time with you, and I like the idea of meeting your family."

She blinks. "Alright, well, okay. I'll text you the address."

"You do that."

And around ten-fifteen, she does. It puts a smile on my face.

THANKS.

SEE YOU TOMORROW, she texts.

I LOOK FORWARD TO IT.

YOU MIGHT WANT TO COME A LITTLE EARLY IF YOU CAN. GAME NIGHT STARTS AT SEVEN, AND IF THE OTHER ADULTS REALIZE YOU'RE HERE, THEY MIGHT MAKE US GO DOWNSTAIRS AND HANG OUT WITH THE BIG PEOPLE.

YOU SAY THAT LIKE IT'S A BAD THING.

LITTLE PEOPLE ARE ALWAYS BETTER THAN BIG ONES.

AS A TALL GUY, I'M TRYING NOT TO TAKE OFFENSE.

I'LL MAKE AN EXCEPTION FOR YOU, BUT I STAND BY MY STATEMENT.

She's adorable.

SEE YOU AT 6:30 THEN.

I try not to read anything into it when she sends me a heart emoji, but I can't help my idiotic smile.

Harrison complains when I call it quits at five-fifteen, but I ignore him. I may have agreed to a little training to blow off steam while I'm here making sure Adriana is okay, but I'm not going to be late for the best part of my day to let some guy choke off my air.

"I'll be back Monday," I say.

"Tomorrow," he counters.

"I've been ignoring my dog," I say. "I can't ignore her all day tomorrow."

"So snuggle with your mutt all morning, and get here around noon."

I shake my head, but I don't argue any further. If I don't come here, I'll probably get bored and end up at the hotel instead. "Fine."

I change my shirt three times before settling on a simple Emory t-shirt. In case I do see Geo or Paisley, I'd like them to remember that I'm a friend so they'll say good things to Anica.

Anica's family has a very nice, tasteful home in a perfect little neighborhood. I admire the flowerbeds as I walk up the sidewalk—and that's not common for me, not here. After Hawaii, very few growing things in Georgia impress me. But the gerbera daisies are stunning, as is the lantana. Add the perfectly round butterfly bushes at the corners, with butterflies darting around them, and it's just exactly the kind of thing I'd plant myself.

If I ever did get married and have kids.

With my luck, it's hardly likely. I lift my hand to knock on the solid wood door, but before I even touch it, it swings open.

"You must be Ethan," a small girl says, one hand on her hip.

"Uh, I am, yes."

"I'm Amy, Aunt Anica's niece. She told me to sneak you up." She winks. "She doesn't want everyone to know you're here."

"Wait, she's serious about that?"

Amy rolls her eyes. "Do you want to have to spend the entire night pretending that the boring stories the adults tell are funny?"

I can't laugh. Or at least, I sense that I shouldn't, so I'm entirely sober when I say, "That sounds absolutely terrible."

"I like you already." Amy spins around and sprints up the staircase at the back end of a beautiful entryway. I look both ways for any sign of other adults and then finding none, I follow her upstairs.

Amy ducks inside a door at the top of the stairs and closes it behind her.

I lean close and tap on it softly.

"What's the password?" Amy whispers.

Is she kidding?

"Uh, *alohomora*?"

"Oh my goodness." Her exasperation is clear, even through a closed door. "That lights things up, Ethan."

"That's *lumos*, unless my Harry Potter game has weakened considerably. I'm pretty sure *alohomora* unlocks things," I say. "But you're the expert, I suppose."

"Whatever. It's not the password." She huffs.

"*Open sesame?*" I ask.

"Just let him in," Anica hisses.

"Oh, fine," Amy says. "But you need to do a better job preparing him next time."

Next time? For some reason my heart lifts at that thought. Most guys might be annoyed by a kid sneaking them upstairs and asking for passwords, but I didn't get anything like this as a kid. Secret operations and passwords? Instead I got an uncle who became my dad when my bio father killed my mom.

I've recovered from losing my mom more or less, and I know I'm lucky to have a dad who cares about me, even if he began life as my uncle. But maybe I never really mourned the loss of a childhood like other kids got. Cousins, and games, and hide and seek.

"So are we really watching the second *Incredibles* movie?" I ask. "Because I loved the first one."

"Did you really watch it?" Anica asks.

"Jack Jack is my favorite," I say.

"Mine too!" A little boy pops up in the corner, his hair sticking out in at least four different directions. "AND I have a little brother named Jack!"

"And your name is?"

"Chase." He holds out a hand to shake. I take it carefully in mine and move it up and down in standard fashion.

And . . . now my hand's sticky. Great. So much for holding Anica's hand later. The room has risers on the back row, making the second line of sofas about a foot higher than the front ones. If I'm lucky, the kids will take the front row. "Are we starting the movie?" I eye the open seat right next to Anica in the back.

"We can't start it until Troy gets here." Amy's remarkably condescending for such a young kid.

"Ethan doesn't know who Troy is," Anica chides. "And maybe you can use a little kinder tone, missy."

"Sorry," Amy says. "Sometimes I forget that some

people don't know everything." Her tone heavily implies that she does, and I should too.

What a hoot. "Well, what shall we do until he arrives?"

"We're building a city out of Legos," Amy says. "But Aunt Anica hates them."

"Maybe I better keep her company back there, if that's a Lego-free zone."

"Do you hate Legos too?" Chase asks.

I shrug. "I don't have a strong opinion one way or another."

"Wait until you step on one," Anica mutters. "You'll develop a strong opinion immediately."

"I imagine that's true." I manage to avoid stepping on one as I wind my way around and up the risers and drop into the spot right next to her. "How did lunch go today?"

"Decent tips," she says. "And I've got my first repeat customer. He insisted on sitting in my area."

Why am I not surprised it's a guy? "Did he happen to ask for your phone number?"

She frowns. "He did."

"Did he tip over fifty percent?"

She shakes her head. "Close, but no."

"Did you give him your phone number?"

She rolls her eyes. "Of course not. I mean, why would I do that?"

"Was he not very cute?"

"Not compared to my brand new boyfriend."

"What?" My shock notwithstanding, the idea doesn't terrify me nearly as much as I thought it would.

She laughs. "Gotcha."

The door bangs open and Anica, in spite of her bold boyfriend jokes, slides almost a foot away from me on the sofa until she bumps into the armrest on the far side. "Oh, it's only Troy." She looks down at her hands and blushes again.

I wish she hadn't been kidding about the boyfriend thing.

Which is totally insane. I haven't had a girlfriend in . . . I can't recall how long. I've dated, of course, but no one special. For the first time in a very long time, I'm not sure I can say that anymore.

Because Anica is special.

I should not be thinking like this at all. I'm not sticking around here once I get things squared away with Phillip and Adriana and Dad, but maybe she would want to come to Hawaii . . . for a visit. She could write there, obviously. And if she wanted to stay a little longer, they have diners on Kauai.

Troy bounds up the risers and toward us. "I'm Troy." He smiles at me, and I forget all about Chase's sticky hands. This kid's entire face is covered in something vaguely orange.

"Uh, you've got—"

Anica cuts me off. "Did you have spaghetti for dinner, sweetie?"

"Yes!" Troy beams.

"Well, you saved some of it for me," Anica says. "Only, I already ate."

Troy's brow furrows.

"Go wash your face," Anica says.

"What did you have for dinner?" Troy asks. "And how did you know I had spaghetti?"

"Your entire face is covered in spaghetti sauce," Amy says. "Duh."

Troy darts out the door, but he forgets to close it behind him.

"Hey, do you guys need anything—" Another blonde woman pokes her head inside and freezes the second she sees me. "Oh."

"Hey, Mary," Anica says. "This is my friend Ethan."

So much for boyfriend. "Hey." I stand up. "Ethan Trainor."

"I'm Anica's . . . " Mary clears her throat. "Well, my husband is her brother-in-law."

Huh? I try to work out how that would work—because Mary seems clear that Anica's not related to her. But she doesn't seem upset about it, just unsure.

"Welcome to our house. You're the very first friend she's ever invited over, and it's been months and months."

"Wait, you live here?" I turn toward Anica.

"I didn't say that?" Anica shrugs. "Yep."

"She's an absolutely indispensable help with her niece and nephew and the new baby," Mary says. "I'm not sure we'd all have made it without her."

"We're good," Anica says.

Troy barrels past Mary then and collapses on the floor, grabbing a whole fistful of Legos like they're a scarce commodity. "I wanna build the tallest tower."

"Too late," Chase says.

"Alright, well, I'll leave you to it," Mary says. "But if you decide you'd like to come downstairs, Paisley's already asking for you."

"We're good," Anica says. "And if you could keep it quiet that I'm up here. . . "

Mary mimes zipping her lips, and waves goodbye as she shuts the door.

"I'm a secret, huh?" I slide closer to her. "I thought you found me attractive."

She bares her teeth in an irritated smile I've never seen anyone else make. "I didn't want to be the one to break this to you, but . . . you're kinda ugly. I think it's the shiny teeth, the perfectly tousled hair, and the washboard abs."

"You've never even seen my abs."

"Oh, I have," she says. "You got pretty sweaty during

that fight, and your shirt clung." She inhales sharply. "What I mean is that all those hard muscles are pretty repulsive."

"Repulsive?" Amy asks. "What does that mean?"

Anica makes a strangling sound.

"It means your Aunt likes me."

"Duh," Amy says. "She's been talking about you for like, hours."

Oh, the blushing. "You don't say." I shift so that I'm leaning against the armrest behind me and I'm staring at her fully. "Tell me again how unattractive I am."

Anica purses her lips.

And now I want to kiss them. Badly. "When are we turning that movie on?"

Her eyes flutter. "Right now."

"Oh, good."

Anica stands up and grabs the remotes. "Kids, find some seats." She dims the lights, but then she comes right back to where I'm sitting, and this time, she doesn't leave any space between us, her leg grazing mine when she sits down again. "Let me find it on here. This Roku is a little confusing."

"If you need help, I bet I can figure it out." My hand closes over hers, and the world tilts when our hands touch. Or maybe it just feels like the world tilts because my heart hammers erratically inside my chest. Either way.

The door slams open again, and Anica's eyes dart to the doorway. I'm starting to hate that door.

"Where's Anica?" A man with an almost predatory look on his face searches the semi-dark room. "Anica?"

"I'm here," she says.

Please don't let this be the guy who made her look all weird when I asked about a secret boyfriend. He's commanding, self-assured, and somehow powerful in a managerial kind of way. I hate him.

"You owe me," he grinds out.

Anica sighs. "Paisley said—"

"Forget what Paisley said. There's no way I'm going to dress as Santa and let them take a photo of her sitting on my knee, looking like a kid."

Anica laughs. "Is that what Trig—"

The man scowls so furiously, I'm almost nervous for Anica, but she seems unconcerned. "Your wife—"

"Yes, yes, she thinks the whole thing is hilarious, I'm well aware. I told her I'd forgive you—if you come down and help us get out of this mess."

His wife. Thank goodness.

"I'm terrible at Fishbowl," Anica says. "Clearly."

"So you can join Trig's team and sink them for us."

"Sink them?" I ask.

The man squints. "Wait, who's that?"

"It's my friend Ethan," Anica says.

"Oh, good, then no one can complain the teams aren't fair." He gestures over his shoulder. "Turn on that movie and get downstairs. Now."

"Or what?" Anica asks.

"Or I'll send my wife up here."

She gulps.

"Who's his wife?" I ask.

"Paisley."

"Oh, I know her," Ethan says. "I'm a little offended I wasn't invited to their wedding, actually."

Anica shrugs. "It was kind of fake at first, or so Mary says. Don't take it personally."

"What?" I'm so confused.

"It's a long story. I can try and tell you what I know, but maybe not right now." She presses a few buttons and the movie starts. She looks at the screen wistfully.

"Maybe she won't come up," I say. "It's not like they can *make* you play."

"Have you met Paisley?" Anica freezes. "Wait, how do you know her?"

"I went to Emory with Paisley and Geo," I say. "And I went to high school at the same place as Trig and his sister Brekka. I was closer to Brekka's age than Trig's, though."

"That's bizarre, isn't it?" I ask.

He shrugs. "My dad's from here, but I got into kind of a lot of fights for a while when I was thirteen. My dad thought it was smart to move before I started high school, and we went to Colorado, where Dad was opening a series of new hotels."

"For a fresh start," Anica says. "And did it work?"

"Hey," Amy says. "You're being loud." It's dark, but I can still make out her scowl, thanks to the light from the opening scene.

And . . . as if on cue, the doors open again. "Anica?" Paisley squints. "Is Ethan up here? For real? Geo *just* told me she ran into him and that you two had a date. I can't believe I'm the last one to know."

Anica laughs. "I surrender." She whispers to me. "Are you ready for this?"

"For what?" I ask.

"We're going into battle."

"Battle?"

"Well, Mary calls it game night if that makes you feel any better," Anica says. Then she stands up and drags me along with her.

✳ 8 ✳

ANICA

The second we reach the light of the hallway outside the movie room, the interrogation starts. So much for a quiet night snuggling on the couch, watching a cartoon.

"Ethan!" Paisley squeals. "It really is you! I could hardly believe it."

When she hugs him, he looks extraordinarily uncomfortable. I'm guessing he doesn't hug many pregnant women. "Congrats on the wedding—and the baby," he says. "It's great to see you."

"You're dating our Anica?" She lifts one eyebrow and somehow manages to look down her nose at him from a foot below his eye level. It's pretty impressive, really.

"You're a princess?" he counters.

"Well-played," she says. "But I'm not done, you know. I've only known Anica for a few months, but I like her. A lot."

"You've known me for years," Ethan says. "Are you saying you don't like me?"

She puts one hand on her hip. "Of course I like you, but

I like her *more*. After all, *she* has *moved* here. I hear you're only visiting."

Ethan glances at me, and I shrug. So I mentioned a few things he said on our failed first date. So what?

Paisley heads down the stairs, clutching the railing tightly, and we trail behind. Ethan touches my arm, and I pause. "Yeah?"

"Did you mention that I'm boxing?" he whispers.

"*Are* you boxing?" I study his face.

It's completely impassive. "I'm not sure yet, but none of them know that I ever did. I'd prefer to keep it that way."

Really? A little part of me feels special, being the only one who knows this secret about him. "Alright."

"Thanks," he says.

"But you'll have some questions to answer later."

He smirks. "I assumed."

"Just don't try and wiggle out of it with more monosyllabic responses."

He raises his hand up like a Boy Scout. "I promise not to wiggle."

I arch one eyebrow. Is he flirting right now? "Funny."

"Finally," James says from the bottom of the stairs. "They're down, so we can pick teams."

"I didn't agree to any kind of follow up bet," Trig says. "I feel good about how things went down." He turns our direction. "By the way, good to see you Ethan."

He waves. "Thanks."

"You're back in Atlanta?" Brekka asks.

"For the time being," Ethan says. "Not sure for how long, exactly."

"Well, don't spend too much time here," James says. "These people are like a plague. They'll worm their way inside and infect you and then you'll never escape. I've been trying and trying to pry Paisley free, but I'm starting to worry I never will."

Paisley rolls her eyes. "Ignore him. He's crabby about the bet we lost last week." She explains it, and Ethan laughs.

"Oh, you can laugh," James says. "But you're not the one being told to buy a Santa suit."

"You'll have to offer me something epic to get me to bet against this," Trig says. "Because right now there aren't many things I want more than the knowledge that all our friends are dying laughing while looking at your photo on their fridge this holiday season."

"Your friends," James says. "I don't have friends."

"Oh, it will be featured prominently on our fridge," Luke says, "and I'm pretty sure we're friends."

James scowls. "What else do you want, Trig?"

"I can't think of another single thing." Trig crosses his arms.

"You can name my baby if you beat us," Paisley says quietly.

The entire room falls silent.

"Are you serious?" Trig asks.

Paisley shrugs and turns toward her husband. He whispers something to her. She smiles, and he nods. "Yeah, we are. But if we win, we're even."

"Deal," Trig says. "Because can I just say how much I love the name Bernard?" He lifts both eyes. "It's an underused name."

Bernard? Is he kidding?

"You wouldn't dare," James says.

"Oh, you can use any nickname you want. But if we win? It'll say Bernard Fulton on that birth certificate."

"What if it's a girl?" Paisley asks. "And maybe we'll give the baby my last name. Did you think of that?"

"Which one?" Trig asks with a smile.

Oh man, they're kind of rough on each other. But Paisley's still smiling and James seems less concerned than he did before.

"What exactly are we playing?" Ethan asks.

I explain it to him while the others pick teams. With her very first choice, Paisley picks me and with her second, she chooses Ethan. Oh, man, the pressure. "Hey, what's the theme this time?" I ask.

"We haven't picked one," Mary says. "What do you think about kids' movies?"

"Good one." Trudy winks at me. "We've totally got this one."

"Mary and Luke are on their team," I point out. "And they have more kids than the rest of you combined."

"But they both work," Trudy says. "I stayed home until not that long ago. I've watched enough Disney movies to break most normal people."

And I've been helping out with Amy and Chase, so I'm up on the latest ones. "Alright, it's on."

"Hey," Trig says. "No fair. You can't stack the game that way."

James looks at Luke and Paul and Rob. "Can't we?"

Rob beams. "I think it's fine."

Trig glares. "You're a traitor."

"I'm on your team, but that doesn't mean I want to call a little girl Bernard for the next twenty years."

Brekka laughs. "You lose the benefit of loyalty when you're being an insufferable jerk."

Trig laughs. "Oh, fine, but you guys better do your best guessing. That's all I'm saying."

We all write down our most obscure kids' movie ideas and drop them into the bowl. Sixty slips this time, thanks to the six couples. Ethan's kind of useless, and Paisley isn't much better, but Trudy and I tear through the pile as though it's tissue paper around a pair of Louboutins.

Paisley smiles at me. "Nicely done."

We're up by almost twenty when we go into the second round. But it's Ethan's turn next. He looks practically pained when he looks at his first slip.

"You can only say one word," James says. "So really think about it."

Ethan's eyes widen. "Reindeer?"

"*Rudolph*!" Trudy says.

Ethan smiles and does the next one. He's not bad, but he's not fast, either. He only gets five, and Trig is up next.

He and Brekka may not have seen many of the movies, but their minds are like steel traps. There's a reason that no one ever wants to allow them to be on the same team.

"They got thirty-seven." James groans.

Trig's a horrible dancer, but even so, it's funny to watch him doing his victory strut.

"Game's not over yet." James stands up.

"Close enough," Luke says grimly. "You can only get eighteen, and that would be a pretty epic turn for you."

James beams. "I don't have to get all of them. If I stop early, that holds you guys to whatever I leave."

That shuts Trig up.

"Doors," James says.

Doors? Paisley and Trudy exchange frazzled glances with me.

"I've seen this one," Ethan says. "*Monsters Inc*."

"Are you kidding me, honey?" Paisley groans. "Doors?"

"Move along," Ethan says.

"Trash," James says next.

"*Ratatouille*," Trudy yells.

And we move through all but four before Rob calls time. If he gives us more than a minute, well, Trig's the only one who complains that it seemed too long. It's nice to see that they're all kind of united on the side of kindness.

Brekka goes next, cycling easily through the last four slips, two of which were duplicates of other movies.

"We need a bigger category next time," Trig grumbles.

"Yeah, we'll take that under advisement the next time you're not trying to hijack the naming of someone's baby," Paul says.

"It's James," Trig says.

"He does have a point," Paul says before standing up for his turn.

"Focus, babe," Trudy says.

"Hey, no speaking this round, so you have to act everything out. Don't forget," Geo says with a twinkle in her eye, "or you'll be disqualified and take no points for the round."

Paisley rolls her eyes. "Like he'd forget."

Paul does a decent job, getting ten using only gestures and movements. Pretty reasonable score for the charades portion, really, especially for him.

Luke is up next. He makes a big production of plucking a piece of paper very slowly.

"Oh, come on," Trig says. "This was a fair bet that they entered of their own volition. If James cares less about the name of his child than wearing a Santa suit for a Christmas card, how is that my fault?"

Luke laughs, and then he tosses a fake head of hair over his shoulder.

"*Tangled*," Mary says. "Good one, sweetheart."

But he can't mime an ogre, apparently, because they're stuck on *Shrek* for a long time and he only clears three for his turn. And . . . now it's my turn again. Now that I know everyone better, even with the looming threat of Paisley's unborn child's name hanging over me, I'm not nearly as scared as last time. I churn through almost twenty movies, leaving only a handful of papers left when my turn ends.

Trig can't win, and he's good enough at math to know it immediately.

"When you guys don't have a hilarious photo of James

and Paisley hanging on your fridge this Christmas, you have no one to blame but yourselves."

Paisley puts a hand on James' arm. "We'll still send you one. How's that?"

Trig cocks his head slightly. "It's better, slightly, but I think you should send one to everyone here."

With her hands around her belly, Paisley beams. "I think that can be arranged, right, honey?"

James grumbles, but doesn't object to a smaller scale photo to mollify his new friends. I lean back in my chair, bumping into Ethan's arm in the process. My heart flies into my throat, and I don't know whether to cry or laugh or close my eyes and savor the moment. Because for a tiny slice of time, *I'm* part of a couple, surrounded by friends and almost-family, and it feels nice. Unbelievably nice.

I fit in, in a way I haven't since Lizzie died.

Guilt and sorrow and regret tear through me. I stand up. "I better get the kids to bed and head that direction myself. I've got the day off tomorrow, which means I really should be writing."

"You have a job?" Paul asks. "Where? Doing what?"

Trudy kicks him.

"She's a waitress not far from the Riviera Grand," Ethan says.

"That's convenient." Geo smirks.

"I think so." His hand squeezes my shoulder and I forget why I wanted to get out of here. I lean into his hand and don't protest as they set up some ridiculously complicated game called Dominion. I lose miserably, but it's entertaining watching James and Trig and Paul act like this game will make or break their lives. Luke acts like he's above it, but he beats them all by a handful of points.

"Your friends are pretty intense," Ethan says.

"My friends?" I whisper. "I think you know them better than I do."

"How do you figure?" Ethan asks. "You *live* here. How exactly are you related to them, anyway?"

"Well, my sister—"

"Speaking of family," Trig says. "How's your dad, Ethan? Is he still the best non-pro golfer in the entire world? My dad still talks about that hole in one he got on hole seven on Ballyneal."

"He's still playing." Ethan's arm tenses next to me. He doesn't like talking about his family, from what I can tell. Not at all.

"And is he still ruling the entire business with an iron fist?"

Ethan shrugs. "Mostly, yeah. I don't see that ever changing."

"Dad still talks about your grandpa's genius in moving from iron to hotels when he did."

"It might have had as much to do with luck as anything else," Ethan says.

And I realize that, unlike me, he fits in with these people. I'm a nobody and the daughter of two nobodies, but Ethan's not. He's a hotel tycoon, son of another hotel tycoon, grandson of a business mogul whom Trig's family respects.

He may feel like the outsider, but he's not.

I am.

"Wait, who's Ethan's family again?" Trudy asks. "Do you know them, babe?"

Paul shakes his head. "He went to school in Colorado for high school with Brekka, right?"

Brekka nods. "Yep, a year ahead of me. I might have had a little bit of a crush on him."

"And I idolized Trig here," Ethan says. He pauses. "In my defense, he was a lot cooler back then."

"Very funny," Trig says.

Brekka can't stop laughing, but when she finally does,

she says, "Your Dad's intense. He kind of makes our mom look easygoing. Maybe those two should've gotten married."

"That's not a horrible idea," Trig says. "Is your dad still single? Maybe a little love in her life with a man she actually respects would loosen Mom up."

"My dad's had the same girlfriend for twenty years," Ethan says. "I don't know your mom well, but I'm guessing she wouldn't put up with being put on hold permanently."

"Yeah, on second thought, maybe not." Brekka giggles. "Although, it would serve her right—let someone else boss her around for a change."

Andy barks by the door, and I leap to my feet. Any excuse to get out of here, because I clearly don't have anything to add in a conversation with these children of business moguls who all have their own enterprises. "I'll take her out."

"We can just put her out back," Mary says.

"It's alright," I say. "I could use a little exercise."

"I'll come along." Ethan stands up. "The few hours between when the sun sets and when it rises again are the only ones that I don't hate Georgia during the summer."

"It's almost September," Trudy says.

"Which is still summer." Ethan jogs toward the door to catch up with me.

Can't argue with that—he's right. I clip Andy's leash to her collar, but before Ethan can duck out with me, I pause. "You can stay," I say softly. "I won't be gone too long. It looked like you were having a good time catching up."

"I'd rather talk to you than any of them." He smiles. "Which is exactly why I needed to catch up with them in the first place. They're old friends, not close friends."

Ah, those dimples. "Alright, if you're sure."

He closes the door behind us. "I am."

Andy usually beelines for the closest patch of grass

to pee, but not tonight. She trots along happily like she was faking a full bladder to escape the house. And if she was, I'd understand it. I can't think of a single thing to say, so I just walk along behind Andy's wagging tail.

"Did you kick the dog?" Ethan asks.

"Excuse me?" I peer up at him, assuming I must have misunderstood.

"To get out of there."

I freeze. "Was it that obvious?"

"Probably not to anyone who wasn't watching you." He chokes. "Or you know, like, paying attention. Something that sounds less creepy than *watching you* does."

I do my best to ignore the tiny zing in my heart and instead force my feet to move—right, then left, right, then left.

He was watching me.

"You're braver than I am," I finally say softly. "The more I like someone, the less I look at them."

"That's good to know. I was worried that I said something wrong."

I look up at him again and realize he's serious. "Not at all," I say. "It's just that I don't fit in with any of them."

"No?" He shrugs. "Could've fooled me."

"Really?"

"First off, they clearly all like you a lot. But beyond that, you're family, right? It doesn't really matter whether family 'fits' or not. They're just part of who you are."

I shake my head.

"How exactly are you related to Mary and Luke again?" The lightness of his tone tells me that he remembers that I evaded the question last time.

My fingers tighten on the leash unnecessarily. It's not like Andy's going to dash away. "I'm not, really."

"I thought you were an in-law."

"I used to be." My eyes are glued on the toes of my scuffed black flats.

"Used to be?" Ethan's voice sounds more unsure than I've ever heard it.

"My sister Lizzie was married to Luke. That's how Amy and Chase are my niece and nephew."

"Wow, they're pretty cool if they hang out with you post-divorce. Does it bug Lizzie?"

"No." I still can't look up at him. "It's not like that." My throat closes up like it always does. For some reason saying it out loud still hurts. "She's dead." The word is always too flat and ugly. Whoever made up that word did a great job. It sounds lifeless and heavy, like tossing a rock into a lake.

"I'm so sorry," he says. "That's terrible. Did it happen recently?"

"Depends on the person, I guess. To me it still feels like it happened last week, but my parents keep telling me I need to get over it already. They're probably right. Lizzie died more than five years ago."

I don't realize that Ethan has stopped walking until I'm almost a dozen feet in front of him.

"Can you look at me for a minute?" he asks.

I lift my eyes to his slowly.

"I know exactly how you feel. I've never quite fit in either, for a very similar reason."

"You lost a sibling?"

His headshake is tight and quick. "Not my sibling, no. My sister Adriana is fine, but my mother."

I can tell that it's hard for him too, to say it aloud. The word is too raw for some reason.

"I hate telling people." His eyes are so big, so empathetic. He really does get it.

My throat is scratchy when I say, "Me too."

He starts walking again, releasing my gaze, and I'm both free and bereft simultaneously.

"People never know what to say."

When he laughs, it's just a little bit bitter. "Talk about a conversation stopper."

"Exactly," I say. "And then if they say anything is dead for the next . . . forever, they get super weird around me. Like, 'That's so funny, I'm dying—' and then they freeze, like I'll be offended."

"Been there," he says. "Talking about my dad is even kind of weird for me because none of them know the truth."

"No?" It's my turn to pause this time.

He exhales slowly. "I never tell anyone. It's easier that way. But for some reason, I want to tell you."

For the first time since Lizzie died, it actually makes me happy that I'm talking to someone about how much it hurts, which of course opens the guilt floodgates again.

"My dad . . . isn't my dad. He adopted us." He exhales in a huge whoosh. "Wow, other than Adriana, I've never told anyone that. People either know or they don't."

"Wait, who is he then?"

"He's my uncle, but when my mom died and my dad wasn't around, he stepped in. It's official and everything. Like his name is on my birth certificate, and Ana and I are his heirs, but it's still weird when I actually stop to think about it."

"Whoa." I blink. "Does that mean your mom and your uncle's names are both on your birth certificate?"

He laughs, and it's a beautiful sound. "Yes! You have no idea how many times I've thought about that, but Ana doesn't find it funny at all."

"Not everyone has a macabre sense of humor," I say. "I confess that mine took a turn toward the morose after Lizzie passed."

"Mine too." Ethan nods. "I mean, probably because Ana

was really young when Mom died, she's always sort of appalled by me and my depressing and twisted jokes."

Maybe he really does get it, how I felt in that room back there. Like a phony—like I'd never really belong. And I hate to admit, even to myself, how much I want to belong somewhere. I long for the feeling I used to have when I was with Lizzie, or talking to her on the phone, or even thinking about something she always did with someone else who knew her too.

Now it's only my parents and Luke who loved her like I did—and they've all moved on.

"How did you end up living with Luke?"

Oh man, I knew this would come up.

"After Lizzie died. . . "

"You couldn't write anymore."

How does he just *get* this stuff? "It felt like something in my brain was broken. Words used to just flow, but it became so *hard*. Like, the more I focused, the lousier my writing became."

"I'm sorry."

Simple, and exactly the sentiment I need to hear. "My bestseller books, of which there are two, are both romantic comedies. But after Lizzie. . . "

"You didn't feel like writing funny."

"Or happy endings, if I'm being honest. I know how much Luke and Lizzie loved each other and watching that end so tragically." I shrug. "I dunno. It kind of shattered my faith in the existence of happily ever after."

"I get it."

For the first time in more than five years, I think maybe someone actually does.

ETHAN

After telling her about my dad, something inside my brain cracks and a lifetime of secrets try over and over to tumble out. I have to stop myself over and over from telling Anica every odd, embarrassing, and bizarre thing about myself.

"Where are we, exactly?" I ask.

Anica stops and looks around as if she doesn't know either.

"Do I need to get out my phone?"

She laughs. "No, just give me a second. I wasn't paying attention to my feet, clearly." She holds her delicate hands out in front of her, spinning a little left, and then a little right, and then she stops and smiles. "Okay. I figured it out. We went a few blocks further than I usually do. But if we turn left up there, we'll walk right back to Orchard Drive and then we're only a block from their house."

"I'll take your word for it."

"You don't look like someone who minds a little phys-ical activity." Her lip curls as though that's the most distasteful thing she's discovered about me so far.

"You don't like 'physical activity'?"

She laughs. "Some things are fine. I don't mind walks, or even hikes if the weather is good. But jogging?" One of her eyes scrunches closed in a pained way, and then she shudders and shakes her head. "Never."

"I'll have to remember that."

"Oh no," she groans. "You're a runner, aren't you? I should've known."

"What about me screams 'runner'?"

"Aren't all boxers runners?" She frowns. "And while we're on this topic, why can't I tell anyone you're a boxer? Do you have some kind of restraining order you're breaking that prevents you from being able to fight?"

"To answer your first question, plenty of boxers hate to run."

"But not you."

I shake my head. "Not me, you're right about that."

"Ugh. Maybe I was right back at the Riviera Grand—we may not have anything in common." At odds with her words, the look she shoots my direction is playful, flirty even.

My pulse picks up in response. "Generally I wouldn't dare to tell a woman she was wrong, but I think you were in that one instance."

"You do?" She pauses at the curb before crossing the street.

"You may hate running," I whisper.

She leans a little closer.

"And I may love it," I whisper.

She leans a little bit closer still.

"But that just means." I pause, my head lowering slowly. "That I'll be more likely to catch you." My lips cover hers, and she whimpers softly.

It does something to me, that involuntary sound, and I

wrap my arms around her, pulling her closer, closer, closer, but still not quite close enough. Her hair is softer than the petals of a lily. Her curves fit perfectly against my chest, and that sound she made, like she's scared and excited and dizzy—I feel the exact same way.

Andy barks, and barks, and barks, and for the first time in my life, I wish I was the kind of person who might kick a dog.

I step back and inhale and exhale several times until I don't want to strangle Luke and Mary's beautiful canine.

"That was. . . " Her voice is breathy and it makes me smile.

"Still upset that I like to jog?"

Her hand strokes my belly, her fingers trailing over the outline of my abdominal muscles. She giggles, and my pulse goes wild. "No, I suppose not, as long as you don't try to force me to run with you."

"I'd never dare," I say.

"I guess I can get over it then," she says. "If you can get over the fact that I'll never in a gazillion years have rock hard abs."

"I like your abs exactly as they are." My arms tighten around her, pulling her toward me again.

Andy barks again.

"That dog is quickly moving up my bad list," I say.

She leans over and ruffles the fur on Andy's head. "She's a pretty smart dog. Maybe she's telling us to take things slow."

My entire life has been a sequence of one slow moment after another—until now. My pulse races, my thoughts spin, and my mind is leaping way too far ahead. Maybe the dog's right. The connection I feel to Anica is undeniable, but I shouldn't let this go too fast or I might scare her—or myself. And I want to get this right.

I really, really do.

"I'll try and forgive her." I lean forward quickly and plant a firm kiss against Anica's mischievous mouth. It's not nearly enough, but for now, it'll have to do. I finally let Anica and Andy drag me across the street. "My dog is far less irritating. That's all I'm saying."

"You have a dog?" The corners of her mouth turn up into a whisper of a smile.

"Actually, my dog is much *more* irritating in most ways, but she knows when to make herself scarce."

"Had a lot of ladies around your dog?" She lifts her eyebrows, and I realize that I've misstepped.

"She's a border collie. I usually take her with me on every long run, and when we make it back, she'll drop into a pile and take a nap. That was my point—she's obnoxious, but when I need a break, she gives it to me."

"Uh, huh." She clears her throat. "And don't think that I forgot that you avoided my other question."

"What?" She asked me a question? When?

"Why can't I tell Luke and Mary and the others that you're a boxer?" She points. "One block to go. Better talk fast. If you don't convince me, I might slip." She covers her mouth and widens her eyes. "Whoops."

She's ridiculous. "After your sister passed, your words went away. But for me, after my mom died, I was angry. Really, really angry."

"Okay."

"My dad thought it would be a good idea—"

"Wait, your dad? Or your uncle?"

I can see why she's confused. "I'll save you some time here. My bio father's name is Phillip. I'll never call him my dad, okay? If I say my dad, I mean my Uncle William. But I always think about him as and call him my dad, pretty much. For some reason, it feels relevant to me that he *chose* that role instead of being my biological father, but it's definitely who he is—my dad. He's been there for every single thing in my life. He's ridiculously controlling, but he does love me completely."

"You're lucky to have him, then."

"I am. I would never contest that, but he's a hard man. He didn't really know what to do with this almost-teenager who landed in his lap. I picked fights at school after school." I shake my head. "It was bad."

"What did he do?"

"He leaned into it, I suppose."

"What does that mean?"

"He told me being angry was fine," I say. "In the right place and in the right ways, but that I had to funnel it into an acceptable channel and never let it control me."

"So you started boxing as a kid?"

I nod. "Yep, but Dad didn't want me to be a 'fighter' to my new friends and family—he didn't want that reputation to follow me. Girls might not care, but teenage boys would definitely see it as a challenge. Whether I wanted to or not, I'd have been a target for any other angry kid who wanted to pick a fight. After we moved from Atlanta to Colorado, Dad had a gym built at the new house. He hired the best trainers to teach me basics after school."

"You've been boxing since you were a kid?"

She has no idea. "I have, and it was a large part of who I was."

"But no one knows."

"Well, I don't do it anymore."

"When did you quit?"

"I missed Atlanta when we moved to Colorado. I was always cold, and I hated skiing."

She laughs. "That's almost a criminal offense in Colorado, from what I understand."

"Practically," I say. "That's one of the reasons I chose Emory for college—from the time I left, I wanted to go back home."

"And now you can't wait to leave and get back to Hawaii. You're a complicated person, Ethan Trainor."

I shrug. "I might be one of those people who always looks back on things a little too fondly. When I was in Colorado, I missed the soft southern accents, the friendly people, and the iced tea. I even missed the warm, humid weather and the swimming in the early fall months."

"And then you got here and remembered that sweating all the time stinks?"

I snort. "Something like that. But even though I didn't really see any of my old friends or live in the same places, I still fell back into some of my old Georgia behaviors."

"Like fighting with people?" She lifts her eyebrows.

"I left my gym and trainer back in Colorado," I say. "But my anger at Mom's death didn't just go away." I can't explain exactly why I needed to come back to Atlanta on my terms or how much fury came back when I did. "I needed an outlet to deal with my . . . frustration, and I met Harrison the first week here."

"You looked up gyms?" she asks.

"I wish." I snort. "I got into a bar fight."

"At eighteen?" She frowns.

"With the bartender who wouldn't serve me a drink because I was underage."

"Uh-oh."

"Punching him would have been really, really bad, except the owner of the bar had spent some time with Harrison Lunger, so instead of calling the cops, he called the man who became my trainer."

"Oh man, really?" She whistles. "Instead of community service, you were asked to punch more people."

"Something like that."

"But why didn't you tell your friends then? Geo told me you were kind of a beach bum who held down a job."

I laugh. "That's not totally wrong. I hadn't been inside a

boxing ring in more than five years when I walked into Harrison's the other day."

"What made you go back inside?"

I shouldn't forget she's an author, at least not until I'm ready for her to know every single thing about my life, which might be nice. But it would also definitely scare her away. "Let's just say that I had a rough week," I say. "I waited too long to deal with some family drama."

"And now that you're back in Atlanta, so is that recurrent anger. Is that why you're so eager to get back to Hawaii?"

Is it? She's far, far too intuitive. I hadn't even considered that, at least not in such plain terms. I shrug. "Maybe."

"But I still don't see why you don't want your friends to know you're a boxer. I think it's pretty cool. I'd tell everyone."

"In high school, Dad pointed out how people would react and encouraged me to keep quiet," I say. "But once I started at Emory, I kept it hidden to keep it from him. He never would have approved of me actually fighting other people in real matches. He came to visit me here pretty often, and I didn't want him to yank his financial support for my schooling, so I kept it a secret from everyone to be safe."

"But now?" she asks. "Your dad still doesn't know?"

I shrug. "I guess I don't really have any reason to hide it anymore. Even if Dad gets mad, it's not like he's paying my tuition."

"Wait." She points at Luke and Mary's house, which is now across the street from us. "Does that mean that I *can* go inside right now and tell them all that you're training at a boxing gym next door to my restaurant? Because it's pretty cool. Not many guys actually know how to throw a punch."

It's probably more accurate that very few guys can take

a real one—or throw an *effective* punch. And she's right that if my dad finds out now, there's not much he can do about it.

And I'm not a kid anymore. I shouldn't have to hide anything—not from friends, and not from my dad.

"Sure," I say. "I guess so. Go ahead." It's an odd feeling, *not* hiding that part of myself.

Anica releases Andy from the leash before we're even through the front door. Andy's clearly eager to be free, and Anica looks almost as eager to share my news. It's kind of endearing, actually. I can't think of a time when I had someone who was proud of me, someone who wanted to brag about me.

"Hey," Mary asks Anica a few minutes later. "What restaurant are you working at? You never said."

"It's called Golden Gloves," Anica says.

"Golden Gloves?" Paisley frowns. "Shouldn't it be white gloves?"

"If it were a fancy place," Anica says, "sure."

"It's not fancy?" Geo asks.

"It's a diner," Anica says with a sneaky grin. "And it's called Golden Gloves because it's next to the best boxing gym in Atlanta. Golden Gloves is a boxing thing—I looked it up." She glances at me sideways.

"It is, yeah," Paul says. "The biggest award an amateur boxer can win."

"That's the reason Ethan's here, really." The gleam in Anica's eye makes me smile. "After an epically bad first date, if I hadn't been interviewing for that job and he hadn't been sparring next door, I'd probably never have seen him again."

That's an unsettling thought. I met her, I took her out, and I almost let her sashay away forever because I was too stupid to see how great she was from the outset.

"Wait, are you serious?" Trig looks at me. "You were *fighting* someone? Easygoing Ethan Trainor? For real?"

"I'm telling you, he's downright scary in a boxing ring with wraps on his hands," Anica says.

Geo and Paisley immediately start laughing.

Trig looks me up and down analytically, trying to decide whether it's all an elaborate joke, probably. Paul tilts his head sideways and narrows his eyes.

"I'm serious," Anica says. "I watched him destroy someone."

Geo stops laughing. "Wait, really?"

Anica nods slowly.

"Oh come on," Paisley says. "No one starts boxing at thirty. What are you thinking, Ethan? That's not safe, and what's the point?"

"To be fair, it's not a safe sport when you're in your twenties either," I say. "But for the record, I'm not just starting. More like, making a comeback."

"A comeback?" Trig asks. "From when?"

"From when I almost won Georgia's Golden Gloves Boxing Championship in 2012."

Paul whips out his phone and starts tapping on it. He looks up at me with the same narrowed eyes, squinched even more tightly closed.

"I'm a light heavyweight," I say, because I know exactly what he's trying to figure out. "I fought right at two hundred pounds."

"You're serious," Trig says.

I shrug.

"You're so much cooler than I realized," Brekka says.

"Why would you hide that?" Rob asks.

I shrug again. "I didn't hide it. I just didn't broadcast it," I lie.

"It says the championship fight that year was between Ethan *Sims* and Jace Blackwell." Paul spears me with a glare.

"You're Ethan Sims? I thought Paisley said your last name started with a T. Trevor or Treager."

"Is there a video?" Anica folds her arms under her chest. "Because if there is, you'll see that it's him." She must have puzzled out that the name difference has something to do with my adoption, but she can't know the truth—that I used Phillip's name to avoid drawing attention to Dad. Beyond that, I always thought Sims was fitting, since Phillip caused the rage that made me so quick to use my fists in the first place.

"I don't see a video." Paul frowns. "Maybe on YouTube."

"Hey, if you don't believe him, you're welcome to come grab some lunch at the Golden Gloves Diner and then go a few rounds with him." Anica's impressively confident in my skills. Paul looks pretty fit. He might shred me. "Just make sure you let me know when you're going so I can watch." She smiles beatifically.

"Please don't let your new boyfriend ugly up my husband. I like all of his teeth." Trudy slings an arm around Paul's shoulders.

Her new boyfriend. I like the sound of that—probably more than I should.

"Ouch," Paul says. "Where's the vote of confidence? I boxed in college too."

"At Harvard." Trig coughs. "Against a bunch of other pansy Ivy League guys."

"Well, I think it's fascinating," Geo says. "You think you know someone after a few dozen study groups, but apparently you don't." She frowns. "What else don't we know about you?"

Trig takes her hand. "Alright, Detective Geode, before you pick a fight with our pugilist friend that I definitely can't win, we better get home."

Geo yawns as if they planned this exit strategy. "Mark is still getting up several times at night."

Trig yawns next. "That kid is a brat already."

Mary laughs. "Stop yawning." She and Luke yawn next, and before I know it, everyone is getting their coats.

"I ought to head home too," I say quietly, reluctantly. "But I agreed to head over to Harrison's tomorrow afternoon. Are you working?"

Anica shakes her head. "Well, not at Golden Gloves, anyway. I'm writing tomorrow."

"Oh, right, you said that." She doesn't look very excited.

"I hope it goes well. It's hard to anticipate whether a writing session will be productive in advance."

"Well, if it's going poorly and you need a break, text me." Play it cool, Ethan. Don't freak her out. "If not, I'm sure I'll see you soon."

"Right," she says. "Sure."

I wish I knew where we were—did Trudy calling me her new boyfriend freak her out? Is she still upset I'll only be here a while? Asking will only make things more awkward. It's better if I drop in on her at Golden Gloves and ask her out again there, probably. Right?

Women should come with some kind of specific user manual, because I never know quite what to do or say.

"Well, see you around." She doesn't even walk me to the door, and I'm not sure whether she's freaked out, or just trying to play it cool around her not-quite-in-laws.

Maybe it's the boxing, or the girl, or the family drama, or some combination of the three, but I can't sleep at all. I toss and turn until the sun comes up and Partner starts licking my face. I groan and pull a pillow down over my head. "Sleep, dog."

Of course that doesn't work. Not with a collie. "Ugh!" I finally throw all the covers on the floor and get up to take her for a jog. Even without much sleep, and even at this absurd hour, and even though it's drizzling outside, I keep thinking of Anica's face when she said, "You're a runner, aren't you? I should've known."

The mock horror. The adorable disdain.

And when her fingers grazed my belly.

I shake off like Partner does and head in to take a shower. A cold shower.

Afterward, I've got a voicemail. It's not a number I know, but I expect it's from work, or maybe Harrison. I tap play, but when the voice emerges, it's not a welcome one.

"Hey there," Phillip says. "I haven't left a phone message for anyone in a long while. This is sort of weird. I'm calling to let you know that Adriana has reached out to me. Twice. I haven't called her back, but she said she was going to come by soon. I'm not sure how to avoid that, and if I'm being honest, I don't want to. I also don't want to upset you. I was hoping to talk to you—maybe even see you. And I have a favor to ask, too. Call me back, please."

I want to hurl my phone against the wall. I want to punch him in the face. And I want to talk some sense into Adriana, or maybe tie her up and duct tape her mouth until she realizes he's a bad, bad man.

I do *not* want to call him back.

But I'm not an angry little kid. I'm an adult, and I do things I don't want to do all the time, so I force myself to return his unwelcome call.

"Ethan!" He answers immediately.

"I'm not calling to chat," I say. "What favor do you need?" Because I have an idea.

"Oh, okay. Well, it's a little weird for me to be asking you this, but I know you're a big business mogul. Adriana tells me you got an MBA from Yale."

"What do you want?"

"I can't seem to find a job."

I swear under my breath. "You want money."

"No, not at all," he says. "I mean, yes. I do want money,

but not from you. I want the chance to earn it. The problem is that without work experience or any references, once I tell any employers where I've been for the last twenty years, I can't even seem to get an interview."

"Eighteen years," I say. "And how terrible for you."

"It is terrible," he says. "Finding a job is a condition of my parole. Usually the government helps you find one, but right now with the economy the way it is, they haven't been able to—they just say we gotta get one in thirty days."

"Or what?" Could he go back to prison? That would solve so many problems.

"I'm not sure, but I think it's not great, and it'll get mighty hard to buy food once this little stipend they gave me is gone."

"Real life is hard, huh?"

"I'm not complaining," Phillip says. "I just thought you might be able to help me find something. Or even if I could list you as a reference, that could help a lot."

"Fine," I say.

"Yes?" Phillip's delight buries itself at the base of my spine and worms its way into my body, gnawing away at me.

I remember what his smile looks like, and that makes me even angrier. If I never make him smile in my entire life, it'll be too soon. "I'll do better than a referral. I'll get you a job, but I have one condition to my help."

"Oh." He coughs. "What's that?"

"You tell Adriana you don't want to see her. You convince her that you want nothing to do with her."

Silence. Complete silence for far too long.

"Are you still there?"

"I'm thinking."

"Well, that probably isn't something you're accustomed to doing," I say. "But I'm not just going to dangle here while you figure it out. Text me back when you know whether you want to take the deal."

"Text?" he asks.

I hang up.

I'm an hour early for my appointment with Harrison, but he takes one look at my face and doesn't risk making a comment.

ANICA

"He is unbelievably handsome," Mary says the second the door closes behind the last guest. "Well done."

"Don't get any ideas," Luke jokes.

The wail of baby Jack's cry emerges from the monitor, and Mary laughs as she stands up. "As if I ever would."

"It's my turn." Luke stands up and waves her back to the sofa.

"And that's why I'll never get any 'ideas,' as you put it." Mary kisses him quickly, and then he jogs down the hall.

"He is hot," I say. "But I want what you've got."

"Luke's taken," Mary says.

I laugh. She's funnier than I gave her credit for at first. "I'm sorry I was so hard on you."

Mary sits up straight. "It's fine. I understood."

"You can be angry with me—you don't have to be perfect *all the time*," I say. "It must be exhausting."

Her shoulders slump. "It is."

I laugh harder. "So let go around me. I don't expect perfection. Heaven knows I'm about as far from flawless as they come."

This is where Mary would normally feel obligated to correct me, and coo about how great I am, and remind me that I'm wonderful. Except maybe she actually listened when I said she doesn't have to be perfect. Because she just says, "Ethan doesn't seem to mind your imperfections." Then she shoots me a devilish look.

My jaw drops.

"You should have seen how he was looking at you," Mary says, "like he hadn't eaten all day, and you were a giant slice of cheesecake."

"Eww," I say. "Gross."

"I'm just saying."

"Well, don't." I stand up.

But even when I go to bed, I can't stop thinking about Ethan and his washboard abs. Who has a stomach like that? No one.

Boxers who like to run, apparently.

Or maybe surfers.

But most importantly, Ethan does.

Gah!

I check the clock. It's almost two a.m., and I still can't sleep.

I finally do what old Anica would have done. Can't sleep? Harness the energy. I open my laptop and pull up a blank word document. I usually write in Scrivener so I can toggle between chapters, but for free writing, nothing beats a blank page.

As I stare at the unrelieved white, the stupid prompt that Henri sent comes to mind. A painfully shy main character . . . like maybe a librarian . . . obsessed with other worlds and terrified of her own.

The pastor bores me. Pastors just don't sound hot.

But what if I wrote a story about a pastor's son? His father injures his leg and sends the son as his emissary. Then what could the son do for a living? Maybe he could be a fireman. Or a police officer. Or a surgeon who just returned from a gig with Doctors without Borders. That seems like something the son of a pastor might wind up doing. And it's hot—way hotter than preaching about heaven and sin and brimstone.

Before I have time to second-guess it, I'm drafting my first romantic comedy in years.

And the hero looks and sounds exactly like Ethan.

So what if he does? It's not like he's ever going to read it. My last boyfriend was an *author* and he never read my books. *Read a romantic comedy?* He had laughed. *Not my thing.*

My fingers fly over the keyboard in a way they haven't in years. I almost forget that this was for an IP project and not just for me.

I write the kind of story I've been desperate to read lately, the kind of story Patrick thought was worthless. The kind of story I have always loved. And then the sun starts to rise, and I stare out the window and blink and blink and blink, half dazed, half drunk-tired. What time is it? It can't already be morning.

But it is.

And I've written four complete chapters. Holy smokes, really? They're rough, but as I skim the opening pages, they're also good. Surprisingly good. My fingers tremble as I click on Henri's email and look over the details. Avon wants a proposal with three sample chapters and an outline.

Before I can second guess myself, I blob out a basic outline of the rest of the story and draft a quick email.

Dear Henri,

I didn't mean to submit something for this, but somehow, I accidentally wrote four chapters. I guess that means I did want to—

No, that's dumb. I delete it.

Dear Henri,

Check out this proposal and tell me what you think.

A

She doesn't deserve a bunch of chatting and explanations. She's clearly not my friend. If it's about the money for her, well it can be about money for me too. Let her make of that what she will.

My finger's hovering over the send button when I notice a new email I somehow missed.

Probably because it's so ubiquitous as to be almost invisible—my daily Publisher's Marketplace email with deals and announcements. I delete it unopened most days, but this morning a name stands out to me.

Patrick McCleve.

My ex.

I can't keep myself from clicking on it to read the full text.

Patrick McCleve's NEVER EVER AGAIN, a literary thriller about a San Francisco power couple that uses a surrogate for their first child, until the wife discovers her husband is a spy for a foreign government and must decide what matters most to her, sold to Martin Lewis at Hachette in a significant deal.

Significant.

I hate Publisher's Marketplace and their stupid code words. Significant deal means Patrick got somewhere between two-fifty and five hundred thousand for his new book. Which means his last three have continued to sell as well as his first.

While I still haven't sold a single new manuscript since my abysmal attempt to write literary fiction. The worst flop of all time. I can still quote the worst of the editorial reviews.

Both forced and contrived, the best part about Maggard's foray into literary fiction was when it blessedly ended. I only wish it had done so more quickly.

A tear leaks from the corner of my eye and rolls down

my face, and I delete the email to Henri with the click of one button. Why was I so excited about an IP project, anyway? It wouldn't even have my name on it, which might be a good thing, actually. Because the name Anica Maggard isn't one that means anything in the literary world. Not anymore, anyway.

I flop back on my bed and finally drift off to sleep.

A persistent buzzing near my elbow finally intrudes on my dream, and I claw my way upward through the fog. Bright light and a ringing phone. I rub my eyes until I can read the tiny little time on the top corner. Just after noon. Which means I've slept... almost five hours.

It's Barbara calling, my new boss, but by the time I try to click talk, it's already gone to voicemail. She doesn't leave me a message, but I get a text message a minute later. YOU ARE SO GOING TO HATE ME. BUT ANY CHANCE YOU CAN COME IN TODAY? I SWEAR WE DON'T USUALLY HAVE SO MANY CANCELLA-TIONS. FLU IS STARTING EARLY THIS YEAR.

In late August? I'd guess it's more of a rash—of flaky employees.

SURE, I text back. IF I COME IN TWO HOURS IS THAT ALRIGHT?

OR EVEN THREE. YOU'RE AN ANGEL.

I shower and make a half-hearted attempt at some kind of makeup, that dumb story about the altruistic doctor rumbling around in the back of my head the entire time. It hardly seems necessary to look my best for work, but it doesn't help my tips to look too haggard. At least our only uniform is an apron. I slide into my favorite work heels—a three-inch wedge that's made of some kind of dark rubber so they're as springy as flats. My calves look great, and my feet don't complain at the end of my shift.

I glance at my clock. I don't have a ton of time, but she did say three hours was fine. I could write a few pages before I leave, if I settle for a protein bar on the way to work, maybe.

I sit down and even though I know this story isn't substantial, even though it's definitely just fluff, I enjoy writing the next scene. By the time I finish the fifth chapter, the hunky doc has realized that he's been trying so hard because something is missing in his life, which is the first step toward fixing himself enough to be ready for real, lasting love.

I'm grinning as I jog down the hall.

A knock at the front door startles me, but I remind myself that it's not my house. If I ignore whoever it is and sneak out the side door, I won't be late.

The door opens. "Anica?"

It's Trudy, so she knocked and then let herself in with the keypad, like usual.

"Hey, there," I say. "I'm just headed out the door."

"Where?" She glances at my purse. "Shopping sounds fun."

I shake my head reluctantly. "Not fun, no. I'm headed to work. They have another server who's out sick so they need me to cover. If you ask me, they ought to hire another new waitress and fire Karina. She cancels more than she works."

"Ah, work drama. It's almost the same no matter what you do."

"Mary's in her room, I think," I say. "And Amy and Chase were in the backyard playing with play-doh on the picnic table."

"Oh, I didn't come for them," Trudy says. "I came to talk to you."

Huh?

"Mary told me she's taking the kids to the park later, but I thought you had the day off. I was going to see if you wanted to get a pedicure."

I glance down at her feet reflexively and she shoos at me with her hands. "Don't look at my toes! They look horrifying. Didn't you hear me say that I need a pedicure?"

Her polish is a little chipped, but clearly her standards are much higher than mine. "I'd love to go," I say, flattered she thought of me. Actually, shocked might be a better word. "But I already told Barb I'd go in."

Trudy sighs. "Oh, alright. I should have texted, I know, but I was driving." She smiles. "Next time?"

"Absolutely." And I mean it. Geo is almost unbearably pretty and driven on top of that. Mary's perfect and beautiful and unfailingly kind. Brekka is brilliant and rich and cultured, plus gorgeous and petite. And Paisley is already best friends with every single person I've met in Atlanta. If I'm being honest, they pretty much all intimidate me.

But Trudy . . . she has been divorced, has a kid, and acts like a real person, but she's also smart and funny. I could actually see myself spending time with her without wanting to cry myself to sleep every night over my failings.

"How about early next week?" I decide I should be more proactive so she doesn't think I'm just being polite. If my former brother-in-law's sister-in-law makes the effort to drive over and invite me to get a pedicure, it's probably my turn to take a risk. "I'm working lunches next week. Could you go after work?"

Trudy smiles. "Paul's not out of town, so I can totally do that. I love that place over by the new frozen yogurt shop. Maybe Tuesday?"

"Pedicure *and* a treat?"

"Even better!" Trudy swipes on her phone and taps on the screen, presumably making note of our agreed-upon girl date. "I'll pick you up—is four-thirty alright?"

"Perfect," I say. "I look forward to it."

"Good luck today. A Saturday dinner shift can't be good."

I shrug. "It's a diner. Could be slammed or kind of slow, depending on how fancy people decide to be."

"Well, good luck getting whichever you prefer."

"Right now, I need tips," I say, "or Mary will be stuck with me forever."

Trudy frowns, but I can't stick around to figure out why. I wave and duck out. The diner is a madhouse when I get there and Barbara sighs when she sees me. "You're a sight for tired eyes."

My eyeballs are actually burning from lack of sleep. I don't do well without a full eight hours, which I know about myself. But another day's tips put me closer to that deposit, so it was the right call. I barely have time to take a bathroom break until around four-thirty when the oddball late lunch rush finally hits a lull.

"You look like you need a coffee and a stack of pancakes," Barbara says.

I laugh. "How did you know I missed breakfast?"

She hands me a plate of pancakes she must have told Ulysses to make and sets a coffee next to it. Then she shimmies. "I hope a man was involved."

If I'd already taken a swallow of coffee, I'd definitely have spit it out all over her. "After a manner of speaking there was," I say. "I spent the night with a super hot doctor who just returned from a tour helping repair cleft palates in Mongolia with Doctors without Borders."

"I thought you weren't working today." Ethan's standing in the doorway. "Someone else came over after I left?"

How did I miss the door jangle? It must have happened when I was laughing. My cheeks heat immediately, and I want to dive behind the counter. Maybe he won't notice.

"I'll let you two talk, but for the record, I called her in last minute." Barb disappears into the back, and I totally want to follow her.

"A doctor?" Ethan frowns. "Are you serious?"

I laugh. "Not really, no."

"You made up some guy?" His eyebrows draw together.

"I couldn't sleep last night, so I pulled out my laptop."

"Chatroom?" Now he thinks I'm a real loser.

"You have got to be kidding," I say. "It's not 2002. No, the doctor I spent all night with is a fictitious character I made up for a book I started writing last night. I wrote four chapters before I finally fell asleep sometime after sunrise."

As realization dawns, his entire face lifts. I should be annoyed, but I can't manage to pull that off. It's too adorable that he was jealous—of a book character I'm writing. He steps closer to me and his eyes drop to my mouth.

"Does it help if I confess that my super hot, charitably minded doctor looks a lot like a certain boxer I know?"

His grin is almost predatory.

"Or maybe you'll be happy to know that I think it's your fault I couldn't sleep."

He kisses me then, but I don't miss the jangle of the bell this time.

"Working," I mumble against his mouth.

He swears under his breath. "I was here first," he says. "So I better get the corner booth."

I roll my eyes, but he gets the corner booth, and he orders two cheeseburgers again. "Really?" I ask.

"I've been eating the same things on my burgers for a decade," he confesses sheepishly. "When I find something I like, I don't get tired of it."

I guess that's comforting in the grand scheme of things. I'm smiling when I take the other customer's order. By the time I bring Ethan his food, he has spread papers out all over the table, and he's working on reports of some kind on his laptop. He camps out in the corner booth until close— alternating between ordering coffee and pie whenever Barb threatens to kick him out. "I'll tip enough to cover it," he says. "Or I can pay a booth fee." He winks at Barb and she giggles as she walks away.

I roll my eyes. "Don't forget my tipping etiquette lesson."

"Oh, come on," he says. "I took up one of your tables all night. If I consumed enough food to make up for that, there's no way I could keep the washboard abs you seem to like so much."

He has a point there. "You can't camp out here every night."

"I know," he says. "But I wish I could."

My heart flip flops in my chest. "And I'm too exhausted to do anything but head home and collapse head first into bed right now."

"Me too," he says. "I didn't sleep well either."

"Family drama?" I ask.

He shakes his head. "I blame a girl."

I hang up my apron.

"She's got the palest cornflower blue eyes. Sometimes they're nearly white."

I blink.

"And the daintiest hands. Sometimes I wonder how she can type fast enough to be an author." He insists on walking me out to my car.

"I'm not much of an author right now," I say.

"Says the girl who stayed up all night and wrote four chapters."

"My ex just landed a huge book deal." I shouldn't have said that. It's not cool to talk about exes this early on in something new. "Never mind."

Ethan wraps an arm around my shoulders and squeezes gently. "Who cares?"

"Huh?"

"You sound upset that your ex is doing well." He presses a kiss to my forehead. "But his success doesn't impact you at all. The woman I'm looking at is doing great, given what life threw at her. Look around at other people less, and worry about your own progress more."

"Do you do that?"

"Professionally?" Ethan asks.

I shrug.

"I'm good at doing that professionally." He smirks. "Less so in my personal life, so don't think I'm lecturing you as some kind of expert. I'm giving you the advice I try to follow myself whenever possible."

I shift and lean my head against his very solid chest. Some of the tightness in my heart eases. "It's good advice."

"People want their exes to do poorly—and I even get that—but it's actually better if they do well. It means you had good taste."

I shake my head. "Oh, he was a catch alright."

Ethan smiles. "So are you. Today. Right now. Waitress Anica. Once you realize that, you'll be an even better catch."

"Good to know."

"Are you feeling caught yet?" His head lowers toward mine.

Like a glow stick that's been cracked, a feeling of giddy joy spreads through my entire body, spiraling outward from my heart. A thrill shoots up and down my spine and then flies out toward my toes and fingers. And then his mouth covers mine and all that bubbly light explodes. My hands reach around his neck and my fingers curl against his slightly shaggy hair.

His lips press against mine eagerly, more insistent than yesterday, and I wish I wasn't quite so tired.

A tiny beeping sound that signals a car unlocking from behind me jolts me back to the real world. "You two are adorable," Barb says.

"I'd better head home before I'm so tired I swerve into oncoming traffic and die," I whisper.

"I'm not sure I've ever been more wide awake in my life." The warmth of Ethan's breath against my face sends a shiver up my body and my head trembles like a leaf in the gusty fall wind. "What are you doing tomorrow?"

"Not working here." Barb winks at me and closes the door of her car.

"I guess nothing," I say. "Although I probably ought to try and write at least a little bit."

"About the hunky doctor?" He lifts both eyebrows.

"Right."

"I suppose I can support that. Any chance you'd send me what you've written?"

I stumble backward, my backside bumping into my car. "Are you serious?"

"Why wouldn't I be?" He lifts one eyebrow.

"You do know I write romantic comedies."

"You said that, yeah."

"I doubt that's really your typical genre."

"It's not my usual selection," he says. "But if you're writing it, I'd love to read it."

I gulp. "I never let anyone read what I'm writing when I'm still writing it."

"That's a shame," he says. "But I'll survive. I've got three other books to read, after all."

I freeze, my arms suddenly heavy, dread sinking into my belly. "What books?" My voice is higher and squeakier than it should be.

"Yours, obviously. I ordered all three of them this afternoon. I'm a little embarrassed it took me this long."

"You can't read them," I blurt. "You can't."

He steps back and sits on my hood, his jaw jutting out defiantly. "Why not?"

"I don't want you to." I cross my arms. "Isn't that enough of a reason?"

"You wrote two best-selling novels and a third book in a completely different genre in the year after your sister died." He frowns. "You really don't want me to read them? More than a hundred thousand people read your first two books."

"Women," I say. "A hundred thousand women."

"Last night, I was thinking to myself that I wish women came with a manual." He drops his voice until it's barely more than a whisper. "See, I didn't want to do anything stupid to mess this up." His hand brushes my cheek and I melt. "And then today I realized that this woman *does* come with a manual. Sort of."

"What does that mean?"

"You've literally written BOOKS about relationships. If I can't learn something from them about how to make you happy, then I really am a dope."

He might be the most adorable guy I've ever met. "Fine. You can read the first two."

"Why not the third?" He straightens. "I've lost someone too, remember? Maybe your book will help me. The blurb says it's about an adopted girl who discovers that although her adoptive parents are idyllic, her birth mother has died, and she spins out."

I nod numbly.

"That sounds fascinating, honestly."

My voice is flat. "Kirkus said, 'Maggard's prose proves as fascinated with its own importance as a Millennial in a hand-painted scarf.'"

"Who's Kirkus? He sounds like a moron."

My laugh comes out more like a sob. "Publisher's Weekly said, 'As impeccably flat as her romantic comedies were effervescent with life.' And—"

Ethan grabs my hand and spins me in a circle. "Stop." He presses a finger to my lips. "No more."

My eyes widen, but I don't try to speak or to squirm away.

"I don't care what a bunch of stupid, overeager critics think. Their only value comes from tearing someone else's work down. What have they ever created?"

I shrug.

"Nothing," he says. "That's what. Stop worrying that I'll be that stupid and trust that I'll find the *Anica* in your stories. Because I can tell you right now—I like Anica in pretty much everything I've seen her in so far."

"Maybe you should write the rest of my story."

He kisses me again, but this time he's the one who pulls away. "I can't have you crashing on the side of the road, can I?" He spins me again, but this time I end up right next to the driver's door of my car. "Go home and stop worrying."

"That's what I do," I say. "I worry, and I know things."

"All right, then do what you do. But don't worry about *me*. I haven't read a word, but I'm already a fan."

At the end of the day, more than washboard abs, more than a shoulder to cry on, more than a thrill that runs down my spine for a second and then disappears, I think that's what I really need. A fan of *Anica*.

I'm so tired when I get home that my eyelids feel like overstuffed bags of groceries, tugging inexorably downward, threatening to burst at any second. Even so, I flip my laptop open and bang out a one-line message to Henri and attach my sample chapters.

Then I click send.

When I wake up the next day and check my email inbox on my phone, there's a message waiting on me.

LOVED IT is the subject line. My heart races and my fingers fumble to open my laptop.

Anica,

Yes, yes, yes, yes, I've been waiting on this for years. I am delighted you replied, and I love those chapters. I'll send an agency agreement over later so we can submit this to Avon.

Have you written anything else you want me to take a look at?
Henri

I collapse back against the pillows and begin to sob. I've been waiting for her to be excited about something I wrote for so very long. More than five years, in fact. It feels good, even if it's only an IP project. Even if there's no way this deal will ever be announced on Publisher's Marketplace, let alone listed as a "significant" deal.

Who cares? Worry about my own life, not anyone else's, right? Ethan's brilliant. It feels good to focus on my triumphs, not my losses for a change. And now that I've got an agent again . . . something feels right about the world.

Before I can second-guess it, I pull up the chapters I've written on *Ashes* and send them to her. I don't mention that it has taken me three years to do those seven chapters, writing only a few hundred agonizing words at a time. Surely with the right incentive, I can finish it faster.

I'm beaming when I walk downstairs.

"Someone's happy," Luke says.

"I sent some sample chapters to my old agent," I say. "And she loved them."

His eyes widen. "That's phenomenal. Really?"

I nod.

"Great work!"

"What?" Chase asks. "What is it?"

"Aunt Anica's writing another book," Luke says.

"Are there cars in it?" he asks. "Oh! Or trains?"

"Not really," I say. "It's not that kind of book."

Chase tilts his head and scrunches up his nose. "What kind of book is it, then? Are there animals?"

I laugh. "Not so far."

"Then what?"

I swallow my bite of Little Bites Frosted Mini Wheats and crouch down next to him. "Well, it's a book with kissing in it."

The look of horror on his face is priceless.

"I wish I had my camera ready," Luke says. "It would have made a great video to play at his wedding someday."

"Right?" I return to my chair. "You'll get it eventually, buddy."

"I doubt it," Chase says. "Dad still likes trucks."

I laugh. "That he does."

"And tools," Chase says. "And trains. Right, Dad?"

Luke ruffles his hair. "Right you are, mate."

"Well, Amy will get it one day for sure," I say.

"Are you working again today?" Luke asks.

I shake my head. "I've got big plans to hide in my room and write on this book while ideas are rolling around in my brain."

"Ideas about kissing?" Chase frowns.

"Exactly," I say. "Unless you guys need me for anything?"

Luke shakes his head. "Not at all. I'll tell everyone to steer clear."

"Thanks."

I send a quick text to Ethan before putting my phone on airplane mode. FEELING INSPIRED. GOING TO WRITE. HOPE THAT'S OKAY.

Luckily he texts back immediately. OF COURSE.

I sigh in relief and settle back into my make-believe world of kissing and shy girls overcoming their hang-ups. When I'm in the groove, I don't sleep. I don't eat. I don't even stop to go pee, unless it gets really unbearable. When I finally take a bathroom break and unplug my headphones, my phone tells me it's almost four in the afternoon.

I check out my total word count for the day. Three and a half chapters—more than nine thousand words. A very,

very good day. One of my best, for sure. I flip my phone back into service and turn my laptop Wi-Fi back on.

DINNER? Ethan texted at some point. WE CAN GO SOMEWHERE OTHER THAN A DINER. ;)

I'm about to send him a response when my email on my laptop loads, and I notice another one from Henrietta. Has she already read my sample of *Ashes*, or is this the agency agreement she mentioned? My knees begin to bounce, and I drop my phone.

I force myself to click the email open.

Anica,

I'm still very excited to submit to Avon, but after reviewing Ashes carefully, I'm not sure I'm a great fit for that project. Since you're still wanting to take your career in that direction, I've attached a provisional agency representation agreement that will only be applicable to the single IP title.

Best,

Henri

A provisional agency agreement.

She hated my other chapters that much?

I know it's not a 'relationship,' but it sure feels like I've been dumped. Again. And for some reason, my absurd hope and glee this morning makes it a rougher gut punch than it was the first time. It feels like she's saying that she'll use me for the kissing books, but if I want anything more, she's out.

I shake my head and try to refocus. It's still good news —an IP project is work.

But all my energy and excitement is . . . gone.

I FEEL PRETTY LOUSY, I text Ethan. RAINCHECK?

PLEASE TELL ME I DIDN'T SAY SOMETHING STUPID. A moment later, Ethan sends a gif of a puppy dog making sad eyes.

If I wasn't so bummed, it would make me smile. NOT

AT ALL. JUST DON'T WANT TO GET YOU SICK IF I'M COMING DOWN WITH SOMETHING.

DON'T WORRY ABOUT ME, he texts back. IF YOU DECIDE YOU WANT COMPANY, I'M NOT AFRAID OF A COLD.

Poor Ethan. All I would do is mope. GOOD TO KNOW, BUT I'M STILL GOING TO STAY PUT TONIGHT.

FAIR, BUT PROMISE ME ONE THING.

?

DON'T GO KISSING ANY HOT DOCTORS, NO MATTER HOW MANY KIDS THEY'VE SAVED WITH EMERGENCY SURGERIES IN SERBIA.

IT'S MONGOLIA, I text. But I'm actually smiling when I do it. AND I'M NOT MAKING ANY PROMISES.

YOU VIXEN. WELL, THEN DON'T FAULT ME FOR MAKING OUT WITH A REALLY HOT BARISTA WHO WANTS TO BE A BROADWAY DANCER.

He's reading my first book, which is ridiculously cute of him. Life is always better when you have someone who tries to cheer you up. I had almost forgotten the feeling.

❧ 11 ❧

ETHAN

When Anica blows me off to write about a fictitious doctor who saves kids in third world countries, I feel adrift. No surfing. No Sunday brunch. Nothing at all to do in this town where I no longer have any friends.

So I call my sister.

"Hey Ethan," she says. "I've been thinking about you, but I wasn't sure whether you wanted to talk to me when you didn't reply to the photo I texted."

Her photo of Phillip with his arm around her. I didn't call her to talk about him. I don't even want to think about him being around her. I grunt.

I can imagine her rolling her eyes at me. Or maybe flopping back on her bed with exasperation. "How was your first week back?"

"Fine," I say. "Dad didn't lie—the hotel's a disaster. Badly mismanaged and coasting on a reputation the current management was working hard to destroy."

"Well, you're great at turning things around."

"I hate firing people," I say. "And hiring new people is always a gamble, but at least a few of them should be as

138

motivated as I am to turn things around."

"I could never fire anyone," she says, "which is probably why Dad never bothered trying to talk me into joining the family business."

"You like what you do," I say. "Don't you?"

"I love it." She sighs. "It doesn't pay well, but we're blessed enough that it doesn't matter."

She doesn't want to fire people, but I'm not sure I could do what she does either, teaching special education at a local elementary school. "Doesn't it depress you at all? All those kids who won't ever have a normal life?"

"Normal is vastly overrated, Ethan. I help them fulfill the maximum of their potential, and for many of them, we have no idea how high they might fly."

Anica should write a book about her. "You want to grab lunch?"

"I would love to," she says, "any time next week."

A sense of unease settles across my shoulders. "Why not today?"

She gulps. "I'm happy to meet you today, but I'm guessing you won't be so happy about it."

My jaw clenches. "Why, Ana?" But I already know.

"If you came to lunch, you might understand. He's not the man you remember."

"People don't change that much," I say. "And even if he has changed substantially, are you really saying you've forgiven him for *killing* our mother?"

Ana sighs. "Ethan, that was a really long time ago, and he can't undo it."

"It wasn't an accident." I force myself to relax my hand where it grips the phone. If I break it, I'll be stuck spending hours at the cell phone store. "He hit her so many times her head flew into the side of the bathtub and she cracked her skull."

I've never said that out loud, not in almost twenty years.

I don't add that I should have stopped him. That I should have yelled, or hit him back, or just taken her place. I don't add that seeing him makes me hate myself even more than I already do at a baseline. She'd never understand, or she'd argue with me and tell me that it's not my fault, blah blah blah. I've heard that from counselors already. They're right . . . and they're wrong.

Phillip is a bad person.

But I'm generally a good person, which makes my failure to do anything for her even worse. I knew she needed help, and I was too afraid of being hit again myself to offer it. Maybe Phillip's going to tell her today that he can't see her anymore. Maybe today will be the last time she takes him to lunch.

Or maybe he'll find a job on his own, and she'll be going to lunch with him forever. Or at least until he hurts her so badly that she can't or won't meet him again. That's what I'd really like to avoid.

"Promise me this, Ana."

"What?"

"If you ever feel threatened by him, if he ever scares you in any way, you will leave immediately and call 911 and then call me, in that order. Promise." And I'll make sure he never sees her again if she ever does make that call, but I can't say that or she won't do it.

"Sure, Ethan. If that makes you feel better, I will absolutely call you if I'm ever afraid. But you're wrong if you really think that will happen. He's not the man he was. He can't even find a job, but he's not drinking. He's not angry, just discouraged. If you gave him a chance, you might find out that the past twenty years have been harrowing for him. He really loved Mom—"

"Ana, I love you, but don't ever say that to me."

She groans. "Fine. Whatever. Let's get together next week, okay?"

"Sure," I say. "Text me a day. I'll drive to you. I know now that school has started, it's hard for you to get away."

"Thanks." She hangs up.

And I have a burning desire to punch something. Again. Every time he comes up, he ruins my day.

I text Anica one more time, hoping against hope that she'll have time to see me today. DINNER? WE CAN GO SOMEWHERE OTHER THAN A DINER. ;) But after half an hour, when she still hasn't replied, I assume she's not going to reply any time soon. Which is good for her, truly. I'm glad she's writing, but I need to do something other than sit around my house or go for another jog.

Harrison's not there when I reach the gym, but there are a handful of guys who are only too happy to demonstrate the many ways they can catch the new guy in yet another hold.

I'm starting to hate wrestlers.

But that helps me. The angrier I get, the better my brain processes stimuli. By the time Chad shows up, I'm spoiling for a real fight—to test how well I'm picking up my new wrestling lessons. And if I read something right that first day, it's that Chad is always happy to spar.

"I've got a big fight coming up next week," he says. "So no blows to the face, and we tap out. Fine?"

I shrug. "Fine with me." I vow to myself not to rely on punches at all, except to keep him away. If I win this, it's going to be with kicks, holds, or a takedown.

Even with him avoiding any blows to my face, fighting him without relying on punches is hard. I suck at kicking, for one. And I have to think way too hard about each hold and how to line them up. My muscles don't know the moves instinctively yet.

Which is how, after a particularly effective blow to my solar plexus, I drop my head and wind up in a guillotine choke. It works by cutting off my air, so it's way slower than the rear naked choke. Knowing that and doing something about it aren't quite the same, but I don't just throw in the towel. I flail and thrash and twist, all the while weakening.

Then when I'm about to tap out, the pressure lessens, just for a second, but it's enough. I shove with my knees to distract him and pop my hand between his inner elbow and my neck, and then I slide out. In spite of my resolve not to punch at all, I pound him with an uppercut, and when his head rocks back, I see my opening. I slide past his guard and throw him into a wicked joint lock—if he pushes at all, I'll break his elbow.

He taps out.

And people around us start clapping. I hadn't realized anyone was watching. Sundays aren't usually big days at the gym, so a six-person audience is surprising. Harrison's smiling bigger than anyone else.

"Nicely done," he says.

"Way better than before," Chad says begrudgingly. "For real. You're getting better fast."

"I lined up a fight for you—in four weeks. A qualifier."

"At the open?" Chad asks.

Harrison nods. "Izzy Volkov."

"Volkov?" Chad whistles. "You sure, coach? With only five weeks' training in UFC?"

"It's not up to me," Harrison says. "I told Whiting it's too soon, but he said his boy's been struggling to find a matchup. He's like a bulldog, that one. Takes people out with holds, and UFC brass is sick of his methods so they aren't giving him many good options." He leans forward and grabs the side of the ring with both hands. "Holds are boring, right? Crowds want strikes—they want boxers. They don't like watching two grown men roll around on the floor gasping for air."

"You told them you had one?"

Harrison shrugs. "An older one, yeah. A comeback story.

Their very own Rocky, except instead of the underdog, I've got a corporate raider who's as comfortable in a board room as he is in a UFC ring."

"Excuse me?" Chad asks.

"I did a little digging on our boy here." Harrison's smile is so big I can see two gold crowns in the back of his mouth. "Turns out he's been using a fake name all this time. You're looking at Ethan Trainor, heir apparent to the Trainor family fortune, including more than ninety hotels across the world."

I groan. There's no way I can fight now. Dad would kill me.

"We'll have to lay some ground rules," a loud voice calls from the entryway of the gym.

Everyone jumps, except for me. It's a voice I've always known. "What are you doing here, Dad?" My voice sounds calmer than I expect.

"There's been an incident at the Riviera we need to discuss," he says. "I came to find you, and imagine my surprise at locating you here."

"You're his dad?" Harrison takes a few steps toward Dad. "Pleased to meet you." He extends a hand.

Dad walks toward him and clasps hands with him, pumping my old trainer's arm up and down. "I'll want to know details on the venue, and I need to approve any and all press releases, obviously."

"That sounds fair," Harrison says, as if my dad's my manager or something.

"Whoa," I say. "What are you doing?"

"We need to talk," Dad says. "Outside."

This can't be happening. How did he even find me here? "I'll get back to you about that fight," I say.

"And we'll need to approve any monikers or nicknames," Dad says to Harrison over his shoulder. "I'll be in touch with a list of options."

The second we clear the gym door, I spin toward Dad. "Why are you here?"

His eyes crinkle up every time he grins. "I could ask you the same thing."

"How did you even know where I was?" I glance around. "Are you having me followed or something?"

"Please." He snorts. "I gave you a car worth more than a hundred thousand dollars. They come with anti-theft monitoring systems, obviously, and I simply tracked you."

All the swear words. And then some creative combinations I've never thought to use before. "I'm not an errant child," I say. "You can't give me a stuffed teddy bear with a tracking chip in it and rationalize that it's for my own good."

"Calm down, Ethan. I did nothing of the sort. I got a call this morning, and I needed to reach you. It didn't occur to me to use the car until you didn't answer your phone, and you weren't at home."

Oh. "What's wrong?"

"We're being audited."

Few words in the English language are as awful as the a-word: audit. "By whom, and for what?" I narrow my eyes at him.

"We just lost our first lawsuit on the OTC taxes."

I blink. "How? They want us to pay taxes on the amount of money that's held back for a booking by the third party booking agency? We don't even ever take custody of that amount."

"The IRS immediately set up an audit of our facilities to determine the exact amount that will be owed if our appeal doesn't succeed."

"How far back are they wanting to go?" I knew there was ongoing discussion, but no one thought the government might actually succeed in clawing back extra taxes from the hotels for the booking company's fees. "We won the other suits, right?"

Dad looks as grim as I've ever seen. "They only need one to set up the audits."

I understand why he tracked me down. "You want preliminary figures for my hotels."

"Yes." He glances back at Harrison's gym.

"And you want me to drop this," I say. "Clearly." I turn to walk out to my car. I'll head for the hotel right away and start to figure out what kind of records we've got on these online travel company reservations.

"Not at all."

I freeze and turn back around slowly. "What?"

"There's something else I've been wanting to talk to you about. Phillip's—" He spins his hand around and around and then waves his arm through the air. "—release, or whatever you call it, that was a convenient excuse to bring you back home."

"Oh?" I fold my arms. "What now? You've been manufacturing weapons on the side? The family home has burned to the ground? You're secretly the Easter Bunny?"

Dad rolls his eyes. "Annelise has tired of waiting patiently for me to give her more attention. She's insisting that if I don't marry her and retire by year end, she'll leave me."

That I did not expect. "Did you try calling her bluff?"

His Adam's apple bobs up and down when he swallows. "I did."

My eyes widen. "And?"

"She left me."

"Did you actually care?"

His lips twist. "Of course I cared. I found it intolerable not to have her in my life."

Intolerable? Wow, Dad. Such an inspiration. "And what are you going to do about it?"

"I'm stepping down in my role as lead for Trainor Hotels International, effective January 1."

He couldn't have shocked me more if he told me he *was* the Easter bunny. "So why did you want me here in Atlanta?" Except that answer is obvious. He wants me to step in to replace him. He always has. I just figured it would be nine thousand years from now, when his cyborg brain replacement finally wore out and he could not possibly locate one more.

"The Board has always been concerned that you lack the . . . ruthlessness necessary to head a multinational corporation like THI."

"They're probably right. You've always been ruthless enough for the entire family."

"But a high-profile corporate executive fighting in the UFC? At the age of thirty?"

"For all you know I'll be decimated," I say. "Is that what you want?"

"Please. The only reason you lost in college is that you got scared."

I splutter. "How did you—you can't have—what?"

"I may not have microchipped your teddy bear on purpose as an adult, but I'm not so stupid that I sent you to Atlanta as a teenager without keeping tabs on you." He lifts one eyebrow. "What sort of father do you take me for?"

"You knew I was boxing all along?"

He shrugs. "You were being smart and as safe as possible, and you weren't brawling in bars, other than that first one."

"Wait—" It's like the sky is spinning and the sun is flickering and the world is all wrong. "You knew about my bar fight?"

"You think that bar owner *just happened* to know the best trainer in Georgia?" Dad laughs. "I forget how naive you are in some ways."

"You *paid him* to put me in touch with Harrison?"

"Your coach never knew," Dad says. "Don't flip out. I reached out to the bar owner and asked him to pass your name along, and offered a generous travel package if he'd do that in lieu of pressing charges."

I shake my head. Even for my dad, this is a new low. "And now you want me to fight so that . . . what does this have to do with the lawsuit again?"

Dad smiles. "So much in life is about perception. You've been the hapless surfer for so long that you've allowed the world to believe it's who you really are. It's time for them to see the iron core of Ethan that has always existed beneath that 'hang ten' façade."

"You want me to impress the board by getting my brains knocked out on television?" It still doesn't compute.

Dad steps closer. "You have always intimidated people, you know."

At six foot three, I've got a few inches on almost anyone in almost every room. With the kind of lean bulk I developed as a boxer and maintained as a surfer, I've always been one of the biggest guys in any group too. I suppose I never thought how that might transfer to the way they treat me. Have I been projecting a laid-back surfer persona so that people don't fear me?

The way I always feared Phillip?

The way I never want anyone to fear me . . . because it would make me like him?

"You lost that Golden Gloves fight because you didn't want to be an alpha," Dad says. "But it's time for you to accept that you can be the scariest person in the room without *doing* horrible things. You aren't like Phillip."

My teeth grind audibly. "With this audit, do you really want my focus split?"

He laughs. "This audit is much bigger than you or I. I've got the best team of lawyers on this—far better than the government's team of reject suits. But with this cloud hanging over us, I won't give the board any reason not to vote for you as my replacement."

"Can't you basically vote me in?" I lift one eyebrow.

"You know I love you," my dad says.

"Of course I do." He sucks at showing it, but he does.

"But when I say I won't give the board a reason, what I really mean is that I'd like you to prove it to me."

Great. He's not worried about the board—he's saying that *he* can't support me until he believes that I'm tough enough to do what it takes. "And if I win some ultimate fighting championship match, then you'll believe that I can do whatever THI needs?"

"It's a start," he says.

I always figured I'd eventually take over, but it never occurred to me that he'd make me perform for the position like a circus dog doing tricks. I'd like to throw the keys to the stupid car he bought me in his face and walk away.

But, surprisingly, I actually want to run THI. "Fine," I say. "But I'm the only one who can approve any monikers."

"I was thinking 'The Shark'."

"You've got to be kidding right now."

"Like the shark tank—you know, a predator, but also a businessman. Think about it."

Fish out of water, limp gills, big fish in a little pond— the horrible metaphors and jokes are limitless. I won't turn into some kind of horrifyingly idiotic media stunt by choosing the worst name ever for myself. "Veto."

I head back to the Riviera to start digging into this disastrous audit—but the second I'm stuck waiting around with nothing to do, I call the local Ford dealership. "Tell me about the new Broncos." Because I'm not about to keep wearing the stupid dog collar Dad threw around my neck, now that I know it's there.

I'm just starting to look into the spreadsheets on the

OTC payments withheld when Anica texts me back. I'd almost forgotten how irritatingly clingy I was being earlier.

I FEEL PRETTY LOUSY. RAINCHECK?

Crap—she's sick? Or . . . is she blowing me off? I think back on how we left things. I thought we were in a pretty good place. Then this morning she says she wants to write. She ignores my invite to dinner all day, and then texts to say she "feels lousy." I better make sure there wasn't some misunderstanding. I just had a metric ton of trash dumped on my plate, but if anything, it makes me want to see her more. PLEASE TELL ME I DIDN'T SAY SOMETHING STUPID.

Does that sound pathetic? I meant it to be funny, but it might be too heavy-handed. I'm too tired for this. I search "uh-oh" on the gifs tab and find one with an adorable puppy making sad eyes. Surely that will signal that I'm playfully asking, but also kind of serious.

NOT AT ALL, she texts back. JUST DON'T WANT TO GET YOU SICK IF I'M COMING DOWN WITH SOMETHING.

Now I want to see her to make sure she's okay—and to ensure I'm not being brushed off. Because, of course, if she is making this up, she would double down and insist she is just sick. DON'T WORRY ABOUT ME. IF YOU DECIDE YOU WANT COMPANY, I'M NOT AFRAID OF A COLD. Although, if I go over there, I'll be up all night working on this. Worth it.

GOOD TO KNOW, BUT I'M STILL GOING TO STAY PUT TONIGHT.

And now I've been too pushy. I should be sitting at home, reading her book. Maybe I'd get some guidance or insight there. Instead I'm stuck here, my eyes crossing at row after row of stupid fees from online bookings. I need to leave things on a playful note. FAIR, BUT PROMISE ME ONE THING.

I imagine her sitting in bed, her hair piled up on the top of her head, tucked under fluffy covers. Maybe she's even writing. What could I ask her to promise me? "Dream of me"? No, too cheesy. "Let me know when you feel better"? No, even worse, because I'm trying to keep tabs on her. "Save me a burger"? Sounds like I'm using her for food.

Ugh, why is this part so hard?

She's a writer, that's why. I'm on high alert all the time, worried I'll use words in an idiotic way. I'm a smart guy, but she, of all people, would be sure to pay attention to the context of which words I use and when.

And also . . . ever since I struck out five minutes into our first date, I've been waiting for her to axe me.

Keep it light, Ethan. Don't let your own insecurities ruin this. A joke we've already had—what about the book she's working on? Who did she say looked like me? A doctor who went to third world countries. Right? Alright, how about DON'T GO KISSING ANY HOT DOCTORS, NO MATTER HOW MANY KIDS THEY'VE SAVED WITH EMERGENCY SURGERIES IN SERBIA. That's not so bad. Playful, and it reminds her that she likes me. And makes her think about our kiss. I click send.

IT'S MONGOLIA, she corrects me. AND I'M NOT MAKING ANY PROMISES.

About not kissing the fictitious doctor version of me. I smile in spite of the lousy day I've had. YOU VIXEN.

Before I called Adriana this morning, I read three chapters of her first book. If I weren't stuck here, I'd be reading the rest right now. I should let her know I'm reading it— bonus points can't hurt if she's thinking about blowing me off permanently. WELL, THEN DON'T FAULT ME FOR MAKING OUT WITH A REALLY HOT BARISTA WHO WANTS TO BE A BROADWAY DANCER. Since that's the main character in that first book—connection drawn between doctor me, and first heroine, Katy, the barista—who is actually quite a lot like Anica.

Or I'm dramatically overthinking this and she now thinks I'm insane. I may not know until the next time I see her—or she successfully avoids me for days and days. I review numbers until my eyes cross, and then I finally head out.

When I reach home, I check the mail on my way inside and discover the title has arrived for my ridiculous Porsche. Perfect. I have an idea of what to do with it, now that I've got a new vehicle on the way. Dad's going to hate it, and that just makes the idea look even better.

The next morning, I go ahead and sign the stupid one-project agency agreement so that Henri can send my proposal to Avon. I'm disappointed, sure, but after a good night's sleep, I'm not depressed. I'm really no worse off than I was before.

Except I may get a decent chunk of money for something I'm enjoying writing.

It won't be much compared to the advances on my last three books, but at least there's no stress over whether it'll sell through. If it doesn't sell well, too bad. That's on Avon. It's sort of like writing ad copy, or like, the text that goes on a website. I just write it, and then they buy the words, and I'm done. No pass pages, no arguing with an editor, none of the miserable stuff. No royalty checks, but . . . even so.

Easy peasy.

Who cares if Patrick McCleve is flying high with his literary thrillers while I'm writing books that will be put out in someone else's name? Not me.

I shower and get ready for work—lunch shift all week— and I can't help wondering whether I'll see Ethan. Maybe he'll stop by for a burger. When I climb in my car, I decide to stop being coy. I'm the one who bailed on our plans yesterday, so I may as well be the one to reach out today.

LUNCH SHIFT ALL WEEK FOR ME. YOU?

He doesn't reply right away, which is a bummer, but I'm not going to be late for work because I sat around staring at my phone for too long. When I reach Golden Gloves and he still hasn't replied, I'm annoyed. Sometimes I wonder whether texting embodies everything that's wrong with the world. No one calls anymore. No one works out any details, and why? Because, no worries! I'll text it all to you. Or, I won't, and you'll be left dangling indefinitely.

Gah.

I'm wiping off my last table in preparation to leave when my phone starts to buzz in my pocket. It's Ethan.

"Hey," I say.

"You at work?"

I scan the parking lot for an ostentatious blue Porsche, thankful for the wall of windows, but nothing. "I'm just finishing up."

He groans. "I'm stuck here until late today. We've hit a bump."

"Uh oh," I say. "That sounds ominous."

"Ominous? Remind me never to play Scrabble with you."

"They never play that on Fridays unless a bunch of people are gone. There are too many people to play most nights."

"You immediately think of game night, huh? Does that mean I'm invited again?" he asks.

I laugh. "I don't even know whether I'm invited. I'm just staying in the house right now, so they feel obligated to make me welcome."

"Well, if we slide in for a few more weeks, they'll probably forget we weren't ever officially invited."

We. His casual use of the word 'we' sends a little thrill

up my spine. "Not a bad plan. But have you considered that *they* might not be cool enough for *us*?"

"Uh, yeah, and that's a fair point. Clearly they aren't, but sometimes you have to do things for the little people. It's called being charitably minded. I'm pretty sure you can deduct it on your taxes."

"Oh man, if Mary could hear you right now, she'd be cringing."

"You're saying she doesn't like tax humor?"

"Oh, she probably does, but I doubt she'd approve of you implying, even in a joke, that you can somehow deduct charitable actions." I hold my phone between my shoulder and ear and untie my apron, then I wave at Barb. "Because how would you even do that? You can't put a price on the value of my company."

"Wait, Mary's a tax person?" Ethan asks.

"Yeah—she's between firms right now, but she's kind of a prodigy."

"I'm not sure you can be a prodigy if you're in your thirties."

"Do you really want to lock horns over semantics with a writer?" I huff. "A prodigy is often used to describe a young person, but it doesn't have to be used for one."

Ethan laughs. "I just like to watch you get all riled up."

"You can't see me," I say.

"Fine," he says. "*Hear* you get riled up. Is that better?"

I unlock my car. "Not really." I hope he can't hear my pout. "Seeing is far preferable."

"I agree," he says. "And a lot happened yesterday. What are you doing tonight, maybe on the late side?"

"Probably writing. Speaking of, I have some news too," I confess. "I sort of have a book on submission with Avon."

"What?" Ethan whoops, and then I hear someone in the background asking him something. "No, I'm fine, it was, just, never mind."

"Thanks for the excitement, but I haven't sold it yet."

"But you're out there with it, right?"

"I guess so."

"I'm proud of you, and before you point it out, I know I have no right to be proud of you. I'm not your dad or your mom or your sibling or whatever, but I'm proud nonetheless."

"Thanks." At least when I'm sitting in my car he can't see me blushing.

"I bet your cheeks are pink right now."

"For the love," I say. "I'm going to hang up on you."

"No you aren't," he says, "but I do have to go. We've hit a tax snag at work." He drops his voice to whisper. "We're being *audited*. My dad is freaking out, although he's officially acting calm. But if we lose our appeal, let's just say we're going to be in trouble."

"You really ought to talk to Mary about it. She's wicked smart and for some reason that stuff just makes sense in her brain. I bet she'd be helpful."

"I'll take it under consideration," he says, "but that's not the only big thing that shifted yesterday."

"We really did have a big day yesterday, huh?"

"I like hearing you say *we*." His voice is low, and again, it sends a zing right up my spine.

"Me too," I say, "but, you know, from you."

"Can you meet me at eight or so, anywhere you choose? Unfortunately that's probably the earliest I'll be able to break away."

"Wow, work is demanding right now."

"It's not only work," he says, "but I'd rather explain in person."

"Cryptic. I like that more than I thought I would." I tap the steering wheel. "Okay, well, I'll already have eaten by then—I get crabby if I get too hungry—but I could meet you for dessert somewhere."

"Name the place."

"There's a pie place that Paisley gushes about right by her old apartment."

"Text me the address?"

"Sure," I say. "I'll meet you there if you promise to park that gosh-awful car far, far away."

He laughs. "Deal." Someone starts to talk to him. "Hang on," he says, I think to the other person. "Hey, Anica, I've got to run. See you tonight?"

"Definitely."

I have big plans to write every second between now and then . . . but after I write one chapter, I get kind of stuck. Which is probably fine. It's not like I even know whether Avon will want it, so there's no rush. Plus, I haven't spent much time with Amy and Chase since I started my new job.

When I emerge from my room, Mary's looking over something on her iPad and softly stroking a sofa cushion that has fallen on the floor with her free hand.

"Um, Mary? Why are you petting a pillow from the couch?"

Mary startles. "Oh." Her hand freezes. "I thought it was Andy—I could swear she bumped my hand." She rubs her eyes. "I might be losing it."

"I think you just need a little break. Would you prefer a nap or an early dinner with Luke?"

Her eyes widen. "Luke!"

Seconds later, he charges into the family room with Jack half cradled in his left arm, scanning for danger frantically.

"Sorry if I frightened you." Mary's smile is suitably chagrined. "Anica said we can go to an early dinner, and I might have gotten a little too excited at the prospect."

"Really?" Luke beams.

"I've got to leave around seven forty or so to meet

Ethan for pie," I say. "But as long as you're back in time, absolutely."

Luke hands baby Jack to me without another word, and Mary grabs her purse. They're out the door before Chase and Amy even realize they're leaving.

"What are you munchkins doing?" I ask.

"I'm making a Play-doh dinner," Amy says. Her hot dog and ice cream cone actually look pretty decent. "And Chase is ruining all the Play-doh by pinching off a zillion tiny pieces for no reason and then grinding them into ugly lumps." She scowls at him. "At least he's wrecking *his* Play-doh this time."

If I ever have kids, my house will be a Lego and Play-doh free zone. "Remember how we talked about using kinder ways to describe things?" Although, I kind of agree with her. What's the point of doing what he's doing?

"I don't care," Chase says. "Amy is always complaining. I just ignore it."

I suppress a laugh. He's not wrong either. Baby Jack starts to fuss, so I make him a bottle. The smartest thing Luke and Mary ever did was splurge on a bottle-making machine. You literally stick the bottle under the spout, press the button for the amount of formula you want, and it dispenses the formula, warmed to the right temperature and mostly mixed, into the bottle. Then seal it up, swirl it around, and bam.

No warming. No measuring. No powdery mess.

Although, I don't have to clean the machine or keep it refilled, so I suppose they're getting the short end of this stick. Oh well. Not my baby. I plonk down on the sofa and stick the bottle in his mouth.

"Mom wants you to try and keep his hands around the bottle at the top," Amy says. "She's trying to teach him to hold it himself."

I lift my eyebrows. "Since when?"

"Since a few days ago."

I love Amy, but she sure is a little dictator. I almost feel bad for her future husband. He's going to be in for it, trying to keep her happy. She's got the exacting standards of Mary and the energy of Luke. Amy leans over and shows Chase how to fill a plastic ice cream bowl with his shreds. "See? You can play too, if you make them into birthday cake ice cream." And the generosity of her mom, Lizzie.

A wave of terrible loneliness washes over me. It's one of the bizarre unknowable mysteries of life that sometimes my loneliest moments take place when I'm surrounded by people I love, but it's inexplicably true. For some reason, when I'm with Amy and Chase, that's when I miss Lizzie the most. She would love to be here, watching them, playing with them, teaching them.

"I miss you so much," I whisper under my breath.

"Are you talking to my mom again?" Amy asks, her eyes as wide and curious as a kitten's.

"Huh?" I sit up straighter, accidentally dislodging Jack's bottle, and he starts to cry.

"I hear you, sometimes," Amy says. "You get kind of a sad look on your face and then you whisper something. I didn't understand why at first, but then I started paying attention and I think you're talking to her. Are you?"

Something heavy presses on my chest and I can barely breathe. "Why do you think that's what I'm doing?"

Amy shrugs. "Well, you always look kind of happy sad when you do it. I usually can't understand much of what you're saying." She looks down at the floor. "But sometimes I talk to her, so I thought maybe you did too."

Oh, God. Lizzie. You're missed by more than just me. "Yes, sweetheart." A tear rolls down my cheek. "When I look happy sad and whisper under my breath, I'm talking to your mom."

"Do you think she can hear us?" Her upturned face is so hopeful.

"I'm sure of it," I lie. "Just like I know that she's proud of you each and every day."

"And me?" Chase asks. "Is she proud of me even though I don't talk to her?"

"Yes, precious boy. She's very proud of you too, and you don't need to talk to her to make her proud."

"Oh good," Chase says. "Because I don't want to look crazy."

Once Jack finishes his bottle, I set him on his play mat and make a deluxe dinner of fish sticks and oven fries. "Oh good," Chase says. "That's my favorite, and Mom almost never makes it because she hates it."

"Well, you're in luck," I say. "Because Aunt Anica has a far less discerning palate than Mary. I actually like fish sticks as long as they're cooked super-duper crispy."

"That's how I like them too," Amy says. "I bet it's because you're my aunt that we like them the same."

"No it's not, idiot." Chase chucks a blob of Play-doh at her. "Everyone likes them that way cuz otherwise they're all squishy and wet."

"Whoa, sir. We don't say—"

"I'm sorry." He folds his arms and his entire face storm-clouds. Lips pulled tight. Eyebrows pulled together. Eyes intent on the ground. Some kids get so embarrassed when they're corrected.

"I think while the food is baking, Aunt Anica needs to get a few loves."

"Yay." Amy runs toward me and hops up onto my lap.

Chase doesn't budge. He's always a harder sell.

"Uh-oh," I say. "I've got a major issue."

Amy giggles.

I wink at her and set her down, and then I drop to my knees and start to shake.

"What's wrong?" Chase walks toward me slowly, the frown sliding away as curiosity takes over.

I sit up quick. "I'm in withdrawals."

He inhales. "What's that?"

"It means," I say, "that I am in desperate, no, *dire* need of loves."

His eyes widen and he tries to run, but it's too late. I snatch him and clutch him to my chest. "Give me hugs you cute little guy. Right now."

He laughs and laughs and laughs, right up until the timer on the fish sticks dings.

I freeze. "What do you think?" I ask. "Do we get them now? Or wait one more minute?"

Chase lifts one eyebrow. "Do I have to give you loves during that minute?"

I laugh. "Of course."

"Then I think we eat them now." He rubs his stomach. "Plus, I'm hungry."

The kids both eat great, and I even get the kitchen cleaned and Jack bathed and changed into jammies before Luke and Mary return.

"Thank you so much," Mary says. "I feel like a real person."

"I should probably inform you that I've deprived you of a fan favorite."

Mary glances at Luke and then back at me. "A what?"

"While you were gone. . . " I lean toward her. "We had fish sticks. I'm terribly sorry you had to miss that."

She laughs. "Is it that obvious that I don't like them?"

"Even Chase knew," I say.

Mary's shoulders slump. "Ah, well. They're smart kids."

"That they are," I say. "And I know it's been hard for you to have me here, but I promise that I'm saving every penny I make and I'll be out of your hair very soon."

She opens her mouth, but I wasn't trying to guilt her, so I cut her off. "I've gotta run, but Jack is ready for bed, and Amy and Chase are too, minus having their bedtime stories."

"Thank you," Luke says. "Truly."

I shrug. "Any time."

"You better run," Mary says. "Your thing with Ethan is soon, right?"

I dart out the door and arrive just in time. And there's no Porsche in sight. He either thought I was serious about parking a long way off, or he's late.

"Hey," a rough voice says from behind me. When I spin around, it's Ethan . . . shutting the door of a tan Bronco and walking toward me purposefully.

"Please tell me you didn't buy a brand new car because I teased you about your ridiculously expensive and fancy sports car."

He laughs. "I hated that Porsche as much as you did, maybe more, and I've been eyeing these since they released. Or re-released? Is that what I should call it?"

I shrug. "All right, well, as long as this isn't my fault."

"Shall we?" He tosses his head at Pleasant Pie. "Because all I had for dinner was a microwave burrito that looked like it had been in the back of my freezer since the last owner found them on sale at Kroger. Last year."

"Eww."

"I'm kidding. I did have a frozen burrito, but I bought it myself last week. I was just going for the pity element and overshot the mark."

I roll my eyes. "Yes, pie." But when we get inside, it's pie overload. "Whoa. How many different kinds of pie are there?"

"We have twelve pies that are available every day," the perky redhead behind the counter says. "But we also have four seasonal pies that rotate at all times. And of course, we have a selection of other pastries and treats, like muffins, croissants, and danishes."

I don't point out that my question was mostly rhetorical as I can see all of those things in the glass case right in front of me. "Okay, well, thanks."

"I vote we get one of each and try them all," Ethan says.

"You know, there are children starving in. . . " I pause. "Where are they starving right now, anyway?"

"Well, I tell you what, whatever we don't eat, I'll have this nice lady wrap up and ship to wherever they are."

"Uh, we don't do that."

The face Ethan makes at me is absolutely priceless. It's a combination of *what the heck is wrong with her* and *I'm glad I have you because you get me*.

And I *so* do, which is why, instead of laughing and confusing the poor girl further, I lean forward until my palms lay flat on Ethan's beautiful chest, and then I go up on my tiptoes and kiss him right on the mouth. "I needed to see you today."

"Rough day? Because I'm still really excited about this cornucopia of pie idea, and I feel like enough pie can fix most anything."

I laugh. "How about we pick three each."

He nods his head slowly. "A three slice day. Got it." He pivots on his heel and drops into a squat to examine the pie more closely through the glass cabinet. "My picks are cherry, chocolate silk, and Dutch apple."

"Those are good choices," the redhead says. "They're my three favorites."

Is she flirting with him? Right after I kissed him? The more time I spend with her the less I like her. "And I'll take a slice of the bourbon pecan, the Snickers, and the pumpkin crumble."

For all her other flaws, she's certainly quick about

popping our slices onto plates, but she mutters as she does. All I catch is "way too early for pumpkin," but for some reason it makes me laugh. As if Ethan's going to dump me because I ordered the wrong pie for the season.

Could he even dump me? Are we actually together? It's not like I can ask on what is probably only our second date.

Moments after we sit, the grumbly girl sets our plates in front of us. "Thanks," I say.

"Yeah, it looks great." Ethan smiles at her and then turns to face me.

"So you've got news?" I ask. "Spill."

"Turns out," Ethan says, "my dad always knew about my boxing. And he found me on Sunday, when you totally ditched me to be a fancy writer, training at the gym."

"Harrison's?"

He nods. "I was finally making some progress on my holds, and Harrison thinks he can get a fight for me in a month. A qualifying fight."

I blink. "Wait, like a real UFC fight?"

"Yep."

"And your dad knows?" I'm struggling to keep up here.

"He had followed me, long story, and yeah, he wasn't even surprised. Like he'd been *expecting* me to be tapped for —" He freezes. Then he shakes his head.

"What? Did your dad completely flip out?"

"No, he was eerily calm about all of it. In fact, he said it would be good for the company—and then he dropped another *huge* bomb."

"The audit thing?"

Ethan swallows. "Yeah, that, and he told me he's stepping down at the end of the year. He wants me to take over and run the company."

"Whoa." I sit up straight. "Is that a shock? Or did you already think it would happen?"

"He's only a few years over fifty," Ethan says. "I figured I had a decade and a half or more."

"Wow. That is a big day—and a lot of information."

"Right?" He takes a huge bite of cherry pie, and his eyes go round. "Oh man, that's good. Paisley's a genius."

I try a bite of the Snickers. It's a little too rich, but it's not bad. "So what does that mean? You're supposed to be a UFC fighter? Or you're supposed to be stepping into . . . what is your dad anyway?"

"He's the executive chairman and the chairman of the board," Ethan says. "And the single largest shareholder."

"But it's a publicly traded company, right?"

He nods. "It is, but he owns such a large chunk of stock that it almost doesn't matter how anyone else votes."

"Almost?"

He shrugs. "It's complicated. There are a few other major stakeholders, but they'd never move against him."

"So it's a done deal? Do you even *want* to take over? Didn't you say you wanted to go back to Hawaii ASAP?"

Ethan's shoulders slump. "I loved it there." He looks up at me. "But I was lonely, too."

He *loved* it? Does that mean he's not planning to go back? Is he saying he wants to stay . . . at least in part . . . for me?

"But Dad also told me he wants me to fight—at least a fight or two, I think. He wants me to prove that I'm scrappy, or something. That this isn't just being given to me, maybe?"

"Weird," I say.

He nods. "I'm not sure how I'm supposed to be training for a fight, which a lot of people literally devote all their time to doing, *and* I'm also supposed to repair the management mess of the Riviera Grand, and I'm supposed to help with this audit mess. All to win him, and presumably the board, over so he'll actually choose me as his successor."

I place my hand over his. "What do you want?"

He sighs. "I'm not sure."

"I think that's the first thing you need to work out." I wish I could help him, but the only person who can decide what Ethan Trainor really wants at the end of the day . . . is Ethan Trainor.

❧ 13 ❧

ETHAN

nica's advice is solid gold. Of course, my first task is to figure out what I *want* to do.

I wish it was as simple to make the decision as it was for her to identify my choice. When I think about taking over the family business—and hopefully running things as competently and effectively as Dad—my heart swells. It has been my end goal since I was in high school, and I've always assumed that someday I would.

I just didn't realize it would be so soon. I'm not sure I'm ready—but maybe I would never have been ready until I was forced to figure it out.

Dad helps me carve out time to train—especially since I've still got a lot of work to do learning how to do holds, and how to effectively counter against them. It's hard for me to trust that Dad's team and the one I've begun to assemble at the Riviera Grand can handle the tax audit without micromanagement. I want to look at every single step of every single review myself—which isn't feasible, especially with the extra things Dad wants me to evaluate and get up to speed on from a business perspective.

That might be further evidence that I'm not cut out for

upper level leadership.

When I step into the boxing ring each afternoon, I feel alive in a way I never have anywhere else. I may not swell with pride, but something deep inside me that never felt quite good enough bares its teeth and roars.

Is it wrong for me to feed that? I wish I knew.

"You're not going to get good enough at kicks in the next few weeks to make a difference," Harrison barks. "We can keep working on them, but focus on boxing strikes and holds for now." He waves Justin into the ring—Harrison's best fighter at the wrestling holds and grabs.

I suppress a groan.

"He's pretty good though, for being such a novice, right?" Dad has taken to coming out and watching me whenever he can get away.

It's irritating.

And I love it.

I'm a mess.

Harrison grunts. "He's a natural at everything physical and always has been, but that doesn't mean he'll be able to evade Izzy Volkov. Once he gets his arm around your throat, you can't break free. There's a reason they call him the Bulldog."

"Made any progress on monikers for our boy here?" Dad asks.

My old trainer scowls. "Just pick one of the ones I sent."

Dad laughs just as Justin swings wide. I can't resist taking a swipe at him, even though I know it brings me close enough for him to sneak around behind me. When my fist connects with his jaw, the risk is worth it. He takes the blow like a champ and shifts cleanly, his arm coming around me like I knew it would.

But I'm faster than him. I've been eating too much pie lately, but I'm still lightning fast. Barely fast enough, but barely counts.

I hate the idea of eliminating pie, but I can't keep eating like I'm in my twenties. At least I don't have to cut out the best thing about the past few weeks—Anica.

I may have avoided the move I saw coming, but thinking about my girlfriend in the ring is moronic. Justin slams the outside of his foot against my lower leg and knocks me sideways. I recover as well as I can, but it's enough for him to grab my wrist and flip it around.

Putting me into an armlock.

I swear under my breath.

"How about the Corporate Chump?" Harrison asks. "Because if he stays that sloppy, he won't last the first round against Izzy."

I tap out, my head twisted sharply enough to the side that I can see when Dad's nostrils flare.

"Again," Harrison says. "And this time, pay attention, boy."

He alternates between calling me old man and boy, but he's always been like that. Push, pull, shove, encourage. Maybe all coaches do that with boxers. Lure, smack. Bait and punish. It's not an ineffective preparation for life in general.

Holds suck, and I hate Izzy Volkov for supposedly being so good at them.

But I remind myself that there's a reason they're pairing me off against him. I need to evade his holds only long enough to take him out with a solid punch. That's always been my strength, and now I just need to be fast enough to play to it.

After more than five minutes of exchanging small blows, which is all I've been tasked to do, Justin catches me again, this time in a rear naked choke hold. I *really* hate that one. If I'd been a split second faster it wouldn't have happened.

To gain speed, I need to cut weight—definitely no more

sweets.

My shoulders tremble and the scrape on my shoulder stings and the inside of my mouth tastes like flop sweat from being shoved to the mat when Harrison finally calls it quits for the day.

"Should he be training like this so close to a match?" Dad asks.

I stumble to my feet.

"Of course not," Harrison says. "With any other fighter, I wouldn't even try it."

"Huh?" Dad opens his mouth to argue more.

"You a trainer now?" Harrison turns around and walks toward the locker room.

"I'm just trying to understand—"

"He's a quick study, but he needs remedial work on holds," he says. "He's jogging on his own, and he swears he's improving his diet." He spits on the ground and wipes his mouth on the sleeve of his shirt. "Normally I wouldn't risk the injury, but we don't got a choice."

"Fine," Dad says. "Fine, if you say so."

"He's right," I say. "If Justin can still trick me, Izzy will roll me."

"Truth," Chad says from the speed bag.

But I have time. Three and a half weeks isn't long, but it's long enough. I hope.

The second we reach my new Bronco, Dad frowns. "Be careful in there, son."

It's not what I expected, but if he's not going to say anything about my new car, I won't either. "I will, or at least, as careful as I can be."

"The auditors are set to arrive at the Riviera Grand in a week. Since it's a recent acquisition for us, there aren't as many fees to review. That's why they want to start here."

"The plan is simple—minimize the numbers as much as possible in case we lose the legal battle, right?"

Dad nods, his mouth working like he's eaten something disgusting. "We'll need to prepare a statement for our investors—they need to be made aware of the risks before the media catches wind."

"There may not be any profits to report this year," I say.

"For the first time in over a decade." Not the best way to retire. It'll almost look like he's leaving because of a failure, instead of because he's ready. He doesn't say any of that out loud, because he doesn't have to—I'd feel the same.

"We'll beat them in court, right?"

He shrugs. "I've been approached by a number of other interested parties."

"Who?" I laugh. "Let me guess. Marriott and Hilton."

He shrugs. "Their representatives won't say, but we've got additional resources if we need them. That's good to know, even if it's miserable luck that we're the man on the ground taking the hits."

He's having way too much fun with these boxing metaphors.

"I've also prepped a press release for the upcoming fight. Can your girlfriend send over a quote for it?"

I practically choke.

"Are you freaking out about the word girlfriend? Or because I want a statement from her?"

I shake my head.

"Look, she's cute, she's funny, she's local, and she's an author, right, which means she's well-spoken? And she's connected?"

I lean against the Bronco. "Do you seriously have someone tailing me? How do you even know about Anica?"

He rolls his eyes. "Check out the tabloids, son."

"I'm not tabloid fodder—they haven't followed me for years."

"Only because you've been unbelievably boring until now. But in the past few days you've been seen at your place of business with your arm around some girl." He leans closer. "The reporter who contacted me said he had a source, and based on the ridiculous details he provided, I'd say the source is your assistant or someone at the Riviera."

Probably that stupid goofy-headed waiter who overheard the setup and recognized Geo. She and Trudy are practically Atlanta royalty—friends with Paisley and James. Married to, well, *almost* to billionaires. "Is this absolutely necessary?"

"If you really want to take over for me, you need to consider that this will be your new life. The stockholders look to your behavior for reassurance. Like it or not, as head of the company, you're the face of the entire brand. You'll be watched all the time, and right now, with the audit news dropping, I'd like to have another news blitz we can release that will distract from that bad news. And if that story includes something that makes the men wish they were you and the girls think you're a solid, family-type man. . ."

I can't quite hide my disgust. "So you're pushing this fight and my new girlfriend as some kind of balanced façade to cover for the damage from the audit?"

I'm not sure why I expect him to deny it, but he doesn't even bother. "Isn't that what I just said?" He's shaking his head as he walks to his car. I can barely hear his last words. "So whatever you do, or however annoying you find her, don't dump this girl until after we've got this mess all worked out."

And for the first time since meeting Anica, I almost *want* to dump her. I don't like being ordered to do things, even things I want to do.

Then I think about her blush. Her laugh. Her snide remarks. Her shy vulnerability about her writing and her sister. Her genuine concern and affection for her niece and nephew. I wish Dad wouldn't order me to do things I have every intention of doing anyway, but I won't let that turn me stupid.

I call her on my way back to the office. "How's your day?"

"Better now," she says. "How'd the training go?"

"My shoulder hurts," I say. "But I survived."

"Back to work?"

"Unfortunately. It's going to be a long month."

"Will it all be over in a month?"

"Maybe," I say. "Maybe not. It's hard to know with legal stuff."

"I meant the fight," she says. "Work stuff won't ever end, especially if you take over for your Dad."

She's not wrong about that, but her actual question is trickier to answer. "I'm not sure. I might lose pathetically, and then, yeah, that's the end of my very short reboot of my fighting career, I imagine. But if I win. . ."

"You could get another fight, and then another."

"It's kind of how it works," I say. "The UFC sort of sets up the fights that people want to pay to see. We're like Vegas performers."

"Savage, brutally scary, and unbelievably hot Vegas performers," she says.

"Speaking of," I say, "Dad asked me for something strange."

"Yeah?"

"I'd rather ask you in person, but with your two jobs and my two jobs. . ."

"I get it. Go ahead. I'm pretty good with weird."

"That bodes well for me," I say, "because Dad wants to cover the negative press of the ongoing audit and the attendant impact on our Q4 earnings with the story about my fight."

"That's smart, actually," she says. "Use the shiny, hot guy to distract them from the bad tax news."

"Except he wants to balance me out—so I don't look feckless I imagine."

"I don't understand."

"Apparently someone snapped a few photos of us at the Riviera." I'll be talking to that stupid blonde idiot. "The news media is already asking whether I'm dating someone."

"Oh."

I have no idea what that 'oh' means. "But if it makes you uncomfortable, I'll tell Dad to shove it. I'll say no comment to anyone who asks."

Her voice is soft when she says, "If what makes me uncomfortable?"

"Dad wants a quote from my girlfriend about the upcoming fight."

She laughs. "That's it? You had me worried."

Worried? Did she think I was upset about the photos? "So you'll do it?"

"Tell me what kind of quote he wants—comedic, serious, supportive, flirty—and I'll send one over."

"You're amazing," I say. "And I think we should go with comedic. The only thing better than a gorgeous babe is a smart and funny gorgeous babe."

"Ooh, that could be a problem. You know about the triangle, right?"

"Huh?"

"You can get hot and smart. You can get smart and funny. You can get funny and hot. But you can't get all three."

"I'm pretty sure you mean you can get work done well and fast but it's expensive, or fast and cheap, but it's going to be low quality, or you can get high quality and cheap, but it'll take forever."

"Oh fine, you've heard of the real triangle."

"I'm impressed you know about it. I thought that was a business thing."

"Clearly you're too smart for me. No one will believe that I'm your girlfriend." She huffs.

"I can hardly believe it," I say. "But if you're not freaking out about being labeled that for the world to see. . ."

"I'm not worried about what anyone calls us," she says. "But I am worried."

Uh-oh. "About what?"

"I know you're tough and smart, and I saw you in that ring. You're clearly good at fighting, but it's risky. I may have watched some stuff online." She gulps. "Please be safe."

My heart swells in my chest. In all the years, with all the dumb things I've done, no one else has ever cared about the cost. No one else has ever been on the sideline, fretting. "Don't worry about that. I've taken plenty of beatings before, and I'm not afraid to tap out if it comes to it. No false pride here."

"I hope that's true—although I don't love the sound of 'taken plenty of beatings.'"

She has no idea. UFC may not have many rules, but it has plenty more than some of the fights I've faced. "So, this week you're on lunch, but what about next—" Another call beeps through. I hold it away from my face to see who it is.

"Ethan? Are you still there?"

"Hey, that's my sister Adriana. Do you mind if I take it?"

"Not at all. I'll text you something your dad can use later."

"Thanks." I press hold and swap. "Ana?"

"Hey Ethan," she says. "You never texted me about getting together."

Oh man. There aren't enough hours in the day. "Right. Well, let's do dinner—"

"I need to do today," she says. "Because I've got plans to drive out to a friend's beach house for the weekend, a million tests and papers to grade Thursday, and tomorrow I'm already busy."

Busy? Vague much? "Please tell me you aren't seeing Phillip again."

"It's none of your business what I'm doing."

"I'm your brother and I love you, Ana."

"It doesn't mean you have a right to decide who I can see."

My blood doesn't boil, but it's a near miss. "Fine."

"So are we on for dinner tonight?"

I don't have much time, and I want to see her. I'm just sick of fighting. "It'll have to be somewhere quick."

"Great," she says. "Where are you right now?"

"I'm almost back to my place," I say.

"Perfect. I'm here too."

"What?"

"I called you on my way over."

"I'm all sweaty, Ana." I pull into the driveway, pass her little yellow Lexus and click the button for my garage door. I roll my window down as I pass. "You can come inside while I shower."

"Okay." She looks at the Bronco. "Dad said he got you a Porsche as a welcome home present."

I shrug. "I don't like Porsches."

"You're kind of exhausting." She smiles. "But I love you."

"I love you too." I park, and she walks through the single car garage door as I get out.

"There it is." She crosses her arms and shakes her head, eyeing the Porsche sitting behind the other, closed garage door, disdainfully. "How could anyone not like that car? It's beautiful."

"It screams 'pay attention to me! I'm important and you should want to be like me.'"

"Isn't that what every man wants?" She bites her lip and

slugs my shoulder.

I walk up the steps to the house. "Not me."

"Oh fine," she says. "I'll take it."

Now it's my turn to laugh. "You have one."

"How did you know?" Her sideways smile is sly.

"Dad told me—last Christmas. He's obsessed with them. It would have been a miracle if you hadn't already gotten one. The only reason he waited this long to buy me one is that I've been so vocal about my distaste."

"He feels like your distaste for Porsches is really a way to express your repugnance for him. You do know that, right?"

I shrug. "I can't be responsible for his feelings. He's a big boy. Maybe he'll figure out that it means I'm *not* him, but it doesn't mean I don't *love* him."

"How are you so wise. . . " She drops her purse on the counter. "And you can't even accept the possibility that Phillip might have changed?"

I grip the corner of the counter. "Can we not talk about this, please?"

"Fine."

I shower quickly, and she keeps her word while we grab sandwiches at a nearby deli—no bread for me.

"You're really going to eat that?" her nose scrunches up.

I brandish my fork and knife above the slab of sandwich meat covered with a slice of cheese, a squirt of mustard, and a pile of lettuce and tomatoes. "What's wrong with this?"

She shakes her head. "It's wrong. You're eating a sandwich . . . with silverware."

I confess that I'm training. If Dad surprised me by his knowledge, Ana surprises me with her complete inability to process it. She blinks and blinks and blinks and swallows several times. "A fighter. Really? Like, you punch people and they kick you and stuff?"

"Well, they can now," I say. "Back when I did boxing before there wasn't any kicking and whatnot, but UFC allows most everything and that's what I'm doing now."

"You're going to, like, be on TV?"

I shrug. "Local channels, probably. But if this fight goes well, maybe broader reach."

"You've been doing this for a long time?" She looks up at me with big, worried eyes. "And you haven't gotten hurt?"

"I haven't had a sanctioned fight in more than five years," I say. "But it's not like I've forgotten how to do it. It's mostly reflexes, muscle memory, and being able to take a punch."

"You're saying you're tough? Like if a big old tough guy punches you, you won't crumple?" She tilts her head skeptically.

I swallow and stare at her. "I learned how to withstand pain at a very early age."

This time, she's the one who changes the subject. "So tell me about this girl Dad says you're seeing."

"You two are like little magpies. What did he say?"

"He said maybe you weren't gay after all."

I laugh so hard my sides ache. "He thought I was gay?"

She shrugs. "The idea had occurred to me, too."

"And you both thought I was hiding it?"

"I wasn't sure, Ethan. You're gorgeous, and you're rich, and you're kind. It was odd that you didn't have any significant girlfriends." She folds her napkin into a square and then unfolds it. "Ever."

"I had a few that I didn't tell you guys about, but geez. It's not like we had a lot of great role models for relationships," I mumble.

"Dad's marrying her," she says. "Finally."

"I heard."

"It doesn't make her our mom." Ana puts her hand on my forearm. "She never tried to be that."

She sure didn't. Annelise wasn't mean, but she was never warm, never supportive, and certainly never welcoming. She was . . . borderline hostile.

"I think she had a rough go," Ana says. "She was dating Dad, hoping and planning for a future with someone who clearly had no plans for kids. She doesn't like children at all, and then suddenly, he's got two kids—children who don't even like her. We were pretty angry and standoffish. At least, you were."

"I don't really care," I say. But maybe that's a lie. Why didn't Annelise even *try* to love us?

"I cared." My poor little sister stares down at her hands, and I realize she's trying not to cry. I've never wanted to punch Annelise, but if she showed up right now, I might.

"It doesn't matter either way, really," I say. "The point is, Dad's actually right. I'm dating someone and I really like her. A lot."

Ana beams. "That's the best news I've heard this month." She doesn't say it's better than Phillip's release, but I know that's what she means. It helps ease some of my frustration with him taking up so much of her time. I don't want him to be a part of her life at all, but at least she cares more about me than him. It doesn't relieve my fear for her and my anger at him, but maybe some of what I was feeling was jealousy. That my sister, the only girl I have ever really loved other than Mom, loves *him* too. Maybe I don't want to share her.

"You will love Anica."

"When can I meet her?"

"When do you get back from the beachhouse?"

"Since we have a county fair day on Monday, there's no school. I won't be back until late that night."

"Next week, then," I say. "If we can find the time."

She beams at me, and I launch into a list of all the things I like about Anica. It's longer than I expected. By the time Ana leaves, I've got almost a hundred work emails to deal with. Taking off afternoons is brutal. I'm slogging my way through them when my phone starts buzzing.

Phillip.

I reluctantly answer. "Yeah?"

"Hello, Ethan. It's Phillip Sims." As if I didn't know who he was. At least he didn't say he was my dad again.

"I know."

"Oh, okay."

He's so awkward. I suppose not being part of the real world for eighteen years will do that to you. "Why are you calling me, Phillip Sims?"

"Last time we spoke, you offered to help me."

"Actually, I offered to get you a job."

"Right."

"And you're ready to give me your answer?"

"I do want a job, clearly," Phillip says.

It's so obvious that he's about to say 'but' that I cut him off. "I think it would be better to talk about this in person."

"Oh," he says. "You do?"

I don't reply.

"Okay."

"Can you meet me if I text you an address?"

"When?"

"Now, or as soon as possible," I say.

"Oh." He seems to be shuffling some kind of paper. "The bus schedule is a little confusing."

The *bus* schedule. I almost can't suppress my smile. I've got him—I can feel it. "How about you text me and let me know when you're close. Then we can talk about it in person."

"Alright," he says slowly. "I can do that."

I text him the address, which is less than three miles from here. I make my way through almost all my emails before he texts.

I'M HERE.

I grab the keys to the Porsche and reach him in under five minutes. He's leaning against a pole at the gas station when I roar around the corner and pull up next to the air compressor. I make sure that I open the door and climb out slowly.

Then I lean casually against the edge of the shiny blue car. Dad outdid himself—it has every bell and every whistle. And Ana said it best—isn't my new sports car what every guy wants?

"Phillip, I'm glad you found the address."

"I'm glad you wanted to meet." He swallows hard and his eyes follow the line of the car. He loves it—I can tell.

"Alright, why don't you tell me, then. You want a job?"

"I do, of course, and it was very generous of you to offer to find me one. But I've had dinner with Adriana twice, and she's—" He shakes his head. "I've had a long time to think about the mistakes I've made. I know I made plenty. More than plenty. I know you can't forgive me for them."

He says he knows, but I can feel that he *hopes* he's wrong, just as Ana is constantly poking me to consider forgiving him, moving ahead as if he didn't ruin our lives and kill our mother. Fury pulses through me. He's right about one thing. I will never forgive him, not for what he did. And I'll never get over what I didn't do. The regret and pain and loneliness and guilt I've hauled around for all these years are all his fault too. "And?"

"It's a miracle that your sister can."

"She was a baby. She doesn't remember anything. Her generosity is a mistake I'll never make. You're the same person you've always been."

The muscles in his jaw work and his face twists. "Maybe I am."

"You know it, deep down. You know it's better for her if she never sees you again. It's better for everyone . . . except

for you. And I know you well enough to know that ultimately, the only person you care about is yourself. So I'm
going to do something that will allow you to do the right
thing. The thing that you're not man enough to do without
an incentive."

His eyes fly up to mine, and there's fear there.

I wish I didn't like the way it makes me feel quite so
much.

"I'm offering you this car." I toss the keys to him.

He catches them on reflex. "I don't understand."

"I've got the title with me. I'll sign it over to you right
now. I even printed up a bill of sale. You'll walk away from
here with a brand new, one hundred and thirty thousand
dollar Porsche—a 911 Carrera Cabriolet. You can sell it, you
can drive it, you can do whatever you want with it. And all
you have to do to get it is something you already know you
should be doing. Walk out of Adriana's life as if you never
existed. Tell her you don't *want* to see her ever again, and
then mean it."

Phillip shakes his head.

"Don't even try to tell me how hard this decision is to
you. I know it's the right call for everyone involved except
for me. I'm the one losing the car."

"You're so much like him."

His words are like a knife twisting in my heart. I love
my dad, but I don't aspire to be like him. "What do you
mean?" As if I don't know.

"Did you know he offered to pay me, too?" His shoulders slump. His face falls. His eyes are hollow, full of only
regret.

"When?" I'm such an idiot. Did he already refuse Dad?
And now here I am, making the same offer.

"Not recently." He smiles, his discolored teeth remarkably sad in a face now lined with age. "But when your
mother and I first fell in love, your uncle approached me,

with full approval from your grandfather. They offered me a hundred thousand dollars to walk away from her, no questions asked."

"You turned that down?" Frankly, I'm shocked.

"You don't care," he says. "I know that no excuse will satisfy you, but my father beat me—he hit all of us regularly. My older brother took it out on me, too. That life, that anger, it was all I knew."

I've studied the cycle of abuse. I hate that he's blaming what happened to him for his decisions. I was beaten, and I've never hit someone who wasn't also spoiling for a fight. And I've never hit a woman or a child. Never.

"I'm an alcoholic," he says.

"Clearly."

"You probably are, too."

"I might be," I say. "If I ever drank."

"You're so smart to avoid the temptation," he says. "I'm proud of you."

I step toward him, my hands clenched at my side. "You don't get to be proud of me. You don't get to feel any way about me. Do you understand?"

He flinches.

"Do you want the car, or not?"

"I turned them down because I loved your mother, and because I was prideful. I thought they were wrong about me." He pulls in on himself then, becoming smaller somehow. Like a toothless dragon. Like a lion with no claws—sick, sad, and broken. I can see what draws Adriana to him. Her whole life is focused on repairing things, healing and teaching and improving. But some things can't be fixed. "I turned them down, but I'll accept it from you, because I'm old enough now to know that you're right."

Adriana might never forgive me if she finds out what I've done, but I'm glad he's taking the car.

So very glad.

ANICA

I haven't been to get a pedicure with anyone other than my sister, which means I haven't been since Lizzie died years ago. I shouldn't be nervous—it's not scary, and yet I'm inexplicably twitchy. Maybe it's because Trudy's running late. I sit on the edge of the sofa, and then I get up and walk past the front door.

"Are you okay, Aunt Anica?" Chase asks.

"Uh, sure," I say. "I'm totally fine. Aunt Trudy's going to take me to get a pedicure."

"A what?"

I point at my toes. "See how the light purple polish on my toenails is all chipped and yucky?"

Chase hunches over and touches my toes. I still forget occasionally how tactile children are. "That's purple?"

I laugh. "It was purple. Now it sort of looks grey."

"Maybe don't do this color again," Chase says. "It makes your toes look like they go on zombie feet."

What a lovely image. "Probably best to avoid that, yes."

Trudy's car pulls up outside, and I'm surprised when she circles to unbuckle Troy.

"Hey," I open the door and wave to her.

Troy waves but then runs straight past me, basically barreling into Chase. Troy hugs Chase like he hasn't seen him in a year every single time he comes over. It's kind of adorable. "I made a Lego dinosaur," Troy says.

"No way," Chase says. "Where is it?"

"Mom said I can't bring it!" Troy glares at Trudy as she walks inside.

"Because you'd have lost the tail or the arms, and then we'd be here for an hour looking. And when we finally gave up and went home, you'd cry the entire way. Chase can see the dino next time he comes over."

Troy kicks the edge of the entry table.

"No, sir." Trudy grabs his arms and turns him to face the corner. "We use our words to express how we feel, not our feet."

I suppress a laugh. Troy's face is priceless, but I really can't encourage him at all. You give a little boy an inch and he'll sprint halfway across the county. "I'm sorry we can't see your Lego dinosaur." I lower my voice and turn pointedly toward Trudy. "Did something come up? Are we not going?"

She rolls her eyes. "Paul had to stay late, but Mary offered to let Troy play here, so we're good."

"Oh no, I feel bad now."

Mary calls from the kitchen. "Anica, do *not* feel bad. It makes my life easier to have Troy here, trust me."

Trudy laughs. "One of the ironies of parenting. Looking after two boys is easier than one." She shrugs. "They entertain each other."

"Until one of them falls off the balcony and breaks an arm," I say.

"Hush, you," Mary says. "There aren't any balconies here."

"Which is why I used that example." I laugh. "I don't want to be blamed for bad juju if something does happen."

A moment later, we're walking back to Trudy's 4Runner. "This is a nice car." I slide into the passenger side. "These seats are amazing."

She glances down at them as if she hadn't noticed. "Paul picked it out. I don't really care much about my car, but he's right that leather seats are way easier to clean. Crusted kid gunk is the worst."

Kid gunk, like that's an actual thing. I like Trudy. I might have to remember her description for a book. "Chase told me I've got zombie toes, so I think it's a good thing you invited me. Or maybe that's *why* you invited me."

Trudy zooms away from the curb and takes a sharp turn. "Please. I need this way more than you do."

"Need this?" I glance down at her toes. They don't look too bad.

"Not the pedicure so much as the break from work and parenting . . . and frankly, I need a friend."

I'm floored. *She* needs a friend? And she wants me? Her sister's husband's ex sister-in-law?

"Uh, well, that's good. I'm kind of surprised, honestly."

"At what?" She takes a corner at what feels like thirty miles per hour.

I grip the edge of my armrest with both hands until my knuckles turn white. "That you'd choose me, mostly, but also that you need a friend. You people have more friends than anyone else I know."

Trudy laughs. "You mean Mary's friends?"

Huh. I'd never considered it that way, but . . . Mary knows Paisley because they work together. She knows Geo because she's Paisley's friend and planned Mary's wedding. She knows Brekka through Geo, who is dear friends with Rob and Geo's husband's sister. None of them have much connection to Trudy . . . except through Mary.

"I didn't even think about that," I say. "You guys are all

so *shiny*, I guess I hadn't considered how you met in the first place."

We stop at a light and Trudy turns to face me. "Shiny?" She giggles. "I love that word. That's totally what they are. Paisley's a secret princess. Brekka's a former Olympian with a dump truck sized brain."

Her word choice is odd, but still strangely apropos.

"And then you have Geo. Don't even get me started on her."

"You don't like her?" I ask.

"Oh, I love her, but she's hard to be around on my good days." She shrugs. "It is what it is. I know that sucks for her, but she's effortlessly stunning and that's a little depressing to us normal humans."

She's totally right. I feel bad thinking it, but it's true.

"She also runs her own event planning business and makes it look like she's doing nothing at all, she's so grace-ful. Then there's Mary—and I love her until the moon goes black, but she's perfection personified."

Also 100 percent accurate.

"You're like a procession of truth bombs today," I say. "I'm terrified what you'll say about me."

Trudy laughs. "You're refreshingly real and normal. The first time I saw you, you had a piece of something green stuck between your two front teeth. I wanted to tell you, but then I thought, hey, she's at home and no one else will see. Why embarrass her? Because I knew then and there that you were *my* kind of people."

I cough. "Your kind? You mean, the single mom who fought her way through college and took down a corporate spy to save her husband's fledgling business?"

She laughs so hard I'm worried she'll actually ram into a fire hydrant. "Oh, that's hilarious. I'm the one in the group who always forgets her wallet, doesn't have a lunch packed for Troy, and forgot to bring baby wipes. But don't worry,

Mary will have an extra lunch and a bag of wipes—even before she had a baby—and she'll do it all with a smile. Me on the other hand, I'm perpetually wearing and saying and doing the wrong things." She pauses at a light and exhales dramatically. "So please, Anica, join me for a pedicure so I won't get a staph infection the next time I put my foot in my mouth."

"At least we're funny."

She pulls into the nail place and blessedly stops the car. My heart slowly slides down from where it has been lodged in my throat. Luckily we're here early enough that there aren't many other customers. "It's too late for most moms with school-aged kids, and too early for most people getting off work," Trudy says as she peruses and then selects her nail polish color. A soft shade of lilac.

"Not that one." I gently push her hand back toward the rack. "Light purple apparently turns your feet into corpse feet when it flakes off."

"Good to know." She puts it back and chooses canary yellow. I doubt that's much better, but I don't bother correcting her. She'll figure it out herself—or Troy will point it out. Ha!

Once we're seated, I confess. "You may feel like you don't fit in perfectly, but at least you've got a group that wants you. I don't have any friends in Atlanta at all."

She frowns at first, but when she realizes I'm serious, she blinks. "Really?"

"It makes me sound a little pathetic," I admit. "I do know that. I've got friends in California, but way less than I realized. A bunch of us used to go out together, but when I stopped barhopping, it was like they didn't have much to say to me anymore."

"You're kidding."

I shrug. "Or maybe I changed too much."

"Changed?"

The woman buffing my toes isn't exactly gentle, but maybe that's on me for having such horrible toenails. I wince, and she eases up a bit. "I was different, before."

She sighs. "Before your sister passed."

"Yeah. Life was so sunny then."

"I'm so sorry," Trudy says. "I've had my share of storms, but mine were always my fault."

"I doubt that."

"I take responsibility for my choices," Trudy says, "always. I chose badly when I married the first time. Mary built herself this little fortress from the world when our parents let us down, but I didn't. Probably because I always had her to protect me. I guess I wasn't as scared to love as she was, although maybe I should have been. I wanted *love,* like the kind I thought my parents lacked. My first husband was so over the top with everything that when he said he'd love me forever, and he gushed and he told me all the right things, I *wanted* to believe him. Without any evidence, and against Mary's advice, I decided to believe every promise he made, no matter how hollow."

"You threw yourself entirely into the care of Mr. Wickham."

Trudy laughs so hard that her feet shake, and the smallish woman doing her nails nearly falls over backward. "Sorry," Trudy says. "I'm so sorry." She wipes at the tears at the corners of her eyes. "I did do that, basically. I love *Pride and Prejudice,* and you're right. I was totally Lydia, which sucks because I despise her."

"But you got Troy out of it at least," I say.

"Which is why I don't regret my naiveté, no matter how difficult the consequences."

"I got nothing from my big mistake."

"You were married?" Trudy almost drops her phone.

"No, nothing that dramatic, but he did take me ring

shopping about a month before Lizzie got sick. I'm sure he's still congratulating himself on dodging that bullet."

"Who was he?"

"Patrick McCleve," I say softly. "You can google him and find out all you need to know. He looks like a taller, younger Tom Cruise, and he's got the same swaggering confidence."

"Some people call that conceit," Trudy mock whispers.

"Sure," I say. "That too, but he really is an excellent writer. I should know. I get regular emails telling me about his new publishing deals."

Trudy's eyes are wide and she leans back as far as she can. "What kind of loser sends emails to his ex to tell her about his books?"

"No, he's not that obnoxious—he doesn't have to be. The publishing world is small. We met because we had debuts the same year with the same publisher. But my career has disintegrated while his has grown exponentially."

"Well, good for him."

"I love that you hate him on principle," I say. "But he didn't really do anything wrong other than be fabulous and love me less when I wasn't."

"You do realize that people, all people, go through phases of life that are great, and other phases that are hard, right?" Trudy shakes her head. "It's the whole reason that wedding vows usually say marriage is for better or for worse."

I shrug. "We weren't married."

"Thank goodness. Trust me, you want someone who doesn't bail at a speed bump."

I guess she'd know. "He tried to help me."

One of her eyebrows arches. "How?"

"He tried to guide my career."

"Guide it?" She stares pointedly down her nose. "Like he tried to tell you what to write?"

"Something like that. I tend to write fluff, for lack of a better word. Romantic comedies. They're easy and fun, but they don't require a lot of depth. He wrote deeper stuff, and I think even before Lizzie died, it bothered him that we weren't equally matched."

Something about that infuriates Trudy. "Who is he to act as a judge of what literature is *worthy*?"

I snort. "My books don't exactly qualify as literature."

"Fine," Trudy says. "You can defend him all you want, but I hate this guy. I wish you'd forget all about his advice."

"I did get—" My phone rings, and I stare at it blankly. The caller ID says Henrietta.

"You can answer it," Trudy says. "We're the only ones in here, and I don't mind."

"It's my agent." I stare, dumbly. Sort of my agent, but that feels like too much to explain right now.

"Pick it up," she says.

So I do. "Hello?"

"Hey, Anica, it's so nice to hear your voice."

"Right," I say. "Same."

"I have great news."

"Oh?"

"Avon loved your proposal and they've sent an offer. It'll pay in two segments instead of three, since it's an IP project. First half on signing, second half on acceptance."

"Okay," I say.

"Did I call at a bad time?" Henri asks.

"Not really," I say.

"What's wrong, then?"

"Nothing."

"You seem upset, that's all."

"Why didn't you like my pages?" I want to kick myself the second I ask.

"It's not that I didn't like them." She huffs. "It's just that I don't sell that type of story."

"You sold my last one."

"Forgive me for being blunt, but it was a total flop, Anica. You know that, I know that, and the publisher knows that—the numbers are what they are."

"I know." And thanks for rubbing it in, but I suppose I did ask.

"And that's not a surprise, because no one wants to read literary tragedies. We aren't French."

"I understand."

"I'm not sure you do." Henri clears her throat. "Anica, you're a very gifted writer, but you lost something when your sister died. I'm not sure what it is—a spark, maybe. These pages for this IP project are the first time I've seen that zing in your writing since she passed. If you wanted to write more of this, I'd take it in a heartbeat."

"You just don't want the stuff *I* want to write." As I say the words, I realize they aren't true. I don't want to write literary tragedy. I *want to want* to write it. But that's not the same.

"I'm sorry if it hurts your feelings. I do like you, Anica, but this is my job. I can't help you drive your career even further into the ground."

"Send the contract." I hang up.

"Whoa," Trudy says. "She sounds horrible."

"I was probably too hard on her. It is her job."

Trudy shakes her head. "You need to stop letting everyone off the hook. It sounds like you do need me. Your other friends are all stupid."

It's so true that it's almost painful, but that makes it funnier. She's right. They all suck. I pull up the email, and I'm shocked by how high the figure they're offering is for an IP project. I explain what's going on to Trudy. "It's not going to be *mine,* but at least it's a paycheck. I'll have more than enough to move out of Luke and Mary's house."

"Why would you do that?" Trudy looks genuinely baffled.

"It's very kind of you to act like you don't know," I say.

"Know what?" She narrows her eyes. "What are you saying?"

"Mary needs more space for her business with Paisley. She's sick of me being there."

Trudy tilts her head. "I'm not part of their super special tax firm club, but no one has said a word to me about wanting you to leave. I'd be shocked if Mary wanted to work out of her home for even a second. As soon as she's ready, she'll have more work than she can handle—plus with her savings and Luke behind her, she can totally pay for office space."

"I overheard—"

"Not that I'm trying to tell you your business or anything, but I'd sooner believe you misunderstood someone than that they want you gone. Luke and Mary have both mentioned how nice it has been for the kids, for them, and just in general, having another adult around now they've had the baby."

Huh. Really? "Well, either way. As an adult, I ought to get my own place soon."

Trudy doesn't argue, and we spend the rest of the pedicure chatting about the kids and her job and Paul. We're almost out the door when she finally brings up Ethan. "How's that going?"

I can't keep the smile off my face after that. "I really like him."

"I am so glad. We all like you two together."

"You've talked about it?"

Trudy has the decency to look a little embarrassed. "Well, not a lot. But when you two ducked out with the dog, it came up."

"He's a lot more complicated than he looks," I say. "And he cares about people and things deeply."

"So it's serious?"

"It's been like a week, so no. But I do really like him. Probably more than I should."

"Time isn't really the barometer for determining what's serious." She sighs and signs the receipt.

I sign mine. "But without time, you don't really see the stuff that matters. How he behaves under stress. How he behaves when someone lies. I can't trust someone until I've been around long enough to test his integrity."

"I hear what you're saying," Trudy says. "But don't place arbitrary limits on things because of time. I didn't set limits with the wrong guy, and I set way too many with the right one."

"But he waited for you," I say.

She nods.

"And that's how you knew he was right."

We climb back into her car. "Maybe," she says, "or maybe I was extremely lucky that he didn't get impatient and give up on me."

That night I think about what she said . . . a lot. I think about it while I review the contract, and when I sign the contract, and when I work on my chapter for the night. I'm almost a third of the way done with the book, which is just bonkers.

And it makes me think about what Trudy said about the fluff, and what Henri said about fluff selling and literary novels having no real place here. I wish I had easy answers. But it seems like the more I think about things, the more questions pile up.

❧ 15 ❧

ETHAN

"What did you do?"

I shouldn't have answered when Adriana called. "Huh?"

"Nice try. Dad met me for dinner tonight and he told me he can't see me *ever again*. He said he feels too guilty when he sees me, and that I look too much like mom. He said a lot of stuff that doesn't make sense, because he was ridiculously happy to see me the last two times."

The fact that she just called him *Dad* is enough for me to feel completely justified. He's not her dad—never has been. He's essentially a sperm donor, and frankly, she's lucky he never did anything more for her. "Slow down." I wish she wasn't quite so smart. If she was a little bit thick, it would make this simpler. "Let me get this straight. I came to you, not once, but repeatedly, and I asked you to cut him off. I said he'd hurt you."

She says nothing, but I can hear murmurs behind her. She must already be at the beach—and if she's this upset while on vacation. . .

"Look, if *Phillip* has realized that he's too big of a loser to see you, that's not on me."

"You did something, Ethan."

"I offered to get him a job," I say. "If he'd promise to stay away from you."

"How dare you?"

"He turned me down."

"He did?"

"Yes, and then he told me that Dad tried to pay him off when he and Mom first got together. But guess what? He said he knew he was bad for you. He said he should have taken that money a long time ago."

"You said he turned it down."

"He did," I say, "but I guess maybe you were partially right. Maybe he has changed, and he realizes that he's horrible for you. Maybe he realized you aren't safe with him, because after a little time to think, when I offered him an incentive to cut you off, he took it."

"That's garbage. I hate you." She hangs up.

She'll come around. Especially if she never really figures out the extent of what I did and thinks all I did was find him a job. At the end of the day, Adriana's angry, but she wants to forgive me. If she can forgive Phillip for what he did, she'll let this go, and then I can sleep easier at night on all counts.

Mostly.

I did have a nightmare last night that Mom came to scold me for my inability to forgive. Which was just my psyche freaking out. I'm doing what a big brother is supposed to do—making the hard decisions and being the bad guy when necessary to protect my sister.

If I hit the guys a little harder during training today, well, it isn't hurting me. "You were on fire," Harrison says. "I need you to channel that for your fight."

And I do. I try to meet Anica a few times a week, either for lunch or dinner. I even make it to a game night, and no one acts like we're usurpers. We're photographed a few times by the paparazzi, which Anica hates. That only makes me laugh harder—her irritation is precious. And other than my time with her, I train. I work. And I train more.

And before I know it, I'm waking up on the day I face off against Izzy Volkov to the sound of someone banging on my front door and Partner losing her crap, barking and barking and barking. I rub my eyes and bolt upright in bed. Who could it be? I drag a pair of jeans on and jog to the front door. "It's fine, girl. Calm down."

I flip the deadbolt and yank the door open.

"Hey." Anica holds up a brown paper bag. "Don't worry. Harrison gave me very specific orders for what you're supposed to eat." Then her eyes drop to my bare chest and she licks her lips.

Which should be hot, but since Partner's doing the exact same thing at my feet, but looking up at the paper bag, it's mostly just funny.

"When you're done training, are you going to get all squishy?" The dreamy, faraway look in her eyes is, however, very hot.

"Um, not unless you ply me with pie." I take the bag out of her hand and set it on the entry table, and then I wrap my arms around her waist and pull her close. "You are about the best thing that I could have seen this morning. Or maybe ever."

I'm not sure what she tries to say, but I might be squeezing her a little too tightly because it sounds like "thamliffa."

I chuckle. "What was that?"

"You are way, way too hot without a shirt on."

Instead of protesting, I decide to use my mouth in a smarter, more useful way. I drop it over hers, my lips stamping her MINE. Her tiny moans are exactly what my heart needs to hear.

Until she starts to bang on my chest with her ineffectual little fists.

I freeze, shifting back enough that I can talk. "Whoa, what's wrong?"

"I got very specific directions from Harrison," she squeaks.

I don't swear about Harrison's interference, no matter how hard it is to remain polite. "And what exactly did he say that made you hit me?"

"He said I shouldn't be doing *this*." She squirms, which doesn't make it easier for me to let her go.

"I'm going to kill him."

"No." She leans up on her tiptoes and kisses me on the mouth. But then she backs away carefully. "You're going to kill Isaac Volkov."

"Him too."

Her smile is dawn on the ocean waves. It's a knockout with a single punch. It's that first bite of cherry pie. "You are the most beautiful woman I've ever seen."

"You're a friggin' Adonis." She shakes her head. "I love looking at you, but I hate the looks I get with you."

"Excuse me?" I grab her paper bag and march toward the kitchen. "What are you talking about?"

"Nothing." She takes the bag from me and points at the skewed kitchen table chair at the end of the table. "Sit."

"You don't have to—"

She presses a finger against my lips and I nip at it before she can roll her eyes and back away. "Stop being naughty. We have time for that later."

"Promise?"

She throws a towel at me. "Go put a shirt on or you might have to kill Harrison for me."

I chuckle, but I do it. Slowly. When I get back into the room, I press. "What were you talking about, the looks you get?"

"Oh, you wouldn't understand."

"Try me. I'm not a genius, but I'm fairly smart."

"You and I are not on par, in terms of appearances."

I throw my hands up. "No, stop right there. You're wrong about that. Believe me. I've seen how the guys at the diner look at you."

"I'm cute. I've always been cute. But I'm not man candy."

"*Man candy*? You're ridiculous."

"All I'm saying is that if we both walked down the street with our shirts off, you'd get more people staring than I would—and men do occasionally jog shirtless, so it shouldn't even be close. But I'm okay with it."

Clearly she's a little bit delusional, but at least it's making her think I'm wonderful. "Well, the only person I want staring at me is you."

"Focus." She sets four fried eggs in front of me. "Eat, don't flatter. Today is a big day."

She's not wrong, so I eat. But if I'm being honest, talking to her does more to center me than anything else could. She stands up to take the plates to the sink, but I stop her. My hand on her wrist is enough to set my heart hammering, but not because I want to rip her clothes off. I mean, I do. I always do, but that's not what practically panics me. No, it's the realization I had when she brought me food and told me to focus—when she took care of me.

"I love you, Anica Maggard."

She's facing the sink, her hands full of dirty dishes, and she goes utterly still.

Oh, no. The first time I ever say that to anyone, and she isn't going to say it back. What's wrong with me? If I just ruined this, then the fight doesn't matter. Nothing does. How can I fix it? My mind flips through possibility after possibility. Make it a joke. Nope. Double down and tell her why. No, that'll probably be worse. Tell her it's fine if she doesn't feel the same. No pressure. Except that sounds so pathetic. No girl likes a sad sack.

Why does anyone ever say they love anyone at all? I've never been this afraid, not in my entire life. She still hasn't moved. Is she going to walk through that door and never come back? Why? What did I do wrong?

She turns then, slowly. She sets the plates on the table, and she pushes me backward.

My heart stops dead in my chest. She's angry?

Then she leans toward me and presses her hands against my chest, palms flattening slowly. "You are the smartest, kindest, bravest, gentlest man I've ever met, Ethan Trainor. I love you more than I've ever loved anyone in my life. Probably too much."

I should have known. My girl's a writer. She'd never simply say, "I love you too."

But when she leans a little farther and kisses me, her fingers curling against the muscle of my chest, I'm gone. I should be terrified, knowing that the power of her words, her feelings, could gut me. She holds my heart in her tiny hands. It's maybe the most terrifying feeling I've ever experienced.

And it's also the most precious.

When I walk into the sports arena, packed with way more people than I expected, even knowing my fight isn't the only one, my heart is utterly calm, because I've already survived the most important part of my day. Having Anica at my side reminds me that ultimately, the result of this match doesn't matter much.

Reluctantly, she leaves my side to sit next to my dad and Adriana. My sister's still not talking to me, but she showed up, which means we'll be alright. I should have introduced Anica to her, but they'll figure that out. I watch them chatting, the two women I love most, and my heart swells.

But too soon, it's my turn. Harrison gives me a pep talk, kind of a pathetic one, but he tries.

"You are, without a doubt, the most talented fighter I've ever trained."

Oh, please.

"But your biggest weakness is your lack of confidence in yourself."

"I feel pretty good about today."

He frowns. "You do?"

I shrug.

"Wait. Does that mean you don't care what happens?"

I shake my head. "Nah, I just think I can take him."

"The Bulldog?" He glances behind me, and I turn instinctively.

He's big. He's bald. He's angry looking. He's got a gold tooth, which personally, I think was probably a mistake. You look equal parts goonish and scary at best. At worst, you look like you're wearing a pirate costume.

"Just remember—"

"Don't drop my head," I say. "I know."

"And no matter what—"

"Don't overextend or he'll flip my arm and I'm done."

He grunts. "I might have said it a few too many times, but you still do it sometimes." Harrison claps a hand on my arm. "Be the powerhouse I know you are, and you've got this, son."

Even if I'm not his son, I like Harrison, and I hope he's right.

I climb into the ring, and the ref walks to the center. Izzy bounces forward too, the scowl lines deep on his face.

"Alright guys, you know the rules," the referee says. "Now's the time to bump fists if you want to."

I hold out my hand, but Izzy's scowl deepens and he bounces back to his side. What an idiot. At least I won't feel so bad taking him out.

The ref claps his hands and we're off. The UFC brass wants something showy? Fine. I won't dance around. I shoot forward and slam a jab into his jaw. It snaps his head back.

And it feels good. Really good.

I think about this guy—who wouldn't bump hands—and I feel myself sinking into the anger. "Hey Blackbeard," I say. "You were too afraid to bump my fists?"

He snarls and swings for me.

I duck and dance sideways, then I plant one on his back, sending him sprawling. If I was Justin, I'd throw him into a lock, but that's not why I'm here. It's not why they took a chance on an old novice. So I give the people what they want.

I've been terrified for the past few weeks, scared that I was outgunned, heading into the fight of my life. But this isn't that. This is fun. This is easy. I run Izzy all over the ring. Up, down, sideways. I knock him pretty good in his jaw again, and he spits blood on the mat.

It's hard to smile around the thick mouthpiece, but I manage to do it.

And he throws a shoulder into my side, knocking me off balance, and wraps his arm around my head. It's the first part of a guillotine choke. Thousands of people screaming, but I hear her through it all.

Anica's shout is pure terror. She's worried about me.

I duck and roll, tossing that stupid pirate off my back before he can lock it in. And then I do something I'd never do in a boxing ring. I hammer into him where he's lying on the ground until the ref calls me off. He's unconscious.

I've won.

I climb out of the ring in a sort of daze.

"One round!" My dad is screaming louder than anyone else. "That was the most exciting five minutes of my life!"

"And the worst five minutes of mine." Anica's arms wrap

around my neck, unconcerned about the sweat and blood spatter, apparently. "I'm so glad you're alright."

"I told you I'd be fine."

She kisses me then. Not for nearly long enough, but it's a start. I pick her up and swing her around, and then I kiss her again. "I want to get out of here," I murmur against her mouth. "Please?"

"Everyone is so happy! We can't just leave."

For the first time, I really look behind me, and I notice that James and Paisley, Trudy and Paul, and Mary and Luke are all milling around behind Anica and Ana and my dad, cheering like lunatics.

"Fine. We celebrate for a bit, and then we leave."

She leans her forehead against mine. "Fine."

If I'd known that 'a bit' would turn into almost two hours, I'd have pushed back harder. Between the press and Harrison and our friends, it feels like we're trying to leave a high school reunion turned family wedding. But finally, we extricate ourselves. I shower the second I get home and then Anica and I head to dinner.

"Please tell me you can eat bread again," she says.

I laugh. "As much as I want."

"Are you done, then?"

I shrug. "I'm not sure, but they never stack fights much closer than a month apart. So even if I'm not, I've earned a cheat meal or two."

She sighs.

"Do you hate it?"

"Not at all," she says. "You were amazing, and clearly you enjoyed it. It's phenomenal you can do that, any of it." She squeezes my hand. "And it's so freaking hot. But. . ."

"But what?"

"I want more Ethan time."

"You've been writing," I say. "Right?"

"I have, actually." Her shoulders relax a bit. "Avon just approved the manuscript I sent, and I started a new one."

"Another IP project? Or is this *Ashes?*"

She shakes her head. "Not *Ashes,* and not another IP project either. This is something new. The idea just kind of came to me."

"Oh yeah?"

She swallows. "It's kind of stupid."

"Try me."

"It's about this guy who's a researcher so he's super nerdy, right?"

"Please tell me this isn't supposed to be based on me."

She giggles. "Well, he works in California, and whenever he's not working, he's surfing."

I roll my eyes, but secretly I'm glad to find that I'm in there somewhere. "Go on."

"Well, he submits a paper, but this person, H.J. Keenan, tears it apart."

"Okay."

"He's so angry that he pulls up that person's papers and picks one. Then he tears it apart in the same publication."

"And?"

"Of course they meet at a conference, and he's shocked that it's a girl. And he hates her on sight."

"And she feels the same way about him."

"Right."

"And then?" I pull into the parking lot of the steakhouse and shove the Bronco into park.

"Well, she gets a research grant, but the person who's assigned to work with her on it—"

"Let me guess. It's me?"

She shakes her head. "Nope, it's the love interest's sister. She's also a scientist."

"Wait, what?"

"So they end up bumping into each other a lot. He

decides to really make her pay for the back and forth they've had and get her kicked off the project. But—"

I kiss her then. "Stop," I say. "You can't tell me any more or it'll ruin the story when I read it."

"You don't think it sounds idiotic?"

"Not at all."

"Oh, good. I'm seven chapters in already." She's so much happier when she's writing.

"Will you quit waitressing?"

"When?" She opens her door and heads for the entrance.

"After you get a new agent and sell this one for a bunch of money."

"Stop," she says. "You're ridiculous."

"I'm serious."

"If that did happen, which it won't, I don't think I would."

"No?"

"I'd see if I could do part time," she says. "Because I like working at Golden Gloves, and not only because it's close to where you're training. It's nice to do something that helps people and to interact with customers, and to see regular families and couples and kids. I think it helps my writing, honestly. Sometimes the conversations and fights and dynamics inspire me too."

"Really?"

She shrugs. "Writing can be kind of solitary. It's nice to be forced out of my room and into the real world."

The hostess seats us right away, and thankfully, no one seems to have followed us here.

After we order, Anica gets quiet. Strangely quiet. "Is something wrong?" Even though she said she loved me, and even though I won the fight, something feels off.

She grimaces, and I know it's not all in my head.

"You can tell me," I say. But I hope it's nothing, because

for the first time in a long time, my life is right where I want it to be.

"What's up with you and your sister?"

My hand freezes on my napkin. "Did Adriana say something?"

"What would she have said?" She tilts her head sideways.

For the first time since we met, I feel like I'm being interrogated. "I don't know. Ana talks about a lot of stuff."

"You two aren't right," Anica says. "That much was clear. What did you fight about?"

I sigh. "I don't like to talk about it."

"That's fair," she says. "But I don't know how to act around her if I don't know why she's mad at you. I feel like this has something to do with your mom and your bio father. If you don't want to tell me, that's fine. But if you love me, you need to know that you can talk to me when you want to."

She's right. Love is trust. I've never told anyone else, but maybe she'd understand. I'm suddenly desperate for her to tell me that I'm right—that I did exactly what I should have to protect my sister.

But what if she doesn't agree?

I look into her wide, trusting eyes, and I take a leap. "My bio father is named Phillip Sims. He beat me and my mom when he drank too much, but he hit my mom a lot more often than he hit me. One night, he beat her pretty severely. I should have stepped in to distract him, but I didn't. I had class pictures the next day and the year before, I had missed them. Mom kept me home because of a black eye. I told myself that's why I didn't try and stop him, but really, I think maybe I didn't want him to hit me."

Anica closes her eyes.

"He killed my mom that night. I could've stopped him, distracted him, something, but I didn't." I stare down at the tablecloth. "He went to prison and I never looked back."

She opens her eyes and stands up. She pulls me up until I'm standing beside her and then she wraps her arms around me. She doesn't say anything, but tears roll down her face. "I'm sorry."

We're still standing up when our food comes.

Anica doesn't even look embarrassed. She simply sits down, wipes her cheeks with her napkin, and places her hand over mine. They leave our plates and walk away.

"None of that is your fault," she says. "Which you either know already, or you won't accept no matter how many times I say it."

"I know it's not my fault that Phillip did that," I say. "But I also know that I could have changed the outcome."

"When we let bad people blame us for their actions, the world is a little dimmer. Don't let his evil steal your light— or your life. Not a second of it."

Something about what she says shakes the bands around my heart loose. It's nothing dramatic, but I breathe a little easier. I smile a little brighter. And she's right. Maybe I've been letting it steal my light, and I know Phillip has stolen too much of my time. And my sister's. I finally realize that she'll get it—why I needed to get rid of him, for my and Adriana's good.

They bring the dessert tray and Anica waves them off. "You can get something," she says, "but I'm stuffed."

I shake my head. "Can we get the check?"

"But why is your sister mad?" she asks. "I'm really happy to know about Phillip." She bites her lip. "Happy isn't the right word. I'm honored you shared. Does that make sense?"

I nod.

"But what does that have to do with Adriana?"

"So, this part is not as horrifying, but it's a little . . . dicier."

"What does that mean?" She quirks one eyebrow.

"I threw away every letter Phillip sent me the entire time he was in prison, but apparently my sister didn't. My dad knew she was talking to him and arranged to get Phillip out early so I could meet with him before she showed up to welcome him into the free world. I tried to convince him to leave her alone."

"That's why you came back to Atlanta."

I nod. "He's not as scary as he was. In fact, he's kind of broken and pathetic."

"Eighteen years in prison," Anica says, like it's no surprise. "I'm sure those years took a toll."

"I guess so."

The check comes and I pay. She doesn't ask anything else while we walk out to the car, but she knows I'm not done.

Once we're both seated, I continue. "Phillip refused to leave her alone."

"He badgered her?" Anica sounds surprised.

"Well, no, but she wouldn't agree not to see him. She yelled at me for my interference, and she got his information and found him."

"What did he do?"

"He met her, for at least one dinner and one lunch, as far as I know. She wasn't very forthcoming with me about any of it, but obviously he didn't tell her that he didn't want to see her." For some reason this is coming out all wrong. I sound like the bad guy as much as he does.

"So Adriana and Phillip talked."

"Right. Then he called me for a job, because he still couldn't find one, and I told him I'd get him one."

"You did?" She frowns. "If he did what?" She's too smart for her own good.

"If he would tell Adriana he didn't want to see her any more."

She groans. "Ethan. Please tell me he said no."

My lips twist. "He did."

"Oh good."

"He killed my mom, Anica." She must not understand what kind of person he is.

"Twenty years ago," she says. "And he paid for that by going to prison."

"She's dead," I say flatly. "He can't pay for what he did. Not ever."

Anica's shoulders are stiff, and her eyebrows are scrunched.

"You think I should have gotten him a job?"

She shakes her head. "I don't think you owe him anything."

"Okay, then."

"But I think you owe Adriana something."

"You're kidding me." I slam my hand against the edge of the steering wheel.

She flinches. "I am not teasing you, clearly, and you can't frighten me into agreeing with you, either. I don't care how awesome you are at laying people out flat."

I inhale and exhale a few times. "I'm not trying to scare you."

"I love you, Ethan. Completely. But it's because I love you that I'm going to say this. You were wrong to try to take Adriana's choices away from her."

"Phillip—"

"You said yourself that you don't know him. You said he's broken. But Adriana is an adult, and she's smart, and she can make her own decisions. Your job is not to take that away from her. If he hurts her, that's on him. You can tell her your beliefs, your thoughts, and your desires, but you have to step back and let her decide what to do with that."

I grit my teeth.

She quiets suddenly. "I know you're upset about all that, but there's more to the story you haven't told me, isn't there?"

"He didn't take the offer of a job, but he did take the Porsche."

I've never heard Anica swear. Until right now.

"I didn't *make* him do it," I say. "He said my dad tried to pay him off too, but he didn't take it back then. He said he was taking it now because it was the right thing to do—to leave her alone."

"I'm glad that the Mayor of Evil has given you his stamp of approval for your actions."

"What does that mean?" I realize that I've driven her straight to Mary and Luke's and I park the car on the curb.

"Ethan." She turns to face me. "You're a brilliant man. I want you to think about this long and hard. Forgiveness isn't for the person you're forgiving. It's for you."

"What are you talking about?"

"We've been raised to believe that we should forgive people who do something to us . . . as though it's some gift for them. My sister Lizzie taught me this. She married an engineering genius, but she was, emotionally, the smartest person I've ever known. She said, from her deathbed, that we forgive others for *ourselves*. If we don't do it, if we hold on to that anger against someone who hurt us, it will eat us up from the inside out. It will destroy us."

I want to hurl something through something else. I want to crush the steering wheel to dust. "What are you saying?"

"I hope you're not so emotionally flooded right now that you can't remember my words. What I'm saying, Ethan, is that while I love you, I no longer trust you. If you would do something like that to your sister, if you would take her decisions away under the label of protection, then you don't know how to love in a healthy way." She inhales deeply and her voice trembles. A tear runs down her cheek. "I'm saying, Ethan Trainor, that until you are able to understand this and my faith that you'll never try to control me, or frankly your sister, is restored, we're breaking up." She flips the car door open before I can stop her and sprints toward the house.

Anica clearly spends too much time reading fiction. She doesn't understand real life or the reality of someone like Phillip. If she understood, if she had been through what I have, she wouldn't think I was controlling Ana. I'm trying to keep her *safe*. Eliminating one option, a dangerous option, isn't the same thing as trying to control what she does. She can do literally anything in the world, except seeing Phillip.

I slam my hand into the steering wheel again, but this time the horn honks and a neighbor pokes their head out the front door. I slam it into drive and peel out down the street.

I could stay and try to go after Anica, or I could call her, or I could . . . I don't know.

But I don't think any of those things will help. She seemed completely calm, composed, and in control of her feelings and thoughts. When I get angry, I always go for a run. Or I get in a fight. Or I go surfing.

By the time I get home, my initial frustration that she wasn't listening wears off and I realize that for once in my life, I'm not angry. I don't need a run. I don't need the calming influence of the ocean. I don't even want to punch someone.

What overwhelms me with its potency is my sorrow. And I don't have a coping mechanism in place for devastating sadness, because I've never felt this way before. I start to think about what she said, but it hurts too badly. I shove it away, and I curl up, and I cry while Partner licks the salty tears from my face.

But no matter how many times I push it away, Anica's words keep coming back to me. She can't trust me—and neither can Ana—because I don't know how to love someone.

As badly as I want to scream and argue and fight, deep down, I know she's right, and like my bio dad, for the first time, it occurs to me that it might not matter whether Anica can forgive me. It might not matter whether she can trust me.

Because despite my flaws, I love her down to my bones. And I'm beginning to realize that she might be better off without someone like me. Sometimes broken things can be fixed, but when something is utterly shattered, you're better off walking away from it. Which is exactly what my brilliant, beautiful, strong girlfriend just did.

I hope I'm strong enough to let her.

16

ANICA

I spend the first week hoping that Ethan's processing what I said. I check my phone every few minutes—and almost text and call him over and over. The only thing that gets me through is focusing on my writing. I may have just lost my happy ending, but I'm going to make double sure this new couple gets theirs.

When the next week rolls around without any word of any kind, something clicks.

I think we're done.

Ethan listened to what I said, and he disagrees with me. He either thinks I abandoned him, or he thinks I'm so clueless that I don't understand. Either way, I'm afraid he's closer to his emotionally constipated father than I can handle. I won't marry someone who will make my decisions for me if he decides that I'm not qualified.

I close my eyes and imagine his utter tenderness. His smile. His laugh. How can he not understand—someone whose parents stole his life with their selfishness—that it's unacceptable to force something on someone you love?

No matter how much time I spend staring at my computer, I can't think of a single happy thing to write.

Which means it's the perfect time to work on *Ashes*.

I pull the manuscript out and realize it's been so long since I wrote on it that I need to read over what I've written.

But when I do . . . it becomes clear that it's awful. It's stilted, and contrived, and forced.

It's not a French-style tragedy, beautiful in its pain. It's more like a Frankenstein-shaped ball of sadness: like I taped together every depressing thing I could think of and I forced them upon the reader in quick succession. No wonder Henri hated it.

My finger hovers over the file for a moment, wondering whether perhaps this isn't the best time for me to make this kind of decision, but then I do it anyway—I delete it. Seconds later, my phone bings. For a split second, I hope it's a message from Ethan.

I hate that I'm still hoping that he'll suddenly *get* it.

But no, it's from my bank—my first deposit for my IP project has hit my account.

I have plenty of money saved thanks to steady work at Golden Gloves, but for some reason this feels like a sign. I've deleted *Ashes*. I've been paid for my new book. It's time for me to leave the comfort of my past—Luke and what he represents—and create a place for myself. Bonus—it won't be a place that's full of memories with Ethan.

I'll still come see Amy and Chase, of course, but I won't have to wallow any more.

I get in my car and I drive, but not to the closest apartments I can find. No, I drive to apartments that are across town. I drive until I see a unit that's perfect. Huge trees. A big pool. A gym, not that I'll use that. I fill out an application on the spot and pay my first month's rent and deposit, pending my background check.

Right around the corner, there's an IHOP.

The universe has a real sense of humor. I stop in and fill

out an application, and the manager offers to interview me immediately. "Things are slow right now," he says. "You timed it perfectly."

Just in case I thought maybe I needed to wait around for Ethan a little longer. . . What more do I want? A signed letter from the guy upstairs? *Anica, move on. Don't waste away like you did last time.*

I hope I've grown enough not to repeat that mistake. When I get home, I look over the two-thirds of a book I've written and I decide it's not epic, but it's pretty good. While I'm high on the momentum of the last few hours, I write a one-page query letter and send it to a dozen agents I've always admired. I could send it to Henri, since I've given up on *Ashes*, but I'm sick of waiting for people who don't support me no matter what.

Conditional love isn't love.

She didn't even have the decency to tell me it sucked and why she thought it sucked. If you're going to do something hard, go all the way.

I stay up until almost three a.m. and write three more chapters. I've got, maybe, three more to go. It feels good. I finally shut my laptop down, only to realize that my blanket is missing. Chase is always taking it and dragging it all over the house. Now that it's officially fall, it's chillier at night and I want it.

I peek out the door and into the hall. I really don't want to wake up Andy, because her barking will wake up everyone else.

So far, the coast is clear, but when I reach the living room, Luke's already there, rocking Jack.

"Anica?"

I swallow.

"What are you doing up?"

If I needed another sign that it's time for me to move. .

. I'm a grown adult who has to account for her behavior like she's a sneaky child. Lizzie would be dying laughing right now. "I think Chase took my blanket."

He chuckles. "You woke up because you're too cold? We can turn up the thermostat, you know."

I shake my head. "I was already awake. I've been writing."

"Oh." Jack starts to wail.

"Need another bottle?"

"Thanks," Luke says.

One magic button later, and I'm handing it to my brother-in-law. "Hope he settles down soon."

"Why are you up writing so late?" That's when I realize he isn't asking for an accounting like a mother might—he's not scolding.

He's worried about me.

Something constricts in my chest and tears threaten. "It's been a rough couple of weeks."

He pats the sofa. "What's going on?"

I sit down. "Ethan and I broke up."

"I figured that when I stopped seeing him abruptly."

"It's a long story, but there's nothing I can do about it."

"What else is wrong?"

"I'm not sure," I say. "But I think it's time for me to move out."

He frowns. "Why?"

"I think I need my own place, Luke. I can never tell you how much it meant to feel like I had a home again, even with Lizzie gone. It's just not the same with Mom and Dad. I can't explain it. They just moved on like nothing had happened at all."

"Eventually, I did too." He jiggles Jack.

"You did and you didn't. You mourned her deeply, like I did, and you didn't settle for half measures."

"What do you mean, half measures?"

I start to bawl then. "Lizzie would be so ashamed of me."

Jack has fallen asleep and Luke sets him in his bouncer and hugs me. "Nothing about you would make her anything but proud."

"I should've made her take that kidney," I say.

Luke lets me go and looks me dead in the eye. "She didn't want it."

"The docs said she could've had—"

"They didn't know how much more time she would've had, but her cancer was terminal. That was a Band-Aid over a bullet wound." He squeezes my knee. "It always was, and she knew that."

"Do you know what I would give right now for another few months with her?" I sob louder, and I clap my hands over my mouth, desperate not to wake anyone else up.

"I would have given anything too," he says, "but you honored her wishes. That was the right decision. She was in a lot of pain, Anica. She put on a brave face when you were there, but they wouldn't have been great months."

"She told me that she wouldn't take it because she wouldn't be able to rest, knowing her life might shorten mine someday." I sigh. "She wouldn't let *me* make that decision, but if she'd listened, she could have known her son."

Luke looks back at Jack. "I understand what you're saying, but there's not a lot to know until they're a little older. A few months wouldn't have made a difference."

"She told me to live brilliantly. She said the world needs my words." I can't stop then—I fold in half and bawl like a baby. Sometimes the pain crashes over me in a wave, like it's just time for the universe to sucker punch me.

Luke wraps an arm around me. "She believed what she said, and I agree with her."

I finally get it together enough to sit up, and I realize

what has killed my ability to write. "But my words aren't valuable, Luke. I write fluff, literary cotton candy."

He grows so still beside me that I turn to face him. "What?"

"Why would you say that?"

"I write love stories, Luke. You know they're nonsense. They're great for, you know, bad days, or whatever. It's women's fiction of the worst kind—like eating a bowl of caramel corn when you feel bad. It helps for a moment, but ultimately, it's filler."

He shakes his head, and then he keeps shaking his head. "You're wrong."

"What?"

"Your sister read your books over and over. She loved them. She has extra copies from that first print run in boxes for Chase and Amy."

"What?"

"She didn't want you to write anything but the stories you love, the 'fluff' as you call it. And I think you should think long and hard about why you think it's not valuable."

"Patrick said—"

"That man was a waste of space." Luke practically growls. "He was the biggest mistake you ever made. I bought a cake the day I heard you broke up. I told the kids we were celebrating freedom. Amy thought March eighteenth was Independence Day for months after that."

I laugh. "You didn't."

"I absolutely did. I did that for Lizzie. She hated him more than I did."

"What?"

Luke leans toward me. "What do you think is the most important decision we make in our lives? What do you think does more to bring us joy and support and peace in our time here on earth?"

"The single most important?" I ask.

He nods slowly.

"Well, I mean, everyone says your wedding day is the best day of your life. Are you saying . . . it's who you choose to marry?"

"Loving someone—that's the most important choice. But what the books get wrong is that it's not a thing you do one single time. You do it every single day. It's a choice, it's an action, it's ongoing. Your books get that right. Your books show girls and boys how to focus on what matters. Home. Family. Nurturing support. They do it in unique and fascinating ways, and that has value. More value than books about social justice. More value than books about scientific research. And in case you never actually read any of that drivel your idiotic ex writes, let me tell you, your stories have a heck of a lot more value than some thriller with a few timely and popular social themes thrown in for flavoring."

"But—"

He shakes his head again. "No buts, not about this, missy. Your sister knew what I know. That you already write stories that matter. That your words, your stories about joy and finding peace and hope and faith and love, those are the best kinds of stories out there. It's the highest form of storytelling. Teach humans how to use their hearts the right way, and how to recognize how to live their lives to the fullest." He stares me in the eye and doesn't look away.

He's serious.

"Thanks," I say.

"You think about what I said," he says. "And you never spend another second thinking that you can't write the stories that brought Lizzie so much joy and pride because they aren't meaningful."

I stand up. "Okay. I'll try."

"You're smart. Once you've had time to think about it, you'll believe me."

I snort. "You try and get some sleep too." I turn and stumble over my blanket. I pick it up with a smile on my face. "You're a good man, Luke."

"And you're a good woman, Anica. Don't forget it."

I'm off the next day, so I plan to sleep in. Until my phone rings and rings and rings. Finally I roll over and pick up. "Hello?"

"Anica?"

Henri? "Yeah."

"I received a strange call this morning."

Weird. "So did I."

"Cute."

"What do you want, Henri? I was sleeping."

"It's almost noon."

"I'm sorry, Mom, what's your point?"

She clears her throat. "One of my colleagues called me at eight a.m. She had been up half the night reading sample chapters she happened to click on at midnight last night."

"Okay."

"They were from you, and she wanted to confirm that I was fine with her offering representation."

"On the basis of *sample* chapters?" I blink and rub my eyes. What's going on?

"Did you or did you not query a romantic comedy yesterday?"

"I did, but pardon my irritation when I say, it's not any of your business that I did. We have a provisional agreement that is now complete."

"This is a very small industry, Anica."

"I know that."

"Why would you send a new manuscript to Phoebe?"

"Um, because I don't have an agent, Henrietta. Why else would I do it? I want to sell it."

"I've wanted to sell romantic comedies for you for *years*."

But she hasn't had my back, not when I needed it. Any guilt I felt over moving on is beyond gone. "I'm going to hang up, Henri, and if I don't get a call from Phoebe soon, I'll sue you." Then I hang up.

It feels unbelievably good to shut her down, even if it was probably a little emotional and immature.

Phoebe calls me twenty minutes later. And two hours after we chat, I get an email from Emery. All told, six more agents contact me, all of them offering representation on a *sample*. I ask for a week to decide. And to finish the book, obviously.

A breakup. A move. Possibly a new job. A new agent. It's been a weird few days.

But after thinking about it and writing a few chapters to clear my head, I eat dinner with Mary and Luke and their beautiful kids.

"I have some news," I say.

"Uh-oh," Amy says. "That's not good."

How sad that my niece assumes any news I have will be bad. "Actually, I think it's good."

Amy glares at Luke. "You said you tried."

"What?" I glance at Luke.

He picks up his fork and takes a bite, and then he points at his mouth. "Full."

"Dad said you wanted to move out but that he'd told you that you shouldn't." She glares at him again. "That's not your news, is it?"

I open my mouth, and then I close it. Amy and Luke *want* me here? They're not just *okay* with me being here. They *want* me to stay?

"We should listen to her reasons for wanting to leave," Mary says. "Maybe she can't sleep well here, or you kids are wearing her out."

"No." I shake my head. "Look, it doesn't have to do

with any of that, but I'm an adult and I ought to have my own place."

"Dad's an adult." Amy crosses her arms.

"But he has kids," I say. "That's different."

"Mary's not a kid," Chase says. "I don't want you to go. We're okay with adults living here too."

I haven't felt wanted somewhere in quite a while. "Alright," I say. "I put a deposit down on an apartment, but I guess I can stay here if you really want me to."

"Yay," Amy says. "Dad, does that mean we can get out the cake?"

Mary nods and Amy and Chase run for the fridge.

"You got a cake?" I pin Luke with my strongest stare.

"We like cake," he says with a grin.

"I can't argue with that."

And Luke did get one thing right—all my problems seem a little smaller when I'm shoveling cake into my mouth.

I call Barbara after I assume the dinner rush is past. "Hey Barb."

"Anica," she says. "I hope you enjoyed your week off."

I worked breakfasts for a week and then took last week off. "Here's the thing."

"It's that guy, I know it."

"Excuse me?"

"He kind of skulks past every day about three times, peering in the windows." She grunts. "Loser."

My heart takes wing. "Has he ever come inside?"

"Is your phone broken?"

I laugh. "No."

"Well, then, does it matter?"

"I suppose not."

"He hasn't come inside," she says. "And it's ridiculous that a man that fine would be afraid to call you. He must've done something very bad."

"Not to me," I say. "But I suppose the principle is the same."

"Please don't quit your job over him," she says. "I'll keep you on breakfasts as long as you want."

"Oh, fine," I say.

"See you tomorrow morning?"

So much for late night writing. "Only three days a week."

"Why?"

"I've been writing, Barb. I need time for that. I can do three five hour shifts a week, no more."

"I'll take it."

Now time to pick an agent. With a finished manuscript in hand, I interview each of them. I ask them about how they would have handled the *Ashes* situation. Two of them have no idea and splutter and make excuses. One says she'd have done the same as Henri. I appreciate her honesty, but she's not for me either. Honesty isn't enough on its own. I want a real advocate—someone who tells me the truth and still does whatever she can to help me, even when we don't agree.

"I wouldn't have shopped your first book," Phoebe says. "I'd have told you my opinions on that one, and on the new one, because I'd have wanted to know if I were in your situation. Think of all the time you wasted on that project."

"I forced myself to reread my last book too, and it was just as bad."

"It was," Phoebe says. "It's a travesty that Henri didn't tell you that. It was sold on the basis of your name, and it devalued your brand."

"Thanks for being willing to do hard things." I think about how, instead of asking me for the full, or offering representation, she called her friend, Henri, and asked if I was available. She clearly approaches things head on. I value that.

"I have a question for you," Phoebe says, "while we're covering hard truths."

"Shoot."

"What made you realize the book sucked? Why are you recommitting to chick lit?"

"I guess I'm doing it for my sister," I say. "I've been a little confused about what matters, but her husband set me straight."

"He sounds like a good guy to have around."

It's bizarre for me to be so involved in his life, perhaps, but she's right. He is a helpful, smart, caring man. It's almost like, in losing a sister, I gained the brother I never had. "I plan to keep him close."

"I look forward to hearing what you decide. I may have already mentioned to a few editors over drinks last night that there may be a new Maggard manuscript in the world soon, and I have two who are already *salivating*."

"You're hired," I say.

"Are you sure?"

"Send me the agreement, but assuming it's standard, yeah. I'm sure." I open up my laptop. "I can send you the full manuscript, too. I finished it today."

"What wonderful news all around."

"This has been a weird and roundabout way to signing a new client, I'm sure," I say. "Like we've done the whole thing backward, but I appreciate your understanding and I like that you called Henri first."

"I never do anything underhanded."

"I appreciate that," I say. "And I look forward to more conversations in the future."

"As do I."

With everything in my life coming up Anica, I should feel amazing. But instead, I can't stop thinking about Ethan skulking by the diner. Why would he do that? What does it mean?

I'm not sure what it says about me that I can write romances that agents are dying to represent, but my own love life is a disaster.

Too bad I can't write myself a happy ending.

17

ETHAN

No matter how long I spend staring at spreadsheets the next day, none of the numbers make sense. I decide to hold the staff meeting early. At least that won't require my brain to analyze data. It has, apparently, called in sick for the day.

"Hannah," I say. "Let's move the staff meeting up."

She blinks at me. "Excuse me?"

"Instead of doing it at ten a.m., let's do it now."

"Um, Mr. Trainor, it's eleven-thirty," she says slowly, like I'm suffering from a traumatic brain injury. "When I came to remind you of the time, you waved me off without looking up from the computer."

I groan. Stupid spreadsheets. "Fine." I wave her off without thinking, and then it clicks. I remember doing that earlier. When I was contemplating whether I need to call Phillip and tell him I was wrong.

I pick up my phone again, but I can't do it.

It's not that I don't believe Anica. She's right, I'm sure. Phillip is a terrible person—or at least, he was. I don't know him at all now, and I'm not sure whether murdering the woman you're supposed to love is forgivable. I'm not sure whether his excuses—alcohol, past abuse, anger issues—absolve any part of his culpability.

But she's undeniably right that my anger doesn't hurt Phillip.

It hurts me.

Now that she's said it, it's clear as day. The long runs, the surfing, the fighting, all of them merely dealt with the fallout. None of them ever addressed the cause. When she looked me in the eye and said that it wasn't my fault—that I can't take any blame for my bio father's actions—I knew she was right about that too, but it has never sunk into my soul.

Knowing that I didn't *do* something and not blaming myself for my failure to change the result aren't the same. This time I pick up my phone, and I actually dial.

"Ethan?"

"Hey, Geo. I have a strange question, and I'd like to ask you to keep this between us."

"Okay," she says. "What do you need?"

"Your fiancé Mark died, right?"

"He did."

"I'm sorry to bring it up, but did you ever talk to anyone about it?"

"About his death?"

"Yes. Or . . . I don't know. Any of it. I never talk about it, but I lost someone too. I'm beginning to wonder whether I ought to discuss it with someone professional."

"I have the number for a wonderful grief counselor."

That may not be quite right, but it's a start. "Can you text it to me?"

"I'd be happy to," she says. "And Ethan?"

"Yeah?"

"I'm proud of you for asking. That's the hardest part. Honestly."

I hope she's right.

But when I finally meet with her psychologist, I know immediately that he's not quite the right fit. He asks me a looooot of questions. I talk and talk and talk. And we haven't even covered anything beyond the night of the incident when the hour is up. "We didn't make much progress," I say. "We'll go a lot faster next time, right?"

Dr. Thayer stands up. "It takes as long as it takes, Mr. Trainor."

"That's not very medical," I say. "I do better with deadlines."

"You can't put a timeline on emotional healing."

I don't groan in front of him, but I decide right then and there to skip my next appointment.

And then I find myself creepily peering inside Golden Gloves. Twice. I decide maybe I ought to go, even if it is a waste of time. It keeps me away from the diner. At my second appointment, we don't talk about my mom's death at all. We talk about forgiveness, and it turns out Dr. Thayer agrees with Anica.

It helps me gather the strength to go to the next meeting.

And the one after that.

I'm headed to my fifth appointment when Dad shows up. "I've got bad news," he says.

I sit down and send a text to Dr. Thayer. NOT BLOWING YOU OFF. SOMETHING CAME UP AT WORK.

"What now?" I ask.

"The court ruled against us." The set of Dad's mouth is grim.

"What does that mean?"

"The news comes out tomorrow that based on our preliminary figures and pending official audit results, we'll report a half million dollar loss this quarter."

I close my eyes. "What will that do to the stock price?"

Dad harrumphs. "Nothing good, but it's been soaring since your last fight."

I open my eyes abruptly. "What does that have to do with anything?"

"I called Harrison. He said you've only been training three days a week."

"Without another fight set up—"

"He said Dana White has offered you three."

I swallow.

"You didn't think you ought to talk to me about it?"

I shrug. "You're not my manager."

He slams his hand down on the table. "You beat that Russian guy, and then you completely freak out and dump your girlfriend, and now I hear you're going to a shrink. Annelise insisted that I give you space, but I think it's time you tell me what's going on."

"Dad, I traded my Porsche to Phillip in exchange for his agreement that he'd completely cut Adriana off."

His eyes widen. "That's brilliant. And it worked? Did you get it in writing?"

I shake my head. "It wasn't brilliant. It was bad, Dad. I never should've done that."

"Darn right, you shouldn't have. Because I should have done it first." He squeezes my shoulder. "And don't worry— I'll get you a new car."

I stand up, shaking his hand away, because for the first time, I get it. I've turned into him—the consuming inferno inside of me left me no perspective. "Dad, are we done here? I have a call to make."

"Look, the real news I needed to tell you is that I set up another fight, with a boxer this time. It's going to be huge. He's ranked near the top, and the media will go crazy for it. The UFC has agreed to wait to announce it until I give them the go-ahead."

"Are you really suggesting that I fight someone way out

of my league to distract from our bad business break? I'm your circus sideshow now?"

Dad rolls his eyes. "Stop painting me to be some kind of villain. You're a natural, he's not out of your league, and you'll get paid a ridiculous amount for agreeing to do this. Besides, if this generates the buzz we're convinced it will, then we're in the clear. Once the bad news hits, we release word of the fight, and boom. It's forgotten. Our stock rebounds, and you can step into leadership as a conquering hero—literally and figuratively. I honestly thought you'd thank me."

"You didn't ask."

"That's not what leaders, do, son. They march into battle and slay the demon."

I ball up my fist to punch him in the nose. And then I think about forgiveness—it's for me, not for him. So I let my anger go, and I walk out of the office. I'm late, but I make it to the last thirty minutes of my appointment.

"Are you going to do the fight?" Dr. Thayer asks. "Or will you refuse?"

I run my hand through my hair. "I want to refuse, but I also want to accept."

"Why do you want to refuse?"

"Because he shouldn't be able to manipulate people that way!" Fury floods me.

"That's how your sister felt," Dr. Thayer observes quietly.

It hits me like a two-by-four. My actions might even have been right. Phillip may have posed a threat, but it wasn't my call. I stole that choice from her, just as my dad stole the decision from me. He didn't ask. He ordered, and I'm not a solider or a child.

"I'll call Phillip today."

"Good, but before we end our session, I'd like to hear you articulate the reasons you want to do the fight."

"Because Dad's right—it would fix our problem. This tax thing isn't a big deal—except that it hasn't been required in the past so we haven't paid it over the past eighteen months. That means it's a blip on the radar in the long run. Anything we can do to instill confidence in our brand with the shareholders is wise. Also, I kind of want to see whether I can compete at that level."

"You could be badly injured."

I shrug. "Maybe, but I doubt it. Fifteen years ago, probably, but they have rules now." Besides, my heart is already slag. What does it matter if I break a rib? Or a jaw? Maybe drinking through a straw for a few months would give me time to think and work through everything.

"You've made marvelous progress," Dr. Thayer says. "And for the record, I credit that young woman, Anica. She was spot on in what she said, and you obviously cared enough about her to listen. That's usually the key."

"I love her," I say without hesitation.

"I believe that," Dr. Thayer says.

I stand up. "Do you think I should fight?" I ask. "Or refuse on principle?"

He grins. "If you do anything 'on principle,' you're handing your power to another person."

By golly, he's right. "Thanks."

"I'm alright taking a few weeks off, unless you need me," Dr. Thayer says. "If you need to focus on training."

"Thanks," I say.

"But definitely send me details." His sideways smile surprises me. I'd never have guessed that buttoned-up Dr. Thayer likes UFC.

"Will do." I shake my head as I leave.

Spending a few hours every day pounding a heavy bag helps me not to fixate on Anica. Knowing that I'm not good for her and staying away aren't quite the same. As the fight nears, I thought it would get easier.

It gets harder.

The day before the match, I wake up thinking about how she came over last time and made me breakfast. A loud banging on the door floods me with hope like I haven't felt in ages. I race to the door, tripping over Partner and falling against the side of the sofa. "Ouch," I mutter. "Partner! Watch out, goofball."

She wags her tail and yips.

The banging resumes.

"I'm coming," I say.

But when I swing the door open, it's definitely not Anica. I haven't been this disappointed about something since she told me we were breaking up. My face falls and I sag against the doorframe.

"Whoa, who were you expecting?" Trig asks.

I don't even bother closing the door. I turn around and shuffle back to my bedroom.

He follows me inside. "Nice place." He snorts.

"Dad picked it out."

"He bought you a suburban cookie cutter house?" Trig lifts one eyebrow.

"Some of us don't collect mansions all over the world." I cross my arms. "What do you want, Trig?"

He purses his lips and sighs. "If I didn't love Geo so much, I wouldn't be here at all, so try not to be such a complete jerk about this. I know that'll be hard for you."

"You're the expert on being insensitive," I say. "So maybe you can tell me."

"Dude, I know I can't fight you, but you don't want to cross verbal swords with me."

I flop into a huge red armchair. "Geo told you I asked for a referral?"

He sits on the edge of the sofa, tiny lines forming between his eyebrows. "Wait. A referral for what?"

I sit up. If Geo didn't tell him about Dr. Thayer, then why is he here? He said he came for her. "Never mind."

"Look, I've been really dumb in the past. Not often, but it's happened. I know sometimes we can get in our own way, alright? So when Geo mentioned that Anica was upset and that it was your fault, I found myself agreeing to come talk to you."

Anica's upset? For some reason my heart soars when I hear that, and it makes me feel even crankier. Like I need *Trig* here to help me deal with my emotions. Please. "I've got a big day tomorrow, and I have some work to do today. Get to the point."

"I'm going to assume you're being such a jerk because you're hurting. I've been there, but my patience has a limit. I'm just going to say what I came here to say." He stares me in the eye. "You're blowing this, dude."

"Blowing what?"

"Everything with Anica."

"There isn't anything to mess up. In case you hadn't heard, she dumped me."

"She loves you."

I try not to blink or look half as panicked as I feel. "I screwed up."

"We all do," Trig says. "Now fix it before it's too late."

"It's already too late." I shake my head. "Trust me, she's better off without me."

"If you're this big of a pansy, maybe she is." He snorts. "For a fighter, you're kind of a dud."

"Why exactly are you here, again?"

"I've watched, patiently, while that girl got her life back on track. It's been hard for her, but she's a good person. She's blossoming again. It makes Geo happy. It makes all the wives happy. Even Luke's giddy."

"Great."

"And now, they're sick of watching her mope around over losing you."

"Okay." I cross my arms.

"So they're setting her up."

"Excuse me?"

"You're not the only good looking guy in Atlanta, Ethan. The past few weeks, she's been miserable, but last week, she didn't just laugh half-heartedly, she actually made a few jokes at game night."

"I'm glad to hear it," I lie.

"You moron, that's a bad thing. It means she's moving on, and you better believe the whole group noticed. Geo asked me if you'd said anything." He shrugs. "About what? I asked her."

"Huh?"

"She wanted to make sure you weren't interested—she said she thought you'd figure out you were an idiot and try to win her back." Trig shakes his head. "I told her I didn't think you had any plans."

"You haven't talked to me at all."

Trig smirks. "So? Was I wrong?"

I shake my head.

"Okay then. So Geo's got a friend," he says. "She knows him from some parties she threw for the Braves. He's their pitcher, and he's a big deal, and she wants to set him up with Anica. She thinks they'd hit it off. Apparently his mom's also an editor for a big publisher, and the guy loves to read."

"A match made in heaven." My voice is flatter than a highway in West Texas and my hands itch to crush something.

"He's a catch," Trig says, "if you'll pardon the pun."

"Great."

"Alright, then." He stands up. "I figured when you

thought about him pressing her up against the brick wall outside Luke's house to kiss her—"

I fly out of the chair and reach for Trig's collar.

He leaps back. "That's what I thought."

"What do you want me to say?" I ask. "That I love her? That you're tearing my heart out right now? I'm trying to do the right thing, here. Do you really have to rub my face in the fact that she's moving on?"

"What's the right thing, Mr. Noble? Hiding in this little house? Making Anica as miserable as you?"

"I'm not right for her," I say. "I'm all broken. I'm trying to fix myself, but if she's ready to move on, she should do it."

Trig shakes his head and steps toward me. "You are the dumbest—" He pauses inches away from my face. "You don't get to sit around and wait until you're fixed. Life doesn't work that way. Fix yourself right now, and then tell her you've done it. Or if you're working on it actively, tell her that instead. She'll work on it with you—that's who she is. But if you sit in the penalty box, that pitcher will walk up and steal your base."

That was officially the biggest bunch of mixed metaphors I've ever heard in my life. Even so . . . is he right?

"You don't learn how to love someone by yourself." He shakes his head and walks toward the door.

"Hey, when is she supposed to meet this pitcher guy?" I ask.

"Tonight."

I swear under my breath. "I'm supposed to leave in a few hours—my fight is tomorrow. You couldn't have given me a little earlier heads up?"

He shrugs. "I don't know what to tell you. I only found out Francisco was coming to game night a few hours ago."

I want to rush over to her house right now. I want to fix

this—tell her I'm working on it. I'm not at peace yet, but I'm working toward it. I want to get wherever she needs me to be. I want to beg her to be patient, but how can I do that without having even fixed things with Adriana?

This time, I don't hesitate. I call Phillip.

"Ethan?"

"It's me, yeah."

"Is everything okay?"

I close my eyes and inhale and exhale.

"Ethan?"

"Yeah," I say. "Look, I'm working really hard to forgive you—"

"I don't—"

"Not for you, for me. You're like a cancer that has eaten away at me for twenty years. Look, that's not the point. I'm calling to tell you that I was wrong." The thought of telling him he can see Adriana cuts me like a blade, but I push forward. "You don't have to ignore Adriana, okay? If she wants to see you, it's fine with me."

"I can't give the Porsche back."

"Oh my—you're kidding right? This isn't about that. I don't want the stupid car back."

"You don't?"

"No, I—look—what I'm saying is that I had no business interfering with whatever Adriana wants to pursue in terms of a relationship with you. Okay?"

He swallows. "Yes. Thank you. I know you don't want to hear it, but I'm proud of you."

I'm making progress, but not that much. I hang up.

I don't call Adriana—I drive to her school. Even though I stop to grab flowers, I'm lucky and I arrive in time for her lunch break.

"Ethan?" She looks around, as if I might be there for someone other than her.

"I'm sorry." I hold the flowers toward her.

"Wait, what are you sorry for now?"

I shake my head. "No, I mean, you were right. I was just like Dad. I've known for a while now, but it took me a while to wrap my head around calling Phillip to rescind our deal. I didn't figure I could convincingly apologize to you before doing that."

"He was willing to trade me for a Porsche," she says. "I think that tells me something valuable."

I sigh. "Look, he was, but it wasn't as much about the car. I think it had to do with his guilt." I know the feeling. "I'm not saying you need to spend time with him. You already know how I feel about that—we're both better off without him. But if it's something you need, well you know better than anyone whether it is. I'm sorry I tried to wade in and force things on you in your life."

Ana steps closer and wraps her arms around my waist. "With mom and dad gone, I needed you to take care of me for a long time. I get it. But I'm old enough now that I only need you to wade in when I ask. Alright?"

I nod. "Yep, deal."

"Nice work," she says. "That was an excellent apology."

"Thanks," I say. "I wish I could take full credit, but I've been seeing a counselor."

Her eyes flutter. "Are you serious?"

I nod.

"That's brilliant. It may be the most impressive thing I've ever heard you say."

Instead of the fury that usually floods my heart, this time it's a feeling of light and air and joy. "Thank you." It's way better than the rage.

"Hey, good luck tomorrow."

"Do you mean tonight?"

She frowns. "Tonight?"

Oh, right, the fight. "Kidding. It's tomorrow. And

thanks." I let her go and step back. "I'd better go," I say. "I've got another apology to make."

"A harder one, I imagine," she says. "But I really hope you do that one right. I like Anica a lot."

"She's way too good for me," I say. "But if I play this right, she might not realize it until it's too late."

Ana laughs. "Play it perfectly, then."

18

ANICA

The editing on the IP project I did was relatively painless. Since the publisher technically purchased the book, they could really change whatever they wanted, so there wasn't much back and forth.

But working with a new agent on my most recent project is strange. Unlike Henri, who mostly sent my manuscript to publishers as it was and then sent me their comments, Phoebe wants to be involved in every step.

"You want me to change what?" I ask.

She explains.

"But if I change that, I'll have to rework the entirety of chapter eight."

"Which is why I'm calling. It'll take some thought and time—"

"You stayed up all night reading it, right?"

"Anica, I *love* your book. That doesn't mean it can't be *better* before we submit to publishers."

After reading over her laundry list of requested changes, it doesn't feel like she loves it. "Alright, let me think about it."

Once I read the sections she's talking about, I realize she's right. The main character isn't acting consistently. It takes me eleven days of almost nonstop edits to fix the problem. I write two extra chapters, but it's better. Much stronger. She calls me the next day.

"It's dramatically improved."

"So are we going on submission?" I shouldn't have to be nervous about asking my agent to do what agents do.

"Of course," she says. "But I had a few more thoughts before we take that step."

Breathe, Anica. Breathe. "Okay."

"I'm emailing you now. When I reread it—and I loved the new chapters four and eight, by the way—I realized that the pacing is a little slow from chapter twenty through the end."

"It's a romance," I remind her. "That's the wrap up."

"Right." She sighs. "I know it is, but think about what we might do to make that move a little . . . faster."

"You want it shorter?" How long are we going to be making dumb little changes like this?

"Not shorter—I want it to have more tension."

Forty minutes later, I get what she's saying and I have a tentative game plan. I hate that she's right again, but I also love that she cares so much. Which is why I spend the next week fixing the pacing issues. Then I send it back one more time . . . and I hold my breath.

Of course she calls me with yet another issue. "We're so close this time," she says. "I just think we could work on dialogue tags a little bit."

This time, I listen carefully, shoving my frustration deep, deep down. And then I make her changes in three days.

"Now," she says the next day. "Now we can go on submission. I'll send you my list tonight."

"Are we going to cast a wide net?"

"I've been thinking about this," she says.

My heart falls. She's only sending it to a few people.

"I don't want you to think this is anything but strategic. I love your book so much that I want to send it to a very curated list, specific editors who I know have latitude to make a deal. I think this is going to be big, Anica. A wide net catches a lot of little fish. We want to use a spear—for the swordfish."

"Significant?" I can't help thinking about Patrick's last deal.

She laughs. "Let's not get ahead of ourselves. This is romance, after all. The advances aren't always as large as other genres that don't have quite as much competition."

"I know," I say. "I know." The list she sends over is killer. She's assembled these publishers with a lot of strategy—competitors, and editors with a lot of seniority and pull. Which means if none of them want this manuscript. . . Breathe, Anica. Just breathe. Someone will want it. I just might not get much. After my last project bombing and then the IP project, I promise myself that I won't be too picky.

I'm a total basket case for two full days, waiting for any word. I keep reminding myself that the publishing world moves slowly—like lichen growing on a rock. It could be weeks before I hear a peep from any of them.

But the next morning while I'm on my way to the diner, Phoebe calls me with news. "We have an offer."

My foot slams into the gas and the car shoots forward. I yank back to avoid slamming into the minivan in front of me.

"Are you there?"

"Yes," I say. "I'm here. Who is it?"

"Lena Paul with Avon."

Why does it always have to be Avon? "Is the offer good?"

"A hundred thousand for world rights, plus standard royalties."

It's not as good as my last rom-com deal, but it's not bad. It's also way more than I got for the IP project I just did with them. They'd know that and assume I'd rush to take it. "What do you think?"

Phoebe sighs. "I knew you'd ask me that."

"A pre-empt means it's a done deal. It sells, and there's no guarantee we'll get that money elsewhere if we wait."

"Yeah, they wanted me to make it clear that they're offering their absolute highest figure because they want to keep you on board. Brett was clear that if we don't take this, we're looking at less for a formal offer."

I hate this part. I like to write the stories, not work the deals. "But?"

"But I think this is a really good book. Unique premise with a main character who's strong on STEM. That's hot right now. It's also got sizzling chemistry, witty banter, an empowered lead and an enlightened man—all the things they're looking for, and you may not have published recently but you're hardly a gamble. You've got an excellent sales record in this genre."

In this genre. That's her subtle reminder of the risk factor. My last book bombed and everyone knows it. It tanks my sales record, which is the reason for the lower offer. That and the time lag. People won't remember me like they would if I'd kept up the momentum.

I should take the pre-empt. Loyalty isn't bad, and that's a lot of money. If it earns out, I'll get more on the next one. Industry standard. I open my mouth to tell her to take it, and my stomach lurches. I never felt queasy like this when I took my past deals. "Can I think about it?"

"Sure," she says.

I pull into the parking lot for work and call Trudy.

"Anica?"

"Hey Trudy. I know you're probably busy, but I've got a big decision to make and I wasn't sure who to call."

"I've got a few minutes. What's up?"

I explain. "And I think I ought to take the pre-empt, but then I felt totally sick when I started to say yes."

Trudy laughs. "I know this one. Your head says to take it, but your heart doesn't agree."

Ugh. "Crap, I think that's right. But what do I do? Head or heart?"

"If I tell you to turn them down, how do you feel?"

"Exhilarated," I say. "I've never done anything like that in my life. I always make the smart move and take the sure thing."

"You're a new Anica," Trudy says. "I'd say go with your gut."

"But what if it comes back to bite me?" I bang the heel of my hand against my forehead. "What if no one else wants it, and I end up getting twenty or thirty percent less from Avon because I'm overconfident?"

"You'll take that bottom paddle as the lesson it was, and you'll do better next time. But if your agent loves it this much, and if several agents called about it based on sample chapters, I'm guessing that's not what's going to happen."

When I call Phoebe back, the fingernails of my hands dig into my palms, I'm clenching them so hard. "Turn it down," I say.

"Atta girl." She hangs up.

My phone taunts me during my entire shift. Not a call. Not a text. Not an email. And then a New York number calls me as I'm wiping down my last booth. Everyone in publishing lives in NYC. My fingers shake as I answer. "Hello?"

"Mrs. Maggard? This is Kevin with Carsure USA, calling to ask you about the warranty on your car. Do you feel as covered as you could? You never know what could happen on the road these days, and you want to make sure you're protecting yourself."

"My car is eleven years old," I say. "I'm guessing you've got the wrong person."

He hangs up, and I slide my dumb phone back into my pocket. So much for my hopes that another publisher would reply quickly or that Avon might realize that I'm playing hardball and up their offer. Even though I know it's stupid, I check my phone twice on the way home from work and again when I get out of the shower.

It sits on my desk and taunts me as I try and work on a list of ideas for my next book. I write up a dozen different opening lines, but none of them really drag me into the story. And every time I close my eyes to imagine how a couple might meet, I see Ethan.

Always Ethan.

It's probably only because he's all over the news right now. They just announced that he'll be taking over his dad's company and the stock price jumped. And he's got another fight coming up, soon. Last time he fought a local UFC guy, someone who had never fought in Vegas—a big deal, but only in the South. This next fight is in Vegas, and everyone in Atlanta is talking about it. It's happening in ten days, which I probably shouldn't know. And have marked with a big red circle on my calendar.

At least it's easy to find images of him online when I get really lonely. Most of them are of him working out at Harrison's—someone there is getting a decent chunk of change selling live images, I'm guessing. None of the photos show him next to any women. I've even found a few articles speculating about what happened between us—most of them blaming me for being too high maintenance.

"Looking at photos of Ethan? Why not just call him?" Luke's not smiling, but I can hear the mirth in his voice.

I slam my laptop closed and spin around. "What's up?"

"You're coming for the game night tomorrow, right?"

"Why not?" I ask.

"Apparently Paisley just told Mary that James can't come, so she wants to claim you as a partner. She was going to call, and I said I'd just ask you." He beams. "I had no idea you were busy." His eyebrows wiggle up and down.

"Knock it off." Although if I'm being fair, Mary and Luke haven't teased me at all since Ethan just disappeared. I expected it, but it never happened.

"I don't get it." He sits on my bed. "I liked him and you did too, I thought. And then bam. Gone."

"You date someone until you find something you can't live with, right?"

"I guess," Luke says. "And you're sure you can't deal with it, whatever it is?"

I exhale slowly. "I thought maybe he'd see that I was right, but . . . " I shrug. "He never called, so I guess not."

"Did you call him?" Luke frowns. "Because with guys, if you yelled at him for something, he might just assume it's over."

I blink. "I—" I shake my head. "No, I was pretty clear." But what if he was too upset to even remember what I said? With Patrick, I stayed *waaaay* too long. Did I bail too fast with Ethan? "I hate dating."

"The only cure to that is to do it long enough that you don't have to anymore. If you keep dumping good guys, though, you could be dating forever." Luke stands up. "But maybe you're right. Maybe it's better you wrote that one off." He pauses by the door. "You know what they say. Rock-hard muscles, brains, generosity, and a good sense of humor aren't everything."

"Who says that?"

"Oh." Luke scratches his head. "I guess no one does. Way to buck the norm." He's chuckling when he walks out.

I'm brushing mascara on before the game night when my phone rings. Phoebe. "Hello?"

"Anica, you genius."

"What?"

"I got an email from St. Martin this morning with an offer—very close to Avon's, so I reached out to everyone else. Four other publishers, Avon not included, want to put in offers. You're going to auction."

I can hardly breathe. "Which ones?"

"So you can obsess over them all weekend, looking up their other books on Publisher's Marketplace?" Phoebe laughs. "I think I'll let that wait until Monday when we look over the numbers together."

"Monday?" I practically wail.

"Three of them asked to have until Monday afternoon to get their best offer together, so it's set for Monday at three."

"That's so long."

Phoebe sighs. "It takes a long time to put together a package—and consult with publicity, marketing, the publisher budgeting people, etcetera. You know that. And also, our agency policy is to reach out to film agents when a book like this goes to auction, which means I'll be busy the rest of today as well."

My heart hammers against my rib cage so loudly that I worry she can hear it.

"Try to enjoy your weekend."

This feels Significant. When I walk into the game night, I'm beaming. I can't help it.

"Someone looks happy." Geo crosses her arms.

I tell them my news.

"I hate you," Trudy says.

"Rude." Mary arches one eyebrow at her sister.

"I'm now the only ordinary person in the group. Again." Trudy scowls.

"She's kidding," Mary says.

"Yeah, don't be ridiculous, Trudy." Geo walks past me and into the kitchen. "There are plenty of us plebeians."

Trudy winks at me. "I was kidding, but not because the rest of you aren't special. It's because I know that I'm special by association. What amazing news."

"This is the happiest I've seen you in weeks," Mary says. "I think maybe it's time." She looks pointedly at Geo.

"What does that mean?" I pour Coke in a glass and take a sip.

"We've tried not to push," Mary says, "but we've all got a few ideas for setups."

I choke.

"My friend Matt is really cute," Trudy says, "and he's smart too."

"But he spends way too much time looking at himself in the mirror in the bathroom," Paul says. "It's not normal."

"Which is why I vote for Geo's suggestion," Luke says.

They've been talking about this . . . together?

"I'm not so pathetic that I need you guys to find me someone," I say.

No one meets my eyes.

"Look, I've been busy with work and—"

"Geo's put together a bunch of events for the Atlanta Braves," Mary says. "And guess what? That handsome Francisco Guerrera? He's not only single, but he also loves books and hates big parties. His last girlfriend was cheating on him—"

"Mary," Geo says. She shakes her head slightly.

"Oh. I thought that was okay to share." Mary's face pales.

Geo sighs melodramatically. "Now that you have, I may as well explain. He found his last girlfriend had been unfaithful right before one of the events I planned. We had to spend some time together to coordinate his media events, and he asked me where I'd suggest he find . . . a higher caliber girl."

"His actual words were that he wanted to find a woman of integrity." Mary winks at me.

"And you said, 'Don't worry. I know the only one in Atlanta'?" I roll my eyes. "For all you know, I'm not a woman of quality either."

"Oh, I'm willing to vouch for you. You can be a little mulish at times, but you hold yourself to very high standards." Mary sits down at the dining table. "Balderdash tonight."

"I am really, really good at Balderdash," I say.

"Then we'll be sure that's on the list for next week," Geo says. "Because I might have mentioned game nights and told him he could come to the next one."

"You're kidding." As I look around the room, I realize they all already knew. "What if I don't find him attractive?"

"I don't think you need to worry about that," Trig grumbles. "These four were all gushing last week."

"I was at game night last week and he never came up." I glance around.

"You were writing last Saturday," Luke says. "Remember I invited you to that fundraiser?"

"Well that's the last time I miss a group event," I say. "I had no idea you'd all be conspiring against me if I skipped."

"Conspiring *for* you," Paisley says. "It's a subtle difference, but a difference nonetheless."

Trudy sits next to me. "They did this to me, too, you know."

"Who did?" I ask.

"Luke and Mary badgered me about setting me up for months." Trudy sighs. "I insisted on finding my own guy."

"See?" I ask. "You get it."

"I ended up marrying the guy they wanted to set me up

with," she says with a smile. "Although, to be fair, I met him on my own first."

I shake my head. "Wait, why haven't I heard this story? I feel like it would make a great book."

"Oh, no," Paisley says. "We aren't writing books about our love lives. I feel like neither James nor I would come out looking very good in that story."

I laugh. "Fine, fine."

By Sunday, I can't think about anything but the auction, so when Mom calls me, I agree to meet them for dinner. I've avoided them for too long. Besides, I should let them know what's going on with the books. I check and double-check my makeup and hair before going over. They've always loved Lizzie so much more than me—no reason to give Mom any excuse to pounce.

"Anica," Mom says when she opens the door. "You look amazing."

"Thanks." I hug her. Dad's waiting for his hug next.

"We were beginning to worry you'd fallen into a hole," Dad says.

"A deep hole, populated with lions," Mom says.

"I kind of did," I say.

"What?" Mom's face falls.

"I've been writing again."

I expect her to beam, but Mom frowns. Typical.

"I actually sold a book six weeks ago to Avon."

"Great, that's great," she says. "Does that mean you'll be heading back to California soon?"

What? I only moved there because of Patrick. "I can write anywhere, Mom."

She nods. "Of course you can. Why don't we go to the kitchen? The meatloaf will get cold."

Dad tells me about his newest project at work while we eat, and I pretend to care about mechanical engineering. See? Not so hard to act like something matters to you when it doesn't—they could try it. But I don't mention that they change the subject every time my writing comes up. There's no reason to point out their flaws and make them like me even less than they already do.

I help Mom clear the table, piling dishes in the sink. "My current manuscript goes to auction tomorrow."

Mom blinks and pushes past me to start loading the dishwasher. "Wait, you can buy it already? Isn't that fast?"

"No Mom, that other book was an IP project. I don't own it—it won't even come out under my name. Remember?"

"I'm sorry, dear. I don't really understand all the book stuff."

But I could explain it if she cared. I start to move along to another topic, but a little rebellious voice inside says NO. I decide to explain what's going on, even if they don't want to know. "Mom, this is another book. I've written two in the last few months."

"That's wonderful," Dad says. "Didn't it used to take you a year to write just one?"

"Yep," I say. "I'm clearly getting faster. These two only took me five months together." I laugh, but neither of them does.

"Okay, so look, auction means that the manuscript I just sent to my agent went out to a bunch of editors, and more than one of them wanted to buy it. It's really rare, and it's a really, really good sign. They all put in their best and highest offer, and then I can pick which one I want to go with."

"So it's not actually an auction," Dad says. "I mean, they can't quite bid up."

I give up. "The point is that it'll be sold on Monday—my fourth book will be out in the world before you know it."

"Technically your fifth," Mom says. "Right?"

I suppose that means she's paying attention. "Right, but that other one won't be under my name. So this will technically be my fifth, but to the world, it's my fourth."

"I think your dad and I are going to go into the family room and watch some television," she says.

Really? I haven't been over in more than two months. "Okay, well."

"You could come watch with us for a bit." My dad's tentative smile breaks my heart. They're awkward and they don't get me, but they're the only parents I have.

"Alright," I say. "I guess so." It can't be worse than researching the list of acquiring editors Phoebe sent and wondering which ones are offering. Or googling updates on Ethan.

My mom is clicking through screens like staying on one too long will set her hair on fire . . . until she finds *Bonanza* —really??—when it hits me.

I'm as big a mess as they are, but in a different way.

Could they act like this . . . because they're as broken about Lizzie's death as I am? They've seemed to handle it totally fine, as though it didn't even faze them, and I've faulted them for it. It's like their daughter died and they don't even care.

But maybe this weird, false joy front *is* them being broken.

I grab the remote and turn the TV off. Then I turn toward them and face it, head on. "You didn't used to watch super old TV shows and never talk about anything. You used to get excited for me when I had news."

"Used to?" Dad swallows and turns toward my mom, for all the world like he's saying 'line' on a movie set. Like he's hoping she'll tell him what to say.

Did aliens replace my parents with pod people? "You can tell me what you're thinking," I say. "Whatever it is. I'd prefer it, honestly."

"We find that we're happier with a routine," Dad says.

So they aren't dead inside. "But your routine hurts me." My whispered words sound so pathetic.

Mom's shoulders collapse and her face falls. "What?"

"Lizzie died and you guys just . . . ignored me." I can't cry, not yet. I need to talk to them about this.

"You stayed in California," Mom says. "Like nothing had changed."

I hurt them, too. "I was bleeding out there," I say. "My world fell apart, and I was so alone."

"You could have called me," Dad says.

"You guys can't even talk to me right here in your own kitchen," I say.

Mom bursts into tears and catapults off the couch and out of the room.

"I'll talk to her." When Dad stands up, he does it slowly, like his joints hurt. They've been aging and I didn't even notice. He walks toward the hall, but stops in the doorway and half turns back toward me. "Can you wait?" His eyes plead with me. "It won't be too long."

I nod.

I've been thinking they aren't here for me, and they've been thinking I didn't care. We're not Ethan's family, but we're not nearly as healthy and whole as I thought. Dad's gone for more than half an hour, but when he comes back, Mom's trailing behind him, her eyes on her embroidered moccasins.

"Can we talk about Lizzie?" I ask.

Mom's eyes fly up to mine, and she nods. "I think that's a good idea."

Dad sits next to me and pats my hand. "I'm sorry we haven't been there when you needed us." His voice cracks on the last word, and I pull him against me for a side hug.

I can't quite keep from crying anymore, but then they both start to cry as well and I don't care about my own tears. We talk about Lizzie for two hours before I notice the time. "You've got to work tomorrow?" I ask.

"He does," Mom says. "And I've got a brunch at the church."

"We need to do this more," Dad says. "We miss you."

"Me too." I stand up. "Thanks for dinner."

Mom walks me to the door and hugs me before I leave. "We're very proud of you." She wipes a tear I can't even see from her cheek. "We don't know quite what to say. I'm a regular person, and so is your dad, and you're a super star."

"I'm just me," I say. "But all you have to say is that you're proud. That's enough."

On the way home, I wonder whether I've done the same thing to everyone—assumed they weren't interested in spending time with me . . . when I'm the one staying away.

Ethan.

But I told him that he should. . . I think about that night. I told him that he didn't know how to love. I told him we were breaking up.

Has he been waiting for my call? Have I been avoiding making it because I was too harsh and I regret acting like I knew everything when I barely know what he went through at all?

When I go to sleep that night, all I dream about is Ethan, telling me he's over me.

Too bad I'm not over him.

The next morning, right after my shift, I walk by Harrison's gym, but it's closed. I'm too early—on purpose. That was the point of the breakfast shifts, after all.

When my phone rings, I jump. Phoebe again.

"You ready to talk strategy?" she asks.

"Uh, sure."

She tells me the list of players, and it's the most welcome distraction. I sink into the details of my book and then I fall into the rhythm of the breakfast crowd, and I hardly think about Ethan at all. By the time three p.m. rolls around, I'm nervous as a tick awaiting a scheduled flea bath.

The chime on my laptop bings, announcing an incoming Zoom call. I answer.

"Okay, I just got the last email," Phoebe says. "You ready to open them?"

I nod.

"Okay, first, Avon. They came in with a hundred and fifty thousand. So much for a hundred being their limit." Her chortle is not very ladylike. It makes me wish I could hug her through the phone.

"Alright, that's good." It's not two hundred and fifty or more, which is 'significant,' but it's not bad at all.

"Now I'm opening St. Martin's. . . It's two hundred and ten thousand, plus they've got an attached offer for the movie rights. They want to lock it in for their Macmillan Film arm." She mutters under her breath for a moment and then says, "Oh, there it is. They're offering another seventy-five for that, and you'll have 'reasonable creative control.' That's nice. They'd like as close to a simultaneous release as possible, which makes sense from a marketing perspective. Usually the movie lags pretty far behind the book."

My mind is swimming.

"Oh man, Hachette's offer is worse than Avon, so they're out." She clicks on something. "And it looks like Simon and Schuster is only offering two hundred flat."

"So does that mean we go with St. Martin?" I ask. "Right?"

"I saved the best one for last," Phoebe says. "Ballantine. Random House has a partnership with RHFilm, which in turn partners with Warner Brothers. They sent a combined offer, two hundred and fifty for the book, and a hundred for the movie, and they've got funding already." She whistles. "I think that's why they asked me to give them until three."

"Whoa, really?"

"We could counter any of these, but I wouldn't. I'll send them all to you now, but I'd suggest taking the Ballantine offer unless we see something concerning in the fine print." She laughs. "This is very, very good news."

The next few days are a blur. I call Barbara and ask for a little time off, since Ballantine wants to meet with me in NYC. I fly out Tuesday morning, review details with Phoebe all day, and then meet with executives from the imprint all day Wednesday and Thursday. By the time I fly home Friday morning, I'm exhausted.

And I've decided that I didn't get my life on track with my writing until I stopped worrying about whether I was writing the right thing and wrote what mattered to me.

I should have realized that and reached out to Ethan before. It's less about whether I was supposed to call him or he was supposed to call me and more about the fact that he's still the only one I want. The second my plane lands, I take the shuttle to my car and head for Ethan's house.

Mary calls me when I'm right around the corner. "Anica?"

"Yeah," I say.

"Are you back yet?"

"I just landed," I say.

"Great. Welcome home."

"Thanks," I say. "Did you need anything?"

"Just wanted to make sure you're coming home for game night," she says.

"Sure, right, yeah, I'll be there soon enough."

"Great." Kids are screeching in the background. "Well, I won't keep you." Which basically means she's busy, but too polite to say that since she called me.

"See you later," I say.

And then I'm parking in Ethan's driveway. His fight is tomorrow, so there's a chance he's not even home, but I can't wait another second. My hands shake as I walk toward the door, but I squeeze my right hand into a fist and bang loudly and clearly. If I got through it with my parents, I can do it with Ethan. Right? I hope.

Only, he doesn't answer.

I sit down on his porch steps and bawl like a toddler.

I know he's likely in Vegas, but it feels like it's a metaphor. I did like I did with Patrick—even though I walked away right off the bat, it took me too long to figure out my crap, and now I'm alone.

Again.

Only, with Patrick it was the right call. This time, I feel like I really had a chance at never being alone again.

And I blew it.

"I will be there," I say. "I said I would."

"You said you'd be here today," Harrison says. "Not the morning of the fight."

"I have a jet," I say. "Or my dad does. I'll be fine, and I'll sleep better in my own bed."

Even though I can't see Harrison, I know exactly which vein in his forehead is throbbing at this very moment. "Leave early. Seven."

"Fine," I say. "I will."

"Don't stay up late tonight," he says. "Do you hear me, son?"

If I had a nickel for every time a guy who *isn't* my dad calls me son. . . "I do."

I have to call my dad next, and he's not pleased either. "I'm almost to the airport," he says. "The pilot is there, ready to go."

"Isn't this why we have a jet in the first place?" I ask. "So that we can go whenever it works for us?"

"It's *my* jet," he says. "You should go at a time that works for me."

"Only for six more weeks," I say. "And I'm the one fighting." Geez, you'd think I was four years old and asking to stay up late to catch Santa Claus. "Look, I told you that I can't get out of this commitment. I'll be there, and everything will be fine. I told Harrison we'd leave at seven."

"Make sure you're asleep by ten p.m. at the latest," he says.

"Only if you promise to come over and tuck me in," I say.

He hangs up.

And I swing right and pull up across the street from Luke and Mary's house. I haven't been this nervous since my last fight. Actually, that wasn't anywhere near this bad. I'm sweating under my arms like a teenager about to ask the head cheerleader to prom. If I hadn't stopped to get a ring, I'd have been here sooner, but I felt like I needed to show her that this wasn't just some random thing. I've thought this through. I want to be with her. I'll do anything—all the work, all the hard stuff. Whatever it takes.

But what if she thinks offering her a ring is just another way to control her? I pull out the box and look at the diamond. I looked at a hundred different rocks today, and most of them looked the same as all the others. This one stood out—this one reminded me of Anica.

It sparkles like the sun.

And it's got five sides.

There were a million squares, emerald cuts, and round diamonds. Quite a few ovals, and plenty of weird marquise cut ones.

This was the only one that had five sides—and I knew I had to have it. She can pick out a setting she likes for herself later. I had it set in a simple platinum band, modified to have five prongs. But somehow, showing up after all this time, it feels wrong to walk in with a ring. Grand gestures aren't the right move—it's the small and consistent things that will show her that I'm changing.

I slide the ring back in the box and stuff it into the dash.

I'm going to marry her—or at least, I hope someday I am. But maybe I'll wait until I'm pretty sure what her answer will be before I ask.

I square my shoulders, inhale and exhale a few times, and then get out of the car. I focus on taking one step at a time as I walk to the front door. Will she be happy to see me? Upset? I'm half an hour early, just like I was that first time. There are a few more cars than usual—Paisley's for one, and a LaFerrari, which must be Trig's—but hopefully I can sneak in under the radar.

I knock on the door and wait.

Amy answers.

"Mister Ethan," she says. "I didn't know you were coming."

I squat down so we're at eye level. "No one did. It's a surprise. Can you sneak me in?"

She bobs her head. "Sure. Good idea. That'll really shock them."

I follow her around the corner, and then she leaps around the edge of the wall and shouts, "Boo!"

Not exactly what I was thinking, but alright. I follow her around and wave. . .

At Paisley, James, Geo, Trig, and some guy I've never seen before—but judging by his build and confusion, I'm guessing he's the pitcher Geo's setting Anica up with. Amy throws me a thumbs up and heads down the hall where I hear Jack crying. I'm guessing Luke and Mary are dealing with some kind of kid-related emergency.

"Ethan." Geo frowns. "Hi."

I meet Trig's gaze. I texted him and told him I was coming—I told him to come up with an excuse to get rid of the ball player. He shrugs.

Thanks a lot, dude.

"Ethan Trainor. Long time no see." Paisley lifts one eyebrow pointedly. "But it's always good to see you." She shakes my hand and turns back toward the other guy. "Ethan and I went to college together. We've been friends for a long time. Ethan, this is Francisco Guerrera, star pitcher for the Braves."

"Great to meet you." I force a smile.

"You too," he says. "Looks like these game nights are a lot of fun."

"Eh." I shrug. "They'll probably be pretty boring for you." Something connects in my brain. "Hey, is that your car outside?" Because Anica's going to *hate* a flashy Ferrari.

"It is," he says. "I figure there's no reason you can't go hybrid when you want speed, right?"

Could I hate him any more than I do right now? "Sure."

"Ethan drives a Bronco," Trig says with a smile. "I wonder how many miles it gets to the gallon."

I should have punched him before I had all these witnesses. "It gets pretty decent fuel economy." I scowl at him. "It's brand new—not one of the old classics."

"That's too bad," Francisco says. "Those classics are pretty great, too."

Does he like the environment or not? "Has anyone seen Anica?" I ask. "I needed to ask her something." As if they don't all know I want to see her. Why else would I be here?

"Ah, Anica." Francisco winks at me. "That's why I'm here. I haven't met her yet—we're being set up. It seems like everyone knows her but me."

My nostrils flare. "You don't say." Paisley and James and Trig and Geo stare at us eagerly. They could throw me a bone here, or they could leave the room so this isn't so awkward. But no, I'm the entertainment, clearly.

"It's actually my first setup," Francisco continues. "I've never agreed to one before, but when Geo told me she had a friend, well. I doubt I'd have survived all the dumb parties and media events last season if it wasn't for her assistance."

Trig doesn't look super thrilled about Francisco, either, which makes sense. Who would want a suave, athletic pitcher gushing about their wife? "Yeah, Geo set me up not too long ago, too." Her head whips back toward me, and I stop short of saying anything more. I'm certainly not feeling like the crew has my back.

Although I suppose that's on me.

"Wait, no one said," I say. "Where is Anica?"

Mary breezes into the room, and then does a double take. "Ethan?"

"Yep, still my name." I need to dial the snark down. I'm the usurper here. "Sorry, long day. How have you been?"

She blinks. "You were asking about Anica?"

I nod.

"She's on her way." She glances from Francisco to me and then back again, then she smiles broadly. "She's just flying back home today. She had to go to New York City."

"For what?" Francisco asks.

I want to strangle him. "Yeah, I'd like to know too." I hate that I'm reduced to asking Mary—alongside a complete stranger—why she went to New York City.

"She just sold her fifth book, and this one went to auction."

Francisco perks up right away. "Which imprint bought it?"

"Ballantine," Mary says. "That's right, your mother works for a publisher, right?"

He swears under his breath. "Wait, is this Anica, Anica *Maggard?*"

Mary nods. "Geo didn't tell you her name?"

Geo walks past me and straight ahead into the kitchen. "I think I need a drink."

"She mentioned her friend Anica, but she said nothing

about books or publishing. I can't believe I'm meeting Anica Maggard. My mom's pretty upset right now, actually."

"Who does your mother work for?" Mary asks.

"St. Martin. She put in a pretty big bid on her next book . . . and lost."

Something is finally going right. "That's too bad." I shove my smile down as far as I can, but I worry it makes me look constipated. I drop it and frown instead.

"She'll be furious I didn't meet her last week," Francisco says, "but I had other plans. There's always her next book, right? With someone as brilliant as Anica, they're never done writing."

It's hard to disagree with him when he's so ridiculously agreeable. Paul and Trudy arrive, which is great. I could use some more people to make this even more awkward. Paisley and James finally come all the way inside and hang their coats. Without a voluminous coat as cover, Paisley looks ready to pop.

"When is your baby due?" I ask.

Paisley beams. "Soon, thankfully."

"Why don't we get started?" Luke asks.

"Maybe I'll wait in the kitchen," I offer.

"No! Don't do that. You can be my partner," Francisco says. "I'll be all alone until Anica gets here."

Fabulous.

And it turns out, he's ridiculously good at Pictionary. "You draw really well," Paisley says as he sits down from his turn. "Like, really, really well."

Francisco shrugs. "I had to choose, sadly, between art and baseball." He leans a little closer, like he's sharing a secret. "Baseball pays better."

I can't even with this guy, but I'm beginning to think I hate him because he's so perfect. That's unlikely to bother Anica in the same way it does me. Of course, it's right after this realization that I hear a key turn in the lock at the front door.

Inexplicably, I wish I could go back in time—because now that she's here, for the first time in my life, I don't want to fight—for her or with her. I just want to run away. Who would pick the tempestuous, controlling, angry mess over the polished, environment-loving warrior poet who's probably fluent in four languages? I bet he owns a pet seal he saved from being clubbed, and lovingly tends in a custom designed icebox room.

Shake it off, Trainor.

Anica said she loved me. That's got to count for something. When she walks through the entry way and into the edge of the family room, Anica's face is puffy and her coat is askew. When she looks up at all of us staring, her eyes widen in alarm. "Oh, game night." She swallows. "I forgot."

"I just called you." Mary glances at her watch. "Although that was more than an hour ago. Did you have car trouble? Where have you been?"

She drops her purse and coat on the floor near the door. "I was—" Her eyes reach mine and she cuts off, her jaw dangling open.

Francisco stands up right next to me. "Anica Maggard. Can I just say what an honor it is to meet you! I had no idea who you were when I agreed to come over, which is probably a good thing." He shakes his head. "Because my mom is a huge fan of yours, and I'd have been hugely nervous if I knew before a few moments ago."

Anica blinks. "Wait, who are you?"

"She's just exhausted from her trip to New York," Geo says. "I told her about you, but I didn't realize what a crazy week she had when I set this up."

"I'm a friend of Geo's," Francisco says. "She told me many great things about you—just not that you write amazing books on top of all of the rest."

"Oh." Anica looks at me again.

"Ah, Ethan," Francisco says. "He did say he needed to ask you something. As excited as I am to get to know you, I'm sure we can all soldier on without you a bit longer, if you two need to talk."

He's a really hard guy to hate. He must realize that, as the only other single guy here, and as someone who's asking to speak to Anica, I must be something to her, and he's sending me off to talk to her gracefully anyway.

I stand up, because I'll take any win I can muster right now. "That would be great. Anica, do you have a minute?"

She blinks. "Uh, sure."

I walk toward the library right around the corner.

"Um." She shakes her head and points down the hall instead.

To her bedroom.

My heartrate picks up. If she was going to kick me out, she could do that in the library, right? For the first time since I came face-to-face with Mr. Francisco Fabulous himself, hope rises inside of me. I trot after her like a lovesick puppy, and I can't even summon the will to care.

She ducks into her room and holds her hand out. "Give me two minutes."

I hear her tossing things and rummaging around with stuff. She's cleaning up. I want to hug her and kiss her and smell her—I don't care what her room looks like. But it bodes well for me that *she* does.

Unless she's disposing of some kind of voodoo doll. . . I tap on the doorframe and peek around. "Ready or not. . . "

"You can come in." She's standing in the center of the room holding a stack of papers, completely still.

I freeze too.

"I was at your house," she whispers.

My brain fills with so many things I want to tell her that none of them can squeeze through. "I. . . "

"If I'd known you were here." She drops the papers and they fly every which way.

"Congrats on your book deal," I say. "That's amazing."

"You have a fight tomorrow." Her eyes widen. "Don't you?"

She's paying attention—following the media coverage, I hope. I nod. "But I had to come over tonight. I had to see you."

"Why?"

"Trig came by," I say. "He said Geo was setting you up."

She frowns. "You're here because of *Francisco*?"

Okay, that sounds bad. "No. I mean, yes, but not like you think. Or maybe like you think, I'm not sure. But Trig —this is coming out all wrong."

She points at the chair next to her bed. "Sit."

I do.

"If I had found you at your house." She sits on the bed and folds her hands on her lap. "Can I tell you what I went over there to say?"

I nod, dumbly.

"I came down on you pretty hard," she says. "And I still think that what I said was essentially true, that you can't force people you love to do things, but I also think that maybe I handled it all wrong. When I was—before—with Patrick, I stayed with him a lot longer than I should have."

"Okay." She seems a little lost. "I'm listening."

"Um, well, the thing was, I guess since I did that all wrong, I didn't want to sit and wait and hope and watch everything fall apart." She looks down at her hands, twisting her fingers together. "So I kind of yelled at you and, I don't know. I was hoping you'd come and tell me that you'd thought about it, and that you were wrong, and that you still loved me."

My heart contracts. "I do still love you."

Her face flies up and her eyes meet mine. "You do?" She blinks.

I nod.

"I love you, too."

I smile then. "I did think about what you said that night. I'm ashamed how long it took me to process all of it, but I did finally work through it. It took me a while to process all of it—and I was doing that, the introspection. I wanted to come and tell you what you wanted to hear when it was all done, when I was finally repaired."

Her head tilts and her eyes are sad.

"But Trig came by to tell me that I was being an idiot. He said that telling you I understood and agreed with you would be enough. He said—" My voice cracks, and I clear my throat. "He said you were moving on."

She laughs, but it's a broken-ish sound. "I went to your house today. Does that sound like someone who's moving on?"

"But Francisco—"

"I'm sure he's great," she says.

"He drives a Ferrari," I blurt out.

She laughs and stands up. "You should have called me the next day."

"I couldn't call him, you know." I shake my head. "I knew you were right, but I couldn't do it. It took me weeks and weeks and a psychologist to call my—to call Phillip—and to tell him that I took it all back."

Her eyes widen and she steps closer. "But you did it?"

"Not until today."

"After Trig came to see you?"

I nod, numbly. It's too late. She'll think it's an act.

But the corners of her mouth turn upward in a ghost of a smile, and I react without thinking. I stand up and reach for her, and she falls into my arms. My head drops toward hers and our lips meet and it's like heaven has met the earth and angels walk among us. I swing her around in a circle, knocking over a stack of small boxes.

"I really need to get my own place," she says. "One little room isn't big enough to contain all my junk."

I want to do it. I want to propose. I want to tell her I'll buy her any house she wants with plenty of room for all our junk, but it doesn't feel right. Everything between us is still too new and too unsure. There's a guy who's here to meet her right outside.

So I kiss her again instead. And for now, that's enough.

My phone rings with an incoming call, but I ignore it. The idiot calls back.

Anica pulls back. "Do you need to get that?"

I groan and pull it out of my pocket. It's my dad. "What?"

"It's nine-thirty. Are you headed to bed?"

I hang up.

He calls me again.

"You have a fight tomorrow," Anica says. "You need to sleep."

I grit my teeth. "I don't even care about that."

"You need to go." She goes on tiptoe to kiss me again, but she pulls away too soon. "I'm not going anywhere."

"Stupid Francisco—"

She puts a finger over my mouth. "Isn't the man I love."

My heart does a backflip. "Okay."

"I'll be here when you get back," she says. "Waiting."

"Oh no you won't," Trig says from the hallway.

Anica's eyes fly wide. "What the—"

Trig and Geo, followed by Luke and Mary, and then Trudy and Paul step into the doorway. "*When he gets back?*" Trig asks. "Are you kidding me?" He glances from Anica to me, and then behind him at Geo. "Absolutely not. If you two are back together, we're going to Vegas, baby!"

I can't even bring myself to be annoyed with him. After

all, that's exactly where I want Anica to be. With me. Always.

"Hey, where's Francisco?" Anica asks.

Oh, shoot. Is he right outside the door too?

"We left him playing monopoly with Paisley and James," Luke says.

"I did try to wave him off," Trig says, "but Geo said he was already on his way over."

"That was like five hours ago," I say.

"Some of us work for a living," Trig says. "I'm just saying that I saw your text, but not until after I finished a big meeting and it was too late at that point."

"Well, I feel a little bad," Geo says. "He's such a nice guy."

"He'll be fine," Luke says. "He's said three words to her."

Paul laughs. "Are we going to stay back here all night?"

"Go away," Anica says. "My boyfriend has to leave in two minutes so he can get his beauty sleep, and you guys are ruining my night."

Her boyfriend. I kiss her again—who cares who's watching?

At least the hoots and hollers move their way down the hall. I might stick around more than the two minutes she mentioned, but some things matter more than huge, paid, televised Vegas UFC matches. Of course, it's not quite the quality time I had in mind, since my dad calls five more times.

I finally groan and straighten. "Dad's freaking out—he's not going to stop."

"Annoying when someone tries to control you, isn't it?" Anica asks.

I laugh. "Yeah, you had a point. Adriana is very grateful too, you know."

"Good." She squeezes my hand and then points. "You better go."

I frown. "So you can finally be alone with Francisco?"

"I hear he drives a Ferrari." She shimmies. "I just *love* fancy cars."

"You know, my dad has one I can borrow if that's really your thing."

"Your dad." She laughs. "That's so hot."

It's hard to force myself to walk away, but I finally do. Francisco even waves at me as I leave. And for the first time in a long time, I sleep really well. The next morning, when I wake up, there's a text waiting for me from Anica.

GOOD LUCK, MR. BALBOA.

The rest of the day passes in a blur of travel and media coverage. This fight is much bigger than the last one, but it's getting a hugely disproportionate share of attention because I'm about to take over my grandpa's company. I try to stick to the canned responses Dad and I worked out, but my eyes scan the edges of the crowd each time, searching, searching.

Until, less than half an hour before I'm due to fight, I finally see her face.

I cut off mid-sentence. "Excuse me." I shove past the never-satisfied reporters. Dad takes over behind me, but a bunch of the cameras turn to follow me.

Anica beams when she realizes I'm coming toward her. "You got the tickets."

"Thanks," she says. "I felt pretty fancy."

"You'll be front row to watch me get my teeth knocked out," I joke.

"Are you afraid Robert 'the Hammer' Jenner will defeat you?" an obnoxious reporter in a blue suit asks loudly.

I roll my eyes and usher Anica toward the locker area. Mary and Luke, Trudy and Paul, and Geo and Trig follow us.

"Where are Brekka and Rob?" I ask. "And Paisley and James?"

"Brekka and Rob aren't leaving the hospital yet—although she did finally have the baby, and Paisley is due like any second," Geo says. "Whereas the rest of us are giddy for a night out."

"We're all flying back tonight, though," Anica says. "Which is *so* strange to think about."

"I bet *Francisco* doesn't have his own jet," I say.

"Yes." Anica pats my arm. "You're definitely the prettiest princess."

"Actually, I think that's Paisley," Trig says. "Sorry, man."

And then it's time for me to weigh in and make my entrance. "I've got to go."

My girlfriend kisses me. "Please don't lose all your teeth or get your head bashed in. I like you beautiful—just as you are."

"I'll do my best," I say. "But I hear surgeons can do amazing things these days. Maybe it's time for an upgrade. I've never loved my nose."

She shakes her head. "Not funny."

"Alright, sorry," I say. "Try not to worry."

"I'll try."

And then I'm walking away from her, and I hate that I agreed to do this. But at least these fights don't last too long.

"You look entirely too happy to be properly prepared for this," Harrison snaps. "Wipe that smile off your face."

"I'm fine," I say.

Harrison grabs my robe. "Boy, you've been the angriest kid I knew for ten years. You're telling me that's not the reason you win?"

I swallow. Is it?

Anica told me I had to let go of my anger . . . for myself. Not for my dad. Not for Phillip. Not for Ana. For me. And

I did it, and I'm just realizing that he's right. For the first time in years, no fury rises inside of me. No hatred fills me with bracing anger. I don't want to punch anyone.

Well, maybe Francisco, but only a little bit. Mostly as a joke.

Dad frowns. "He's skilled and his reflexes are great."

Harrison grunts.

And then it's time for me to go. I walk down the stupid fighter runway and head for the ring, the audience cheering and shouts rising as Robert approaches from the opposite side. He seems to be hopped up on enough anger and buzzy energy for both of us.

The thing that stands out to me as I walk into the ring is that Ana and Anica are holding hands—and this moment feels strangely transfixed opposite the last fight, the one that preceded our break up. I shake my head and listen to the ref. He's calling us to the middle.

"We're going to have a nice, clean fight today, boys. You know the basic rules." He rattles them off anyway. Then he glances from me to Robert. "Bump fists if you want."

Robert, unlike that Izzy idiot, jams his fists forward in a sportsmanlike manner. Which, of course, does nothing to help me find my anger.

The quick jab he lands on my jaw helps a little, as does the immediate pummeling I take on my midsection. I spin away, trying to regain my bearings, but Robert effing Jenner never eases up. He's everywhere at once—in front of me, on the left, then spinning to the right. I block as fast as I can, but I can't seem to land a single solid hit.

I'm losing badly when the first round finally ends.

The media is hardcore loving this. I try to tune out the jeers, the shouts, and the incessant questions, but I can't stop thinking of the headlines. The corporate raider can handle local fights, but he gets demolished when faced with a real fighter.

I expect Harrison to bring me some water, some silver nitrate, and a slap in the face.

He sends Anica instead.

"Harrison said you needed to see me." She blinks at the corner where Robert's glaring at us.

"The media will have a heyday with this," I say.

"Don't worry about that," she says. "They're a flash in the pan, believe me." She touches my face. "Ouch." She shakes her head. "But listen, Ethan, there's something I forgot to tell you earlier. I know I told you that you had to let go of your anger."

I blink, which hurts on the right eye. I can already feel it swelling.

"What I forgot to say is that it's a process. Those old feelings of fury are going to flare up again every time you think about the things that made you angry to begin with. All that hatred is going to resurface over and over." She shifts a little closer. "You'll have to learn to put it away regularly, to surrender those feelings each time, and that's how you'll find your inner peace." She stands up. "But maybe for the next few minutes . . . " She leans close and whispers. "Don't surrender." She tosses a look over her shoulder. "Because that guy is a smug piece of crap and I'd love to watch you beat the ever-loving junk out of him."

I love her so much.

After she leaves, I dig down deep. I think about the night Phillip lost his job. He had been playing pretty steady at a local restaurant, but someone complained about how long his break lasted and he yelled at that person and then the owner fired him. He didn't come home to tell Mom the news—he went out and got plastered instead. I was asleep when he got in, but the sound of a loud crash woke me up.

He had run into the end table and knocked Mom's favorite lamp—a Tiffany lamp her parents had given her—to the floor. She didn't even yell at him. She knew better than that by then, but his anger was a defense mechanism, so it didn't matter. Mom went to get the broom, and Phillip took it from her, wrenching it out of her hands. He slapped her across the face and she fell onto the glass, cutting her hand.

Which made her cry.

And pissed him off worse.

That night was the first time I got up in his face and told him to leave my mom alone.

It was also the first time he hit me. Beat me half to death, actually. That memory disintegrates any feelings of peace I've found, leaving me standing in the middle of an ocean of wrath. I stand up and walk to the center of the ring.

Somehow, looking at Robert Jenner—I refuse to call him 'the Hammer'—I see myself that day. A little boy, scared, taking a beating, and then watching as his mother gets slammed around anyway. My fury at Phillip transfers to Robert, and when the ref claps his hands, I lean back and then slam forward into him, a jab, a cross, and then a right hook in quick succession.

He was already sprawling backward when my cross hit, and his head went flying to the side. I'm on him that very second, hitting him as he goes down, but the ref grabs my arms.

"He's out, that's it."

A knockout in five seconds. The crowd goes completely wild.

I shake my head and back toward my corner. Did that really just happen? I blink and turn back toward Robert. Still down.

Boy, was Anica right. That rage is still right there—which means it's on me to let it go every single day, or I'll turn into the same monster I was.

The media swarms the second I emerge from the ring.

"What's his next fight?" "How long will he rest?" "How will he continue to manage the fights and the demands of his new job?"

I wave and the cameras move from Harrison toward me. "Hey there, adult human right here."

A few of them laugh.

"I think this is a good time to announce that I'm retiring from fighting, effective immediately." I open my mouth to tell them that it's because I'm in love and I want to marry my girlfriend, but something feels off about it.

Because tonight is about me—about me and the company. It's my spotlight, and asking Anica to marry me on an evening that's about my stuff feels wrong. So I just keep repeating that my decision is final, and that I have thought it through, and that yes, I do know that there have only been a handful of knock outs that took place that fast, and that yes, I appreciate their support, but I'm not fighting again.

"Why?" the reporter in the blue suit asks. "Is it because of your girlfriend? We all noticed that you're back together."

I scowl. "Anica has brought nothing but peace into my life." And then I pause. "So yes, I suppose you could say I'm giving up fighting *thanks* to her. She brought me what I was always missing, and that's the reason I fought. With her in my life to remind me of what matters, I don't need it anymore."

Then I walk away, ignoring any other questions and demands. And I walk toward the smiling, beauteous face of my future.

❧ 20 ❧

ANICA

The wind against my face is almost warm, but I still shiver and sink into the little cocoon my sweater has made around my body where I'm slouched in the chair on the back porch. I squint at my laptop screen, worrying about the right word to finish my sentence.

I reach down to scratch my knee, and Partner rushes over to lick my hand.

"You know what your dog's problem is?" I ask.

"Hey, are you done?" Ethan drops his book and sits up straight. "Not that I'm rushing you, but the weather is finally warming up."

I roll my eyes. Spring keeps taunting us. "I'm not done, but I have reached a stopping point."

Ethan leans across the table and kisses me. "I'll take it. Wanna go for a walk with the fur babies?"

Since Partner can't be trusted around the chickens, we have to keep her on the front porch on a leash if we want to be outside at Mary and Luke's. Andy's a patient dog, but Partner's incessant bouncing and licking and enthusiasm wears her out.

"Sure, but maybe we leave Andy here." Ethan opens the front door and Andy shoots through, Partner at her heels. "Not you, goofball." Partner stops and looks up at him with complete adoration.

Sometimes I catch myself looking at him with the same dopey look on my face. Eh, at least he loves us both back. There are worse things than occasionally being rendered a dope by love. I stand up and stretch.

"You shouldn't sit still for so long," Ethan says.

"Occupational hazard," I say. "No way around it."

"Dictation software gets better every day."

I wiggle my fingers. "Not nearly as good as these babies."

"I do like watching you type, and I swear I've gotten used to hearing the clackety clacking all the time."

"I promised Phoebe—"

He shakes his head. "We are taking a break from work." He takes my hand. "And going for a walk. You need to enjoy something other than the light of a computer screen."

I roll my eyes, but I know he's right. Sometimes I worry I'll turn into a pod person. "Just don't try to make me jog."

"We've been together for almost five months now," he says. "And you think I'd be dumb enough to try that?"

"Oh, so now you're not counting that first month?"

He squeezes my hand. "Fine, six with a break in the middle."

"A break for you to figure out how to find your inner peace."

Partner takes off at a run, and then is yanked back when the leash pulls tight. She barks and barks and barks.

"Squirrel," Ethan says.

"I figured."

He tells me about his dad's upcoming wedding and how overblown it has become as we round the bend. And then he freezes. "That spot right there—" He points. "That's where we had our first kiss."

"I remember." I stop and run my hand through his hair. And I kiss him again. "And this one is even better."

"Mm," he says against my mouth. "I agree."

Partner yanks and he stumbles back, dropping the leash. "Partner." She sits immediately and he crouches down on one knee to grab the nylon cord.

Only, he doesn't get back up. He reaches one hand into his pocket. "I hope you know how much you mean to me."

My heart stutters inside my chest. Is he about to propose?

"I thought I had everything under control." He's still kneeling. "But then I met you and you showed me that I was basically held together by scotch tape, twine, and Elmer's glue."

He is.

I can barely breathe.

"So I wanted to ask you something." He pulls his hand out of his pocket.

And offers me a stick of gum.

"Did you want any gum?"

My jaw drops and I shake my head.

He stands up and starts laughing. "Your face. That was so funny."

I whap his arm. "You're a jerk."

"You love me."

I do. He's right. Even if he almost gave me a heart attack with his stupid prank.

The next morning, while I'm working at Golden Gloves, he sails in and takes his normal corner table. He eats his usual, an omelette and a glass of orange juice, and then he pays his bill. "This is more than fifty percent," I say.

"Oh please, it's fine. We're almost engaged."

My jaw drops. "Excuse me?"

He stands up. "Attention, gathered patrons of Golden Gloves! I have a very exciting announcement."

Everyone in the restaurant stops eating and turns toward us, including Barbara, with a knowing smile on her face. What's going on? Is he proposing now? Here? Was yesterday's joke just to prime the pump?

"Most of you have met my girlfriend here, Anica. You've seen how beautiful, graceful, bright, and hard-working she is. You can easily see how she captured me and brought me under her spell."

Oh my gosh, is it really happening? Is he about to propose? He's such a . . . I don't even know how to describe what an adorable little punk he is, and I'm an author. Heat floods my cheeks.

"Without Anica, my life would be . . . well, I wouldn't be up here making this announcement. That's for sure." He reaches into his bag and pulls out a roll of paper. "Although to be fair, I need someone else up here with me. They're arguably more important than I am in all this."

What's he doing with that paper?

"Barbara, come up here, you little schemer."

My boss ducks from behind the counter and comes toward us.

"I've heard a lot of you mention that this place has gotten crowded lately, and as you know, I run a bunch of hotels in the area. One of them needs a new restaurant, as it happens."

He's not proposing at all. What is wrong with me? Is my brain broken? I need to stop seeing proposals everywhere I look like a desperate lunatic.

"So we're going to be partnering, Barbara and I, to open a second Golden Gloves, and if my girlfriend agrees to transfer there, she'll be able to work a lot closer to my new office." He winks at me.

Good grief. "We can talk about it," I say.

A few of the customers cheer, but it doesn't look like quite the excitement he was hoping for. He kisses my cheek and heads for the exit. "I'm leaving in a few hours for New York—the Goodhampton negotiations are wrapping up. I'll see you at game night and we can talk more about this then."

"Or you can call me and give me details tonight, mister," I say.

He nods. "I will."

And he does, but it turns out he doesn't really care which location I work at—or if I quit. "I was just teasing Barbara in there," he says. "She's paranoid that if we open this new location, you'll abandon her. She wants to hire someone to manage the new spot so she doesn't have to step out of the familiar into the unknown. I think the new location will need her there at least a few days a week."

"I know I said I wouldn't quit," I say. "But with all the writing I've been doing lately, I've actually thought about surrendering my apron."

"Oh, wow." Ethan's quiet. "I had no idea."

"You can still get omelettes without me there."

"But it's the company I love."

I laugh. "I'll be able to go *with you* to get food."

"I do like that idea," he says.

He's so busy that week that I get a lot of writing done. Phoebe's delighted. "This one is even better than the last. Oh, Anica. I see another auction in your future, and I am not going to let this one go so low."

"Maybe we sit on it for a bit," I say. "Better not to flood the market with Anica Maggards."

She laughs. "We can discuss it—but there are other imprints who are still annoyed that they missed the last one."

I take my time getting ready for game night, since I

haven't seen Ethan since Monday. But then Amy pokes her head through the door. "Hey, Aunt Anica."

My hand pauses, the mascara brush suspended in midair. "Is everything okay?" She doesn't usually just shoot into my room like that.

"Yeah, but Mom's kind of freaking out. I thought you might be able to help."

"Of course." I stuff my makeup back in the bag and run a brush through my hair. Good enough.

I follow the noise into the kitchen where Mary—calm, cool, collected Mary—is crying over a bowl of half-mixed guacamole.

"Hey, Mary, are you okay?"

She looks up at me and blinks. "None of these avocados are alright. This guacamole is trash."

"Uh, why are you crying, though?"

"Because I don't have any other snacks." She throws her hands up in the air. "I'm the only one who ever hosts! Why is that?"

I walk the rest of the way across the room and gently take the bowl away from her. She's not wrong—the guacamole looks disgusting. I scrape it into the trash. "I'll come up with something, but people bring stuff too, usually."

She hiccups and a thought hits me.

"Hey." I wrap an arm around her shoulders, trying to soothe her from what is undeniably an overreaction. "Is there a chance you might be pregnant again?"

"Excuse me?" Her eyebrow pops up so fast I almost scramble away from her in fear. When Mary pins you with the eye, you don't last long.

"I'm sorry." I step away. "It's just that when Lizzie was expecting she got a little moody."

She scowls. "I'm sorry, I have a bad day and suddenly I'm pregnant?"

I shake my head. "No, I have no idea. I was just asking."

"I'm still nursing," she says. "So, no."

Uh. "Please tell me that you're also using birth control."

"I'm *nursing*," she says.

Hm. "Okay." I'll have to mention the possibility to Luke.

"Oh, no." She leans against the counter. "Am I pregnant? I can't be pregnant. Jack isn't even a year old yet." Her face looks white.

"I'll just run grab a test," I say. "If you want me to, that is."

She waves at me, and I rush to my car. Which, of course, since this is important and I'm in a hurry, won't start. I sneak back inside. "So, any chance I could take your car? Mine won't start."

"Oh my gosh, you have got to get a new car. That thing is a total piece of junk." Mary practically chucks her keys at me.

I really hope she's pregnant. Otherwise she's had a complete personality lobotomy without any reason. Luckily, the local drug store is close. I'm getting back just as Rob and Brekka show up, baby Ruth in a car seat, Rob swinging her back and forth like she's weightless. "Hey guys."

"Whatcha got?" Rob looks at my bag.

Luckily, I've already come up with an excuse. "Bean dip and queso. None of the avocados were any good." I shrug.

"Good call." Brekka smiles at me. "I feel like a mean game of monopoly tonight. How about you?"

Playing her at monopoly sucks. It's like the root canal of game nights. "Only if Trig is playing too." Watching those two lock horns is actually pretty entertaining.

"Duh."

I smile. "Then, sure."

Moments later, I've made up an excuse and ushered

Mary into her room. "Don't go." She grabs my arm. "Can you wait in the room while I take this?"

"You can't cheat on this test," I say.

"No jokes."

Okay, no sense of humor about this. Right.

I wait. And then I wait. And then I wait more. "Oh, man. Oh, man. How? Anica?" She shoots around the doorway to her bathroom, brandishing the test. "How?"

"Uh, so it's a little awkward to explain this to you, but the guy has—"

"Eww, no. Stop. I said no jokes." She tosses the test in the trash and sinks onto the bed, dropping her face in her hands. "I love Jack. So much. And Amy and Chase too, of course."

"But you're tired."

She looks up. "I only started feeling like a person again a few months ago." She closes her eyes. "And the nausea."

I sit down next to her and take her hand. "It's temporary. The shape of your family will last forever."

She sighs. "You're right." She squeezes my hand again. "Of course you are. Luke will be giddy. Nothing makes him happier than kids. Babies. Whatever." Her shoulders slump. "I may have to hire help, you know. We barely survived Jack."

"Luckily, if you need to, you can afford it." Oh, but I'll need to move out. Which I can totally do. "It's going to be a blessing, I promise."

She nods. "I just need a minute. Can you tell them I'm on a call or something?"

"Of course. Should I send Luke back when he's done with Jack?" Putting Jack to bed has become a whole ordeal. No one manages it as well as Luke.

"Yeah, please. I'm sure I'll be able to summon some excitement by then." She looks up at the ceiling. "Why am I such a dud?"

"It's easy for me to be excited," I say. "My body isn't being taken over and I'm not the one who's going to be puking."

"Oh, the puking." Mary groans. "But the baby smiles and the tiny outfits."

"There are a lot of good parts," I say. "And I'll be here for whatever you need."

She looks up at me. "You have been a Godsend, Anica. I mean that. Thank you. For being my friend. For being a great aunt, and for being a support for Luke, too. Your approval means a lot to him." And she's crying again.

"I'm not going anywhere. I'll be here for whatever you need."

"I know that, too." Mary smiles through her tears.

A moment later, when I hear a shout, I know that Luke's delighted. It's good at least one of them is happy. I'm sure Mary will come around, eventually.

"Is something going on?" Paisley asks as she crosses from the entryway into the kitchen.

"We've got a roach problem," I say. "We're looking into it."

She drops the chip she was picking up back into the bowl. Ha! Paisley cracks me up.

Ethan shows up a few minutes later, and suddenly my day brightens by a factor of ten. He hands me a gorgeous bouquet. "I know I'm late, but I figured I should make time to bring you these." Gerbera daisies. I hug them to my chest, and then head to the kitchen for a vase.

"Are you trying to make us look bad?" Paul asks. "Geez, dude. Knock it off."

"I've been gone all week," Ethan says. "I'm trying to make up for abandonment."

"James was gone all week." Paisley arches one eyebrow. "Are you taking notes, honey?"

He wraps his arms around her waist. "Totally. I am so

excited to learn everything I can about how to keep my wife happy . . . from the guy who isn't even engaged."

Ouch, that one hurts a little. I jam the flowers into the vase and plonk it down in the center of the kitchen table.

"Alright." Brekka rolls up to the counter. "I was promised a Monopoly game."

James reaches for the box. "I call the do—"

"You always get the dog." Paisley snatches it out of the box.

Before I can even reach the table, Geo, Brekka, Rob, Paul, Trudy, Trig, and Ethan have snatched all the pieces out of the box, leaving me with nothing. "I guess I'll go cut up fruit or something," I say. "Geez."

"Or," Ethan says. "Maybe you could play with this." He drops something on the table. I lean closer.

And then my heart skips a beat. And then another.

It's a diamond ring.

"If you were willing to marry me, I mean." Ethan drops down on one knee.

I open my mouth.

"Ah, ah, ah. Do you have any idea how much pressure there is when you're proposing to a bestselling author? You might even try to lay the groundwork a bit by making her think you're doing it several different times. Just so she doesn't see the plot twist coming."

I inhale.

"Wait, did we miss it?" Mary comes running down the hall.

"We delayed as long as we could," Brekka says. "Geez, how many cockroaches do you have in there?"

"Cockroaches?" Luke asks. "What are—"

"I'm kind of in the middle of something here," Ethan says. "C'mon."

"Right," Luke says. "Sorry. Carry on, mate."

Ethan takes my hand. "I have wanted to marry you

since the day we got back together. I actually bought this ring that day and I've been carrying it around in my car, my pocket, and my briefcase. I thought I lost it twice." He chuckles. "But I wanted to wait until I knew that you had faith in me."

"Faith?" My eyes well with tears.

"You told me something the day after we got back together. You said that my fury would rise up, over and over, and I would have to learn to let it go. I didn't want to ask you to build a family with me until you could trust that I always would, and that you were safe with me. But you know what I've decided?"

I shake my head.

"It wasn't nearly as hard to let it go as I thought it would be, and I think it's because *you* are my peace. From the day you came into my life, it was like all the crappy things that have happened to me didn't matter anymore. If there is some kind of balance sheet in heaven, I think you more than offset the misery allocated to me. So for you, each and every day, come what may, I promise to set aside any anger, any irritation, any fury, any judgment and choose to forgive. For you, for our kids, and for the family we'll create. Together." He scowls playfully at Luke and the gathered audience. "And I guess for our friends too. I promise to keep my peace and my joy and my happiness with me forever . . . with you by my side. Please say you'll marry me, Anica Maggard. Be my happily ever after."

"Yes," I say. "Yes, I will. Gladly."

❧ 21 ❧

ANICA

"**I** can't believe you wanted to have the wedding here," Geo says. "When your fiancé owns more than a hundred hotels, several of them much nicer than this."

"Next month he'll own a hundred and forty, once the acquisition goes through," I say proudly.

"Who can keep up?" Mary asks.

"Not me," Trudy says. "But believe me, James is keeping count. That guy never cared about hotels before, but he talks about them all the time now."

"He's too competitive," I say. "That's James' problem."

"It makes him who he is." Paisley shrugs, but she likes it.

"I picked the Riviera Grand because it's where we first met." I look around and think about that day. Everything was so new then—my friendships tentative, my faith in myself almost nonexistent, and I judged Ethan by all the wrong measurements.

"You're too sentimental," Geo says. "I did the best I could, but. . . " She looks around and shrugs. "We could have done a much nicer job at—"

285

"Hush." Mary takes my arm. "It's time."

I follow her out into the hall where my dad is waiting. He looks so nice in his black tux. "Anica." He kisses my forehead. "You're even more beautiful than usual."

"Thanks, Dad."

My mom is next to him, her eyes alight with joy. "I'm so happy."

"You look beautiful," I say.

She waves her hand at me. "That's my line." But she's smiling in a way I haven't seen much since Lizzie died.

"Time," Geo points.

And as if she's somehow omnipotent, the wedding march begins. Most brides would have to gather up a train, but not me. I had my dress custom made to be cute and short, with a fluffy skirt, and pure white, including the tiny apron detail over the top. To remind me of the hours we spent together in the diner, falling in love one tiny bit at a time. As I served him, and he learned to trust me.

I walk, one steady step at a time, toward my beautiful-beyond-belief fiancé. He beams when he sees me. And I keep my eyes on him the entire walk to the front. My dad passes me off slowly. "Take care of my girl."

"Of course," Ethan says. "With everything I am."

And then the pastor starts in with the service. I try to listen to every word, but I keep getting distracted by Ethan. He keeps squeezing my hand, raising his eyebrows at me, making wry faces, and winking.

"Knock it off," I hiss.

"You love it."

He's right.

"If you two have prepared vows?" The white-haired pastor pauses.

Ethan jumps right in. "The first thing I knew about Anica is that she was a bestselling author. At the time, I thought, cool." He laughs. "I had no idea how hard her job would make every event and every situation. Who wants to have their vows compared to the ones written by someone who literally writes *love* for their job?"

The audience laughs.

"But I long since gave up on any pretense of having insight or words that will compare to hers. So I'll keep my vows short. Anica has done more than love me. She has repaired me. I thought I had been unlucky before meeting her, that I just hadn't met the right girl. I didn't realize that I wasn't ready to love until she taught me *how*. She taught me that love isn't just liking something, or even taking care of something. It's forgiveness, and faith, and trust, and growth. It's like growing a plant, except even more delicate. So my promise to her today, in front of all these witnesses, is that I'll never allow the hectic nature of life to distract me from what matters more than anything else: earning her trust."

I pause for a moment to drink in his words. He's learned from me? I've learned so much more from him. "Ethan may have been stressed about what to say," I start. "But imagine being an author and the expectations that the audience will have for what I share." I laugh. "Most of you know that the tragic death of my sister wrecked every part of my life. I couldn't write. I couldn't love. I could barely function. Ethan's crediting me with fixing him, but he had to do that himself, because it was all I could do to wake up and shower and comb my hair when we met."

I look around the room. "I know this is my wedding, but one thing I've learned is that a wedding is about more than just two people getting married. When you choose to create a family, you're taking on more than just one person. You're taking on their family, too. I bet if you talk to Luke, he'll tell you that's absolutely true. Lizzie's not even here anymore, and he's still stuck with me."

This time the audience laughs, but it's soft, as if they feel guilty about it.

"I'd like to say thank you to the people who supported me, who built me up, and who showed me the importance of family and love and trust, so that I was able to find that with Ethan. And to you, my dear husband, I'd like to promise you that I will always and forever be there to yell at you when you mess up. Except unlike my first attempt, when I do it in the future, I'll stick around to make sure you understood what I said."

This time the laughter is real.

"And I promise that no matter how bumpy or circuitous the road ahead of us, we'll take the trip together, every mile of the way."

The pastor waits for a breath or two to make sure we're done, and then he nods. "And do you, Miss Maggard, take Mr. Trainor to be your lawfully wedded husband?"

"I absolutely do."

"And do you, Mr. Trainor, take Miss Maggard to be your lawfully wedded wife?"

"I do."

"Then I now pronounce you man and wife."

Ethan's smiling when he slides a ring on my finger alongside my engagement ring. And I'm beaming when I slide his over his knotty, callused finger. "Caught ya," I whisper.

And then he kisses me.

He doesn't stop kissing me until the pastor clears his throat.

Which is not nearly long enough, but luckily we've got plenty of time for that—a lifetime really.

The dancing and the cake go by in a blur, but I make sure to eat my burger and fries carefully so I don't get ketchup stains on my dress.

"You forgot your salad." Ethan sets a strawberry spinach

salad next to me. "The spinach is full of vitamins. It almost offsets the metric ton of sugar in the dressing."

I laugh. "You are always looking after me like that, Mr. Trainor. Many thanks."

"Gladly, Mrs. Trainor."

"I hate to interrupt," my new father-in-law says. "But I have a little something for you."

"Dad," Ethan says, "you didn't—"

He clears his throat. "It's not for you. Sorry if I was unclear. It's for Anica." He extends his hand and drops keys into my lap.

Porsche keys.

My laughter rings from the rafters.

"I think you might like it, if you give it a chance," he says. "It's not a 911—it's a Cayenne. The nicest one they make."

His new wife, Annelise has one arm around his waist. "It thanks you for driving with it," she says. "I love mine."

Of course she does. "Thank you both. It's a very thoughtful, and humorous, gift." And it runs, so it's better than the one I keep refusing to replace. I only wish Lizzie was here to name this one, like she named Cashew so many years ago.

"By way of warning," Ethan's dad says as Annelise wanders off. "She insisted we get you a car seat, too." When he turns to walk away and winks over his shoulder at us, he looks exactly like Ethan. He may not be perfect, but I'm grateful my love had a parent who cared for him, albeit an imperfect one.

When I look up at Ethan, I do see his imperfections. I'm not oblivious to them, but I choose to focus on his many strengths. And I embrace the joy in my life.

I think Lizzie would be proud of me—for my words, and for the family I've found since she left.

"We've never talked baby names," I say. "But now that we have a car seat. . ."

"I was thinking Elizabeth," Ethan says.

"Gosh, I hope we have a girl first," I say.

He swings me around and leads me out to the dance floor to celebrate with all our friends and family. Amy's chiding Troy, who keeps stepping on her feet. Geo looks half asleep on Trig's shoulder. Paul's spinning Trudy with a smile on his face. And Brekka's holding baby Ruth on her lap and swaying to the music while Rob stands behind her. Even Mary, poor sick Mary, is here, holding Luke's hand. When I glance her way, she smiles.

"I know there are more exotic locations we could have chosen," I say. "You wanted Hawaii, and it would have been a stunning place to get married." I swallow the frog that has crept into my throat. "Thank you for letting me have it here."

"I get it," Ethan says. "Once you've found a real home, you never want to leave."

"Yes," I say. "That's exactly it, and now that you're here, this is home for me."

"Me too," he says. "Finally and forever."

<<<<>>>>

I hope you enjoyed the story as much as I enjoyed writing it! I have another contemporary romantic women's fiction series planned for next year. . . but it won't be out right away. If you're looking for another read right now, you could check out my fantasy series, the Birthright Series, which starts with Displaced (if you keep scrolling you can check out a sample chapter!), or my post apocalyptic series, the Sins of Our Ancestors Series, which starts with Marked.

Or I've also got a standalone romantic suspense story, Already Gone. If you'd like to get Already Gone FOR FREE, you can sign up for my newsletter at www.BridgetEBakerWrites.com.

And if you'd like to join a fun group of readers (and me!) on a facebook group, check out "Bridget Baker's Binge Reader Recovery Program" right here: https://www.facebook.com/groups/750807222376182 I'm currently working on writing some exclusive content for each of my series—short stories about things that happen AFTER the series end. So if you want some FREE short stories that will let you catch up with the characters you love, join the group today.

SAMPLE CHAPTER OF
DISPLACED

My mom should have killed me the day I was born. In her nearly nine-hundred-year reign as the Empress of the First Family, sparing my life seventeen years ago was her single act of mercy.

Evians around the world refer to me as "Enora's Folly."

It's no wonder I'm fatally flawed, a blemish among the shining population of evians Mom rules. I spent my childhood running away from my twin sister's taunts. Maybe that's why no one on the island can catch me. On days when life feels too heavy and my heart struggles to beat without melancholy, the Kona wind blowing against my face reminds me the world is vast and full of possibility. And on days when I need that wind, but my mom's too busy to run with me, there's always Lark.

"Wait up," she calls from dozens of yards behind me.

I stop at the top of the northeastern cliffs, the highest point on Ni'ihau, and scan the horizon while I wait for her. Dolphins leap energetically in the distance. I've been on this island the majority of my life, yet every single time I stop to take in the lush island of Kauai in the distance, and every time I stand at the highest point of Ni'ihau, the majesty of my surroundings astonishes me. When Lark finally reaches my side, her lungs heave in great, gulping breaths and she bends over double. "We should've taken the horses."

"Are you okay?" I lift one eyebrow.

She waves her hand at me absently and wheezes. "Fine, you idiot. Not all of us are machines. You've got to ease up for the little people."

"You're the one who suggested we take this trail."

"I guess that makes me the idiot." She straightens next to me, her heart rate decelerating back to normal.

"As your best friend, I officially disagree with you." I grin. "You're smart and talented, Lark. People like you. Now repeat that until you believe it."

"Speaking of how much you love me..." Lark won't meet my eye.

"What's up?" I ask.

"I need help."

Most evians don't do favors, not without negotiation and *quid pro quo*, or at least a few moments of analysis to weigh the impact and risk to them. But I'm the broken heir, the defective twin, the one who doesn't view friendship as a commodity like I should.

Which is why I immediately say, "Anything. You already know that."

Lark's voice drops to a whisper. "The intelligence subsection is getting more competitive every year."

She's a year older than me and recently completed her training, which means placement for her first work assignment happens in the next few days.

"Right," I say. "Balth said it's gotten popular." Not that I care, since I'll never be placed anywhere. I'm stuck here forever.

"A few years ago, Mom could've gotten me a spot for sure."

"But now?"

"Well." She clears her throat. "She can't do much now. But if I could defeat a seventh gen in a challenge. . ."

Lark wants to fight me. And more than that, she needs to beat me. Publicly.

"You want to stab me with a sword in front of everyone we know?" That's a pretty big ask. I mean, I heal lightning quick, but it still hurts. Plus, Lark is tenth gen. Losing to her would be a new low, even for me.

"I really don't want to get stuck working for Uncle Max."

"Oh come on. He loves fostering the young minds. He's always talking about it."

"He is." Lark groans. "The idea of restructuring corporations all day long. . ." She closes her eyes. "I'll die of boredom."

Lark has always been melodramatic. "Just submit your DNA and you'll be auto-admitted into intelligence. It's not *that* competitive. I mean, you suck at appearance modification, and your mom is pretty well known, so you'll probably be stuck human side initially, but you can buckle down and practice your modifications and you'll cross over eventually."

"But if I defeat you, I'd be automatically ranked number one in Alamecha's class."

And I'd look pathetic, losing to someone with three generations more genetic deletions. I open my mouth to tell her no, but her quick inhalation stops me. She can test right into a top tier Security placement with a simple blood draw. Usually only candidates below fifteenth gen resort to theatrics like a public challenge. Why would she ask me to destroy my reputation for something she doesn't even need?

"You're absolutely positive you want a Security placement?" I ask.

Her gray eyes widen and her breath hitches again. This request matters to her. She might have even orchestrated this run to ask me without interruption. Heaven knows she never wants to go jogging, so this suggestion came out of the blue. My oldest friend has never asked me for a single thing, not in seventeen years. She probably knows better than anyone else how hard things are for me, and now she's asking me to do something she doesn't really need, knowing Judica will never let me forget my defeat.

Why?

I want to shove the thoughts away and ignore the nigglings at the back of my mind. But I can't. I'm not wired that way, and I keep circling back to the same conclusion. "I can only think of one reason you'd ask me to throw a challenge."

Lark's heart rate spikes and the scent of her perspiration rises, almost as strongly as when she was running full tilt.

Unfortunately, that's the confirmation I need. "You can't do the blood test."

Her nostrils flare. "Of course I can."

She's lying to me, but I hope I'm wrong about why. Because I think she just asked me to commit treason, and she didn't even plan to tell me I was doing it.

Why does she need me to throw a fight? I rarely train in earnest, whereas she spends hours every morning with her mom. Actually, she's rumored to be one of the best fighters on the compound. "Why not simply challenge me?"

Lark's gray eyes widen.

"Come on Lark, you can tell me. What's going on?" Please, please come clean.

"Never mind. It's fine." Lark turns away from me and picks at non-existent lint on her pants.

When I grab her hand, she jumps like I electrocuted her. "Tell me."

She yanks her hand away with wounded eyes. "There's nothing to tell."

"You're half human." My words hang in the air like a cloud of gnats, impeding my vision of the future, clouding my memory of the past, a plague on my heart. I wish I could wave my hand and dissipate the reality of my accusation, but I can't. Only Lark can fix this, by denying my wild claim.

I need her to deny it.

I'm afraid she can't.

When she doesn't say a word, I struggle to breathe. Lark's father must have been human. She's only half evian. Every moment of our seventeen years as best friends shifts, recharacterized by my new knowledge. Her heaving when we run, her training alone, her reticence to travel with me. The ground beneath my feet feels unsteady, like there's been an earthquake.

"Why didn't you tell me?" I whisper. "Why didn't you confess years ago?" The realization that she didn't even tell me now slaps me hard. I had to figure this out, about my own best friend.

A tear streaks down her face and she wipes it away ruthlessly. "What will you do now you know?"

"Look at me."

She doesn't.

"I can't believe you're asking me that right now. I'd never turn you in. You think I could ever watch your execution? Lark, *look at me*."

Her lower lip wobbles. "I should never have asked in the first place. Mom was right. Why did I try to outsmart you? I'm deficient."

I can't even imagine living with that kind of fear. Why didn't her mother leave with her or adopt her out? The idea of life without Lark shatters my heart into pieces. All this time and she couldn't even risk telling her best friend.

That's reason enough for me to throw one fight. No one should live like she's had to live, and if I can create a safer space for her in our world, I'll do it.

This time it's my voice that wobbles. "Your mistake wasn't in asking, it was in withholding the relevant information. Of course I'll do whatever you need. You'll get into Security and select intelligence and then you'll leave." I realize one reason I didn't want to help her before is that her Uncle Max lives here, and I didn't want her to leave.

But she has to go.

If she stays on the island, it's only a matter of time before someone else figures it out. "Then no one will ever know."

She shakes her head. "If you figured out why I asked, someone else might guess too."

"So we stage your challenge. Someone optimistically throws one down on me at least twice a year, you know, seeing as I'm the useless twin. I always turn them down flat, but maybe you'd make me mad enough to accept. Best friends know exactly which buttons to push, right?"

The corner of Lark's mouth turns up slightly. "Even so, Balthasar might figure it out," she says. "During the match I mean. It's dangerous, too dangerous to risk, which is why Mom said not to even ask you." She drops her face into her hands. "Mom's going to kill me when I tell her about all this."

"Tell your mom that you have an ally now." I smile and take her hand in mine. "I may not be *the Heir,* but I'm an heir, and beating me will be enough. Besides, once you're in the field working from the human side, you'll be away from all the evian politics. And working on the human side, you'll be safe."

"That's the plan," she says. "But when Mom finds out you know..."

"So don't tell her."

Lark shakes her head. "I can't lie to my mom. I can't. I lie to everyone else."

Her life has been harder than I ever realized. "How slow are you, exactly?"

Lark balls her fingers into a fist and swings at me. I duck easily. Her reflexes probably put a human to shame, but they're notably slower than mine. Ugh. How will we pull this off?

"I think the only way people won't notice your speed is if I'm truly horrible," I say. "Which shouldn't be too hard. I haven't reached the point of integrating active combat into my training yet, so I'm sure I'll be convincingly terrible."

"You're saying your mom's insistence on training you in old school melodics might save me?" Lark's smile reaches her eyes this time, and when her stormy gray eyes sparkle, I decide we can pull this off.

We don't have a choice.

And if you enjoyed that, grab Displaced right now.

ACKNOWLEDGMENTS

As always, the biggest thanks go to my ridiculously supportive husband, and my sweet and super duper supportive kiddos. They have all been tremendous... and complained very little at my neglect while writing and editing.

I also appreciate my copy editor, Carla Stuckey, and my proofer, Carrie Harris. Love to both of you ladies—especially for the quick turn arounds you always pull.

And for my readers: I straight up LOVE you guys. You have no idea. You make all my dreams come true. Thank you for your kind reviews, your emails and notes and comments of support. When you recommend me to your friends and family, it means the WORLD to me.

ABOUT THE AUTHOR

Bridget loves her husband (every day) and all five of her kids (most days). She's a lawyer, but does as little legal work as possible. She has three goofy horses, one very busy dog, two spoiled barn cats, two lion's head rabbits, and more chickens than she cares to admit. She makes cookies too often, and believes they should be their own food group. In a (possibly misguided attempt) to level the scales between consumption and exertion, she kick boxes every day. So if you don't like her books, her kids, or her cookies, maybe don't tell her in person.

Suppressed (2)

Redeemed (3)

Renounced (4)

The Anchored Series:

Anchored (1)

Adrift (2)

Awoken (3—releasing July 15, 2021)

Capsized (4—releasing September 15, 2021)

A stand alone YA romantic suspense:

Already Gone

Children's Picture Book

Yuck! What's for Dinner?